DRACULA

Abridged

By

Bram Stoker

Abridged

By

Alex Cristo

InAmerica Press

Published in the United States by InAmerica Press

a division of InAmerica, Inc.

POB 2645, Valley Center, CA U.S.A.

InAmerica and colophon are registered trademarks of InAmerica, Inc.

Library of Congress Cataloging-in-Publication Data

ISBN 978-1-934613-33-7

Cristo, Alex, author.

Dracula Abridged

Alex Cristo

First U.S. Edition

[First Printing]

InAmerica Press website address: www.inamericapress.com

Printed in the United States of America.

http://alexcristo.com

Introduction

Welcome to my abridgement of Dracula! Enter freely and of your own free will! You will find every scene and character from the original still included in these pages with all the horror and drama. This version of Stoker's classic has been edited to be more friendly to a modern reader and is about half the length of the original. I have done my best to keep the characters, themes, and interactions as true to Bram Stoker's original as possible, including his deliberate grammatical errors and spelling mistakes...but in half the pages. Enjoy!

Contents

Jonathan Harker's Journal, 3 May

Bistritz. Left Munich at 8:35 P. M, on 1st May, arriving at Vienna early next morning; train was an hour late. Buda-Pesth seems a wonderful place.

The impression I had was that we were leaving the West and entering the East; the bridge over the Danube, which is here of noble width and depth, took us among the traditions of Turkish rule.

We came after nightfall to the Hotel Royale in Klausenburgh. I had for supper a chicken done up some way with red pepper, which was very good but made me thirsty. (Mem. get recipe for Mina.) It was called "paprika hendl," and it is a national dish found along the Carpathians.

I found my smattering of German very useful here, indeed.

I had visited the British Museum, and made search among the books regarding Transylvania; it had struck me that some foreknowledge of the country could hardly fail to have some importance in dealing with a nobleman of that country.

The district is in the extreme east of the country, just on the borders of three states, Transylvania, Moldavia, and Bukovina, in the midst of the Carpathian mountains; one of the wildest and least known portions of Europe.

I was not able to find on any map the exact locality of the Castle Dracula, but I found that Bistritz, the post town named by Count Dracula, is a fairly well-known place.

In the population of Transylvania there are four distinct nationalities: Saxons in the South, and mixed with them the Wallachs, who are the descendants of the Dacians; Magyars in the West, and Szekelys in the East and North. I am going among the latter, who claim to be descended from Attila and the Huns.

I read that every known superstition in the world is gathered into the horseshoe of the Carpathians, as if it were the centre of some sort of imaginative whirlpool; if so my stay may be very interesting. (Mem., I must ask the Count all about them.)

I did not sleep well, for I had all sorts of queer dreams. There was a dog howling all night under my window, which may have had something to do with it; or it may have been the paprika.

I had for breakfast more paprika, and a sort of porridge of maize flour which they said was "mamaliga", and egg-plant stuffed with forcemeat, which they call "impletata". (Mem., get recipe for this also.)

I had to hurry breakfast, for the train started a little before eight.

All day long we seemed to dawdle through a country which was full of beauty of every kind. Sometimes we saw little towns or castles on the top of steep hills such as we see in old missals.

At every station there were groups of people in all sorts of attire. Some of them were just like the peasants at home, with short jackets, and round hats; but others were very picturesque.

The women looked pretty, except when you got near them, but they were very clumsy about the waist. Most of them had big belts with a lot of strips, but of course there were petticoats under them.

The strangest figures we saw were the Slovaks, who were more barbarian than the rest, with their big cow-boy hats, great baggy dirty-white trousers, white linen shirts, and enormous heavy leather belts, nearly a foot wide, all studded over with brass nails. They wore high boots, with their trousers tucked into them, and had long black hair and heavy black moustaches.

It was on the dark side of twilight when we got to Bistritz. Being practically on the frontier--for the Borgo Pass leads from it into Bukovina--it has had a very stormy existence, and it certainly shows marks of it. Great fires, a siege, and the loss of 13,000 people: the casualties of war, famine and disease.

Count Dracula had directed me to go to the Golden Krone Hotel, which I found to be thoroughly old-fashioned.

I was evidently expected, for when I got near the door I faced a cheery-looking elderly woman in the usual peasant dress--white undergarment with a long double apron, front, and back, of coloured stuff fitting almost too tight for modesty. When I came close she bowed and said, "The Herr Englishman?"

"Yes," I said, "Jonathan Harker."

She smiled, and gave some message to an elderly man in white shirt-sleeves, who had followed her to the door.

He went, but immediately returned with a letter:

"My friend.--Welcome to the Carpathians. I am anxiously expecting you. Sleep well tonight. At three tomorrow the diligence will start for Bukovina; a place on it is kept for you. At the Borgo Pass my carriage will await you and will bring you to me. I trust that your journey from London has been a happy one, and that you will enjoy your stay in my beautiful land.--Your friend, Dracula."

4 May--I found that my landlord seemed somewhat reticent, and pretended that he could not understand my German.

This could not be true, because up to then he had understood it perfectly.

When I asked him if he knew Count Dracula, and could tell me anything of his castle, both he and his wife crossed themselves, and, saying that they knew nothing at all, simply refused to speak further. It was all very mysterious and not by any means comforting.

Just before I was leaving, the old lady came up to my room and said in a hysterical way: "Must you go? Oh! Young Herr, must you go?" She was in such an excited state that she seemed to have lost her grip of what German she knew, and mixed it all up with some other language. When I told her that I must go at once, and that I was engaged on important business, she asked again:

"Do you know what day it is?" I answered that it was the fourth of May. She shook her head as she said again:

"Oh, yes! I know that! I know that, but do you know what day it is?"

On my saying that I did not understand, she went on:

"It is the eve of St. George's Day. Do you not know that to-night, when the clock strikes midnight, all the evil things in the world will have full sway? Do you know where you are going, and what you are going to?" She was in such evident distress that I tried to comfort her, but without effect. Finally, she went down on her knees and implored me not to go; at least to wait a day or two before starting.

It was all very ridiculous but I did not feel comfortable. However, there was business to be done, and I could allow nothing to interfere with it.

She then rose and dried her eyes, and taking a crucifix from her neck offered it to me.

I did not know what to do, for, as an English Churchman, I have been taught to regard such things as idolatrous, and yet it seemed so ungracious to refuse an old lady meaning so well and in such a state of mind.

She saw, I suppose, the doubt in my face, for she put the rosary round my neck and said, "For your mother's sake," and went out of the room.

I am writing up this part of the diary whilst I am waiting for the coach, which is, of course, late; and the crucifix is still round my neck.

Whether it is the old lady's fear, or the many ghostly traditions of this place, or the crucifix itself, I do not know, but I am not feeling nearly as easy in my mind as usual.

If this book should ever reach Mina before I do, let it bring my good-bye. Here comes the coach!

5 May. The Castle.--The gray of the morning has passed, and the sun is high over the distant horizon, which seems jagged, whether with trees or hills I know not.

I am not sleepy, and, as I am not to be called till I awake, naturally I write till sleep comes.

There are many odd things to put down.

I dined on what they called "robber steak"--bits of bacon, onion, and beef, seasoned with red pepper, and strung on sticks, and roasted over the fire, in simple style of the London cat's meat!

The wine was Golden Mediasch, which produces a queer sting on the tongue, which is, however, not disagreeable.

I had only a couple of glasses of this, and nothing else.

When I got on the coach, the driver had not taken his seat, and I saw him talking to the landlady about me.

Some of the people who were sitting on the bench outside the door-- came and listened, and then looked at me, most of them pityingly. I could hear a lot of words often repeated, queer words, so I quietly got my polyglot dictionary from my bag and looked them out.

I must say they were not cheering to me, for amongst them were "Ordog"--Satan, "Pokol"--hell, "stregoica"--witch, "vrolok" and "vlkoslak"--both mean the same thing, one being Slovak and the other Servian for something that is either werewolf or vampire. (Mem., I must ask the Count about these superstitions.)

When we started, the crowd round the inn door, which had by this time swelled to a considerable size, all made the sign of the cross and pointed two fingers towards me.

With some difficulty, I got a fellow passenger to tell me what they meant. He explained that it was a charm or guard against the evil eye.

Everyone seemed so kind-hearted, and so sorrowful, and so sympathetic that I could not but be touched.

I shall never forget the last glimpse which I had of the inn yard and its crowd of picturesque figures, all crossing themselves.

Then our driver, whose wide linen drawers covered the whole front of the boxseat,--"gotza" they call them--cracked his big whip over his four small horses, which ran abreast, and we set off on our journey.

I soon lost sight and recollection of ghostly fears in the beauty of the scene as we drove along. Before us lay a green sloping land full of forests and woods. In and out amongst these green hills of what they call here the "Mittel Land" ran the road, losing itself as it was shut out by the straggling ends of pine woods, which ran down the hillsides like tongues of flame. The road was rugged, but still we seemed to fly over it with a feverish haste. The driver was evidently bent on losing no time in reaching Borgo Prund. It is an old tradition that the roads are not to be kept in too good order, lest the Turk should think that they were preparing to bring in foreign troops.

Here and there seemed mighty rifts in the Carpathian Mountains, through which, as the sun began to sink, we saw now and again the white gleam of falling water. One of my companions touched my arm as we swept round the base of a hill and opened up the lofty, snow-covered peak of a mountain, which seemed, as we wound on our serpentine way, to be right before us.

"Look! Isten szek!"--"God's seat!"--and he crossed himself reverently.

As we wound on our endless way, the shadows of the evening began to creep round us. Here and there we passed Cszeks and slovaks, all in picturesque attire. By the roadside were many crosses, and as we swept by, my companions all crossed themselves.

Now and again we passed a leiter-wagon--the ordinary peasants's cart. On this were sure to be seated, the Cszeks with their white, and the Slovaks with their coloured sheepskins. Sometimes the hills were so steep that, despite our driver's haste, the horses could only go slowly. I wished to get down and walk up them, as we do at home, but the driver would not hear of it. "No, no," he said. "You must not walk here. The dogs are too fierce." And then he added, with what he evidently meant for grim pleasantry--for he looked round to catch the approving smile of the rest--"And you may have enough of such matters before you go to sleep." The only stop he would make was a moment's pause to light his lamps.

When it grew dark there seemed to be some excitement amongst the passengers, and they kept speaking to him, one after the other, as though urging him to further speed. He lashed the horses unmercifully with his long whip, and with wild cries of encouragement urged them on to further exertions. The crazy coach rocked on its great leather springs, and swayed like a boat tossed on a stormy sea. We were entering on the Borgo Pass. One by one several of the passengers offered the sign of the cross and the guard against the evil eye. Then, as we flew along, the driver leaned forward, and on each side the passengers, craning over the edge of the coach, peered eagerly into the darkness. No one would give me the slightest explanation. And at last we saw before us the Pass opening out on the eastern side. There were dark, rolling clouds overhead, and in the air the heavy, oppressive sense of thunder. It seemed as though the mountain range had separated two atmospheres, and that now we had got into the thunderous one. I was now myself looking out for the conveyance which was to take me to the Count. There was on the road no sign of a vehicle. The passengers drew back with a sigh of gladness, which seemed to mock my own disappointment. I was already thinking what I had best do, when the driver, looking at his watch, said to the others something which I could hardly hear, it was spoken so quietly and in so low a tone, I thought it was "An hour less than the time." Then turning to me, he spoke in German worse than my own.

"There is no carriage here. The Herr is not expected after all. He will now come on to Bukovina, and return tomorrow or the next day, better the next day." Whilst he was speaking the horses began to neigh and snort and plunge wildly, so that the driver had to hold them up. Then, amongst a chorus of screams from the peasants and a universal crossing of themselves, a caleche, with four horses, drove up behind us, overtook us, and drew up beside the coach. I could see from the flash of our lamps as the rays fell on them, that the horses were coal-black and splendid animals. They were driven by a tall man, with a long brown beard and a great black hat, which seemed to hide his face from us. I could only see the gleam of a pair of very bright eyes, which seemed red in the lamplight, as he turned to us.

He said to the driver, "You are early tonight, my friend."

The man stammered in reply, "The English Herr was in a hurry."

"That is why, I suppose, you wished him to go on to Bukovina. You cannot deceive me, my friend. I know too much, and my horses are swift."

As he spoke he smiled, and the lamplight fell on a hardlooking mouth, with very red lips and sharp-looking teeth, as white as ivory. One of my companions whispered to another the line from Burger's "Lenore".

"Denn die Todten reiten Schnell." ("For the dead travel fast.")

The strange driver evidently heard the words, for he looked up with a gleaming smile. The passenger turned his face away, at the same time putting out his two fingers and crossing himself. "Give me the Herr's luggage," said the driver, and with exceeding alacrity my bags were handed out and put in the caleche. Then I descended from the side of the coach, as the caleche was close alongside, the driver helping me with a hand which caught my arm in a grip of steel. His strength must have been prodigious.

Without a word he shook his reins, the horses turned, and we swept into the darkness of the pass. As I looked back I saw the figures of my late companions crossing themselves. Then the driver cracked his whip and called to his horses, and off they swept on their way to Bukovina. As they sank into the darkness I felt a strange chill, and a lonely feeling come over me. But a cloak was thrown over my shoulders, and a rug across my knees, and the driver said in excellent German--

"The night is chill, mein Herr, and my master the Count bade me take all care of you. There is a flask of slivovitz (the plum brandy of the country) underneath the seat, if you should require it."

I did not take any. I felt a little strangely, and not a little frightened. The carriage went at a hard pace straight along, then we made a complete turn and went along another straight road. It seemed to me that we were simply going over and over the same ground again, and so I took note of some salient point, and found that this was so. I would have liked to have asked the driver what this all meant, but I really feared to do so.

I struck a match, and by its flame looked at my watch. It was within a few minutes of midnight. This gave me a sort of shock, for I suppose the general superstition about midnight was increased by my recent experiences. I waited with a sick feeling of suspense.

Then a dog began to howl somewhere in a farmhouse far down the road, a long, agonized wailing, as if from fear. The sound was taken up by another dog, and then another and another, till, borne on the wind which now sighed softly through the Pass, a wild howling began, which seemed to come from all over the country, as far as the imagination could grasp it through the gloom of the night.

At the first howl the horses began to strain and rear, but the driver spoke to them soothingly, and they quieted down, but shivered and sweated as though after a runaway from sudden fright. Then, far off in the distance, from the mountains on each side of us began a louder and a sharper howling, that of wolves, which affected both the horses and myself in the same way. For I was minded to jump from the caleche and run, whilst they reared again and plunged madly, so that the driver had to use all his great strength to keep them from bolting. In a few minutes, however, my own ears got accustomed to the sound, and the horses so far became quiet that the driver was able to descend and to stand before them.

He petted and soothed them, and whispered something in their ears, as I have heard of horse-tamers doing, and with extraordinary effect, for under his caresses they became quite manageable again, though they still trembled. The driver again took his seat, and shaking his reins, started off at a great pace. This time, after going to the far side of the Pass, he suddenly turned down a narrow roadway which ran sharply to the right.

Soon we were hemmed in with trees, which in places arched right over the roadway till we passed as through a tunnel. It grew colder and colder still, and fine, powdery snow began to fall. The baying of the wolves sounded nearer and nearer, as though they were closing round on us from every side. I grew dreadfully afraid, and the horses shared my fear. The driver, however, was not in the least disturbed. He kept turning his head to left and right, but I could not see anything through the darkness.

Suddenly, away on our left I saw a fain flickering blue flame. The driver saw it at the same moment. He at once checked the horses, and, jumping to the ground, disappeared into the darkness. I did not know what to do, as the wolves grew closer. But while I wondered, the driver suddenly appeared again, and without a word took his seat, and we resumed our journey. I think I must have fallen asleep and kept dreaming of the incident, for it seemed to be repeated endlessly, and now looking back, it is like a sort of awful nightmare. Once the flame appeared so near the road, that even in the darkness around us I could watch the driver's motions. He went rapidly to where the blue flame arose, and gathering a few stones, formed them into some device.

Once there appeared a strange optical effect. When he stood between me and the flame he did not obstruct it, for I could see its ghostly flicker all the same. Then for a time there were no blue flames, and we sped onwards through the gloom, with the howling of the wolves around us, as though they were following in a moving circle.

At last there came a time when the driver went further afield than he had yet gone, and during his absence, the horses began to tremble worse than ever and to snort and scream with fright. I could not see any cause for it, for the howling of the wolves had ceased altogether. But just then the moon, sailing through the black clouds, appeared, and by its light I saw around us a ring of wolves, with white teeth and lolling red tongues, with long, sinewy limbs and shaggy hair. They were a hundred times more terrible in the grim silence which held them than even when they howled. For myself, I felt a sort of paralysis of fear.

All at once the wolves began to howl as though the moonlight had had some peculiar effect on them. The horses jumped about and reared, and looked helplessly round with eyes that rolled in a way painful to see. I called to the coachman to come. I shouted and beat the side of the caleche, hoping by the noise to scare the wolves. How he came there, I know not, but I heard his voice raised in a tone of imperious command, and looking towards the sound, saw him stand in the roadway. As he swept his long arms, as though brushing aside some impalpable obstacle, the wolves fell back and back further still. Just then a heavy cloud passed across the face of the moon, so that we were again in darkness.

When I could see again the driver was climbing into the caleche, and the wolves disappeared. I was afraid to speak or move. The time seemed interminable as we swept on our way, now in almost complete darkness, for the rolling clouds obscured the moon.

We kept on ascending. Suddenly, the driver was in the act of pulling up the horses in the courtyard of a vast ruined castle, from whose tall black windows came no ray of light, and whose broken battlements showed a jagged line against the sky.

Jonathan Harker's Journal Continued, 5 May

I must have been asleep, for certainly if I had been fully awake I must have noticed the approach of such a remarkable place. In the gloom the courtyard looked of considerable size, as several dark ways led from it under great round arches. I have not yet been able to see it by daylight.

When the caleche stopped, the driver jumped down and held out his hand to assist me to alight. Again I could not but notice his prodigious strength. His hand actually seemed like a steel vice. Then he took my traps, and placed them on the ground beside me as I stood close to a great door, old and studded with large iron nails, and set in a projecting doorway of massive stone. The stone was massively carved, but worn by time and weather. As I stood, the driver jumped again into his seat and shook the reins. The horses started forward, and trap and all disappeared down one of the dark openings.

I stood in silence where I was, for I did not know what to do. Of bell or knocker there was no sign. Through these frowning walls and dark window openings it was not likely that my voice could penetrate. The time I waited seemed endless, and I felt doubts and fears crowding upon me. What sort of place had I come to, and among what kind of people? Was this a customary incident in the life of a solicitor's clerk sent out to explain the purchase of a London estate to a foreigner? Solicitor's clerk! Mina would not like that. Solicitor, for just before leaving London I got word that my examination was successful, and I am now a full-blown solicitor! All I could do now was to be patient, and to wait the coming of morning.

Just as I had come to this conclusion I heard a heavy step approaching behind the great door, and saw through the chinks the gleam of a coming light. Then there was the sound of rattling chains and the clanking of massive bolts drawn back. A key was turned with the loud grating noise of long disuse, and the great door swung back.

Within, stood a tall old man, clean shaven save for a long white moustache, and clad in black from head to foot, without a single speck of colour about him anywhere. He held in his hand an antique silver lamp, in which the flame burned without a chimney or globe of any kind, throwing long quivering shadows as it flickered in the draught of the open door. The old man motioned me in with his right hand with a courtly gesture, saying in excellent English, but with a strange intonation.

"Welcome to my house! Enter freely and of your own free will!" He made no motion of stepping to meet me, but stood like a statue. The instant, however, that I had stepped over the threshold, he moved impulsively forward, and holding out his hand grasped mine with a strength which made me wince, an effect which was not lessened by the fact that it seemed cold as ice, more like the hand of a dead than a living man. Again he said.

"Welcome to my house! Enter freely. Go safely, and leave something of the happiness you bring!" The strength of the handshake was so much akin to the driver, whose face I had not seen, that for a moment I doubted if it were not the same person to whom I was speaking. So to make sure, I said interrogatively, "Count Dracula?"

He bowed in a courtly way as he replied, "I am Dracula, and I bid you welcome, Mr. Harker, to my house. Come in, the night air is chill, and you must need to eat and rest." As he was speaking, he put the lamp on a bracket on the wall, and stepping out, took my luggage. He had carried it in before I could forestall him. I protested, but he insisted.

"Nay, sir, you are my guest. It is late, and my people are not available. Let me see to your comfort myself." He insisted on carrying my traps along the passage, and then up a great winding stair, and along another great passage, on whose stone floor our steps rang heavily. At the end of this he threw open a heavy door, and I rejoiced to see within a well-lit room in which a table was spread for supper, and on whose mighty hearth a great fire of logs, freshly replenished, flamed and flared.

The Count halted, putting down my bags, closed the door, and crossing the room, opened another door, which led into a small octagonal room lit by a single lamp, and seemingly without a window of any sort. Passing through this, he opened another door, and motioned me to enter. It was a welcome sight. For here was a great bedroom well lighted and warmed with another log fire, also added to but lately, for the top logs were fresh, which sent a hollow roar up the wide chimney. The Count himself left my luggage inside and withdrew, saying, before he closed the door.

"You will need, after your journey, to refresh yourself. I trust you will find all you wish. When you are ready, come into the other room, where you will find your supper prepared."

The light and warmth and the Count's courteous welcome seemed to have dissipated all my doubts and fears. I discovered that I was half famished with hunger. I went into the other room.

I found supper already laid out. My host, who stood on one side of the great fireplace, leaning against the stonework, made a graceful wave of his hand to the table, and said,

"I pray you, be seated and sup how you please. You will I trust, excuse me that I do not join you, but I have dined already, and I do not sup."

I handed to him the sealed letter which Mr. Hawkins had entrusted to me. He opened it and read it gravely. Then, with a charming smile, he handed it to me to read. One passage of it, at least, gave me a thrill of pleasure.

"I must regret that an attack of gout forbids absolutely any travelling on my part for some time to come. But I am happy to say I can send a sufficient substitute, one in whom I have every possible confidence. He is a young man, full of energy and talent in his own way, and of a very faithful disposition. He is discreet and silent, and has grown into manhood in my service. He shall be ready to attend on you when you will during his stay, and shall take your instructions in all matters."

The count himself came forward and took off the cover of a dish, and I fell to at once on an excellent roast chicken. This, with some cheese and a salad and a bottle of old tokay, of which I had two glasses, was my supper. During the time I was eating it the Count asked me many question as to my journey, and I told him by degrees all I had experienced.

By this time I had finished my supper, and by my host's desire had drawn up a chair by the fire and begun to smoke a cigar which he offered me, at the same time excusing himself that he did not smoke. I had now an opportunity of observing him, and found him of a very marked physiognomy.

His face was a strong, aquiline, with high bridge of the thin nose and peculiarly arched nostrils, with lofty domed forehead, and hair growing scantily round the temples but profusely elsewhere. His eyebrows were very massive, almost meeting over the nose, and with bushy hair that seemed to curl in its own profusion. The mouth, so far as I could see it under the heavy moustache, was fixed and rather cruel-looking, with peculiarly sharp white teeth. These protruded over the lips, whose remarkable ruddiness showed astonishing vitality in a man of his years. For the rest, his ears were pale, and at the tops extremely pointed. The chin was broad and strong, and the cheeks firm though thin. The general effect was one of extraordinary pallor.

Hitherto I had noticed the backs of his hands as they lay on his knees in the firelight, and they had seemed rather white and fine. But seeing them now close to me, I could not but notice that they were rather coarse, broad, with squat fingers. Strange to say, there were hairs in the centre of the palm. The nails were long and fine, and cut to a sharp point. As the Count leaned over me and his hands touched me, I could not repress a shudder. It may have been that his breath was rank, but a horrible feeling of nausea came over me, which, do what I would, I could not conceal.

The Count, evidently noticing it, drew back. And with a grim sort of smile, which showed more than he had yet done his protruberant teeth, sat himself down again on his own side of the fireplace. We were both silent for a while, and as I looked towards the window I saw the first dim streak of the coming dawn. There seemed a strange stillness over everything. But as I listened, I heard as if from down below in the valley the howling of many wolves. The Count's eyes gleamed, and he said.

"Listen to them, the children of the night. What music they make!" Seeing, I suppose, some expression in my face strange to him, he added, "Ah, sir, you dwellers in the city cannot enter into the feelings of the hunter." Then he rose and said.

"But you must be tired. Your bedroom is all ready, and tomorrow you shall sleep as late as you will. I have to be away till the afternoon, so sleep well and dream well!" With a courteous bow, he opened for me himself the door to the octagonal room, and I entered my bedroom.

I am all in a sea of wonders. I doubt. I fear. I think strange things, which I dare not confess to my own soul. God keep me, if only for the sake of those dear to me!

7 May.--It is again early morning, but I have rested and enjoyed the last twenty-four hours. I slept till late in the day. When I had dressed myself I went into the room where we had supped, and found a cold breakfast laid out, with coffee kept hot by the pot being placed on the hearth. There was a card on the table, on which was written--

"I have to be absent for a while. Do not wait for me. D." I set to and enjoyed a hearty meal. When I had done, I looked for a bell, so that I might let the servants know I had finished, but I could not find one. There are certainly odd deficiencies in the house, considering the extraordinary evidences of wealth which are round me. The table service is of gold. The curtains and upholstery of the chairs and sofas and the hangings of my bed are of the costliest and most beautiful fabrics, and must have been of fabulous value when they were made, for they are centuries old, though in excellent order. I saw something like them in Hampton Court, but they were worn and frayed and moth-eaten. But still in none of the rooms is there a mirror. There is not even a toilet glass on my table, and I had to get the little shaving glass from my bag before I could either shave or brush my hair. I have not yet seen a servant anywhere, or heard a sound near the castle except the howling of wolves. Some time after I had finished my meal, I do not know whether to call it breakfast of dinner, for it was between five and six o'clock when I had it, I looked about for something to read, for I did not like to go about the castle until I had asked the Count's permission. I opened another door in the room and found a sort of library. The door opposite mine I tried, but found locked.

In the library I found, to my great delight, a vast number of English books, whole shelves full of them, and bound volumes of magazines and newspapers. A table in the center was littered with English magazines and newspapers, though none of them were of very recent date. The books were of the most varied kind, history, geography, politics, political economy, botany, geology, law, all relating to England and English life and customs and manners. There were even such books of reference as the London Directory, the "Red" and "Blue" books, Whitaker's Almanac, the Army and Navy Lists, and it somehow gladdened my heart to see it, the Law List.

Whilst I was looking at the books, the door opened, and the Count entered. He saluted me in a hearty way, and hoped that I had had a good night's rest. Then he went on.

"I am glad you found your way in here. These companions," and he laid his hand on some of the books, "have been good friends to me, and for some years past, ever since I had the idea of going to London, have given me many, many hours of pleasure. Through them I have come to know your great England, and to know her is to love her. I long to go through the crowded streets of your mighty London, to be in the midst of the whirl and rush of humanity, to share its life, its change, its death, and all that makes it what it is. But alas! As yet I only know your tongue through books. To you, my friend, I look that I know it to speak."

"But, Count," I said, "You know and speak English thoroughly!" He bowed gravely.

"I thank you, my friend, for your all too-flattering estimate, but yet I fear that I am but a little way on the road I would travel. True, I know the grammar and the words, but yet I know not how to speak them.

"Indeed," I said, "You speak excellently."

"Not so," he answered. "Did I move and speak in your London, none there are who would not know me for a stranger. That is not enough for me. Here I am noble. I am a Boyar. The common people know me, and I am master. But a stranger in a strange land, he is no one. You come to me not alone as agent of my friend Peter Hawkins, of Exeter, to tell me all about my new estate in London. You shall, I trust, rest here with me a while, so that by our talking I may learn the English intonation. And I would that you tell me when I make error, even of the smallest, in my speaking. I am sorry that I had to be away so long today, but you will, I know forgive one who has so many important affairs in hand." Of course I said all I could about being willing, and asked if I might come into that room when I chose. He answered, "Yes, certainly," and added.

"You may go anywhere you wish in the castle, except where the doors are locked, where of course you will not wish to go. There is reason, and did you see with my eyes and know with my knowledge, you would perhaps better understand." I said I was sure of this, and then he went on.

"We are in Transylvania, and Transylvania is not England. Our ways are not your ways, and there shall be to you many strange things. Nay, from what you have told me of your experiences already, you know something of what strange things there may be."

This led to much conversation, and I asked him many questions regarding things that had already happened to me or come within my notice. Sometimes he sheered off the subject, or turned the conversation by pretending not to understand, but generally he answered all I asked most frankly. Then I asked him why the coachman went to the places where he had seen the blue flames. He then explained to me that it was commonly believed that on a certain night of the year, last night, in fact, when all evil spirits are supposed to have unchecked sway, a blue flame is seen over any place where treasure has been concealed.

"That treasure has been hidden," he went on, "in the region through which you came last night, there can be but little doubt. For it was the ground fought over for centuries by the Wallachian, the Saxon, and the Turk. Why, there is hardly a foot of soil in all this region that has not been enriched by the blood of men, patriots or invaders. In the old days there were stirring times, when the Austrian and the Hungarian came up in hordes."

"But how," said I, "can it have remained so long undiscovered, when there is a sure index to it if men will but take the trouble to look?" The Count smiled, and as his lips ran back over his gums, the long, sharp, canine teeth showed out strangely. He answered.

"Because your peasant is at heart a coward and a fool! Those flames only appear on one night, and on that night no man of this land will, if he can help it, stir without his doors. And, dear sir, even if he did he would not know what to do. Why, even the peasant that you tell me of who marked the place of the flame would not know where to look in daylight even for his own work. Even you would not, I dare be sworn, be able to find these places again?"

"There you are right," I said. "I know no more than the dead where even to look for them." Then we drifted into other matters.

"Come," he said at last, "tell me of London and of the house which you have procured for me." With an apology for my remissness, I went into my own room to get the papers from my bag. Whilst I was placing them in order I heard a rattling of china and silver in the next room, and as I passed through, noticed that the table had been cleared and the lamp lit, for it was by this time deep into the dark. The lamps were also lit in the study or library, and I found the Count lying on the sofa, reading, of all things in the world, English Bradshaw's Guide. When I came in he cleared the books and papers from the table, and with him I went into plans and deeds and figures of all sorts. He was interested in everything, and asked me a myriad questions about the place and its surroundings. He clearly had studied beforehand all he could get on the subject of the neighborhood, for he evidently at the end knew very much more than I did. When I remarked this, he answered.

"Well, but, my friend, is it not needful that I should? When I go there I shall be all alone, and my friend Harker Jonathan, nay, pardon me. I fall into my country's habit of putting your patronymic first, my friend Jonathan Harker will not be by my side to correct and aid me. He will be in Exeter, miles away, probably working at papers of the law with my other friend, Peter Hawkins. So!"

We went thoroughly into the business of the purchase of the estate at Purfleet. When I had told him the facts and got his signature to the necessary papers, and had written a letter with them ready to post to Mr. Hawkins, he began to ask me how I had come across so suitable a place. I read to him the notes which I had made at the time, and which I inscribe here.

"At Purfleet, on a by-road, I came across just such a place as seemed to be required, and where was displayed a dilapidated notice that the place was for sale. It was surrounded by a high wall, of ancient structure, built of heavy stones, and has not been repaired for a large number of years. The closed gates are of heavy old oak and iron, all eaten with rust.

"The estate is called Carfax. It contains in all some twenty acres, quite surrounded by the solid stone wall above mentioned. There are many trees on it, and a small lake, evidently fed by some springs. The house is very large and of all periods back, I should say, to mediaeval times, for one part is of stone immensely thick, with only a few windows high up and heavily barred with iron. It looks like part of a keep, and is close to an old chapel or church. I could not enter it. There are but few houses close at hand, one being a very large house only recently added to and formed into a private lunatic asylum. It is not, however, visible from the grounds."

When I had finished, he said, "I am glad that it is old and big. I myself am of an old family, and to live in a new house would kill me. I rejoice also that there is a chapel of old times. We Transylvanian nobles love not to think that our bones may lie amongst the common dead. I seek not gaiety nor mirth. I love the shade and the shadow, and would be alone with my thoughts when I may." Somehow his words and his look did not seem to accord, or else it was that his cast of face made his smile look malignant and saturnine.

Presently, with an excuse, he left me, asking me to pull my papers together. He was some little time away, and I began to look at some of the books around me. One was an atlas, which I found opened naturally to England, as if that map had been much used. On looking at it I found in certain places little rings marked, and on examining these I noticed that one was near London on the east side, manifestly where his new estate was situated. The other two were Exeter, and Whitby on the Yorkshire coast.

It was the better part of an hour when the Count returned. "Aha!" he said. "Still at your books? Good! But you must not work always. Come! I am informed that your supper is ready." He took my arm, and we went into the next room, where I found an excellent supper ready on the table. The Count again excused himself, as he had dined out on his being away from home. But he sat as on the previous night, and chatted whilst I ate. After supper I smoked, as on the last evening, and the Count stayed with me, chatting and asking questions on every conceivable subject, hour after hour. I felt that it was getting very late indeed, but I did not say anything, for I felt under obligation to meet my host's wishes in every way. I was not sleepy, as the long sleep yesterday had fortified me, but I could not help experiencing that chill which comes over one at the coming of the dawn, which is like, in its way, the turn of the tide. They say that people who are near death die generally at the change to dawn or at the turn of the tide. Anyone who has experienced this change in the atmosphere can well believe it. All at once we heard the crow of the cock coming up with preternatural shrillness through the clear morning air.

Count Dracula, jumping to his feet, said, "Why there is the morning again! How remiss I am to let you stay up so long. You must make your conversation regarding my dear new country of England less interesting, so that I may not forget how time flies by us," and with a courtly bow, he quickly left me.

I went into my room and drew the curtains, but there was little to notice. My window opened into the courtyard, all I could see was the warm grey of quickening sky. So I pulled the curtains again, and have written of this day.

8 May.--There is something so strange about this place and all in it that I cannot but feel uneasy. I wish I had never come. It may be that this strange night existence is telling on me, but would that that were all! If there were any one to talk to I could bear it, but there is no one. I have

only the Count to speak with, and he-- I fear I am myself the only living soul within the place.

I only slept a few hours when I went to bed, and feeling that I could not sleep any more, got up. I had hung my shaving glass by the window, and was just beginning to shave. Suddenly I felt a hand on my shoulder, and heard the Count's voice saying to me, "Good morning." I started, for it amazed me that I had not seen him, since the reflection of the glass covered the whole room behind me. In starting I had cut myself slightly, but did not notice it at the moment. Having answered the Count's salutation, I turned to the glass again to see how I had been mistaken. This time there could be no error, for the man was close to me, and I could see him over my shoulder. But there was no reflection of him in the mirror! The whole room behind me was displayed, but there was no sign of a man in it, except myself.

This was startling, and coming on the top of so many strange things, was beginning to increase that vague feeling of uneasiness which I always have when the Count is near. But at the instant I saw the cut had bled a little, and the blood was trickling over my chin. When the Count saw my face, his eyes blazed with a sort of demoniac fury, and he suddenly made a grab at my throat. I drew away and his hand touched the string of beads which held the crucifix. It made an instant change in him, for the fury passed so quickly that I could hardly believe that it was ever there.

"Take care," he said, "take care how you cut yourself. It is more dangerous that you think in this country." Then seizing the shaving glass, he went on, "And this is the wretched thing that has done the mischief. It is a foul bauble of man's vanity. Away with it!" And opening the window with one wrench of his terrible hand, he flung out the glass, which was shattered into a thousand pieces on the stones of the courtyard far below. Then he withdrew without a word.

When I went into the dining room, breakfast was prepared, but I could not find the Count anywhere. So I breakfasted alone. It is strange that as yet I have not seen the Count eat or drink. He must be a very peculiar man! After breakfast I did a little exploring in the castle. I went out on the stairs, and found a room looking towards the South.

The view was magnificent, and from where I stood there was every opportunity of seeing it. The castle is on the very edge of a terrific precipice. A stone falling from the window would fall a thousand feet without touching anything! As far as the eye can reach is a sea of green tree tops, with occasionally a deep rift where there is a chasm. Here and there are silver threads where the rivers wind in deep gorges through the forests.

When I had seen the view I explored further. Doors, doors, doors everywhere, and all locked and bolted. In no place save from the windows in the castle walls is there an available exit. The castle is a veritable prison, and I am a prisoner!

Jonathan Harker's Journal Continued

When I found that I was a prisoner a sort of wild feeling came over me. I rushed up and down the stairs, trying every door and peering out of every window I could find, but after a little the conviction of my helplessness overpowered all other feelings. I behaved much as a rat does in a trap. When, however, the conviction had come to me that I was helpless I sat down quietly, as quietly as I have ever done anything in my life, and began to think over what was best to be done. I am thinking still, and as yet have come to no definite conclusion. Of one thing only am I certain. That it is no use making my ideas known to the Count. He would only deceive me if I trusted him fully with the facts. So far as I can see, my only plan will be to keep my knowledge and my fears to myself, and my eyes open. I am, I know, either being deceived, like a baby, by my own fears, or else I am in desperate straits, and if the latter be so, I need, and shall need, all my brains to get through.

I heard the great door below shut, and knew that the Count had returned. I went cautiously to my own room and found him making the bed. This was odd, but only confirmed that there are no servants in the house. When later I saw him through the chink of the hinges of the door laying the table in the dining room, I was assured of it. For if he does himself all these menial offices, surely it is proof that there is no one else in the castle, it must have been the Count himself who was the driver of the coach that brought me here. This is a terrible thought, for if so, what does it mean that he could control the wolves, as he did, by only holding up his hand for silence? How was it that all the people at Bistritz and on the coach had some terrible fear for me? What meant the giving of the crucifix, of the garlic, of the wild rose, of the mountain ash?

Bless that good, good woman who hung the crucifix round my neck! It is odd that a thing which I have been taught to regard with disfavour and as idolatrous should in a time of loneliness and trouble be of help. Is it that there is something in the essence of the thing itself, or that it is a medium, a tangible help, in conveying memories of sympathy and comfort? I must find out all I can about Count Dracula, as it may help me to understand. Tonight he may talk of himself, if I turn the conversation that way. I must be very careful, however, not to awake his suspicion.

Midnight.--I have had a long talk with the Count. I asked him a few questions on Transylvania history, and he warmed up to the subject wonderfully. In his speaking of things and people, and especially of battles, he spoke as if he had been present at them all. This he afterwards explained by saying that to a Boyar the pride of his house and name is his own pride, that their glory is his glory, that their fate is his fate. Whenever he spoke of his house he always said "we", and spoke almost in the plural, like a king speaking. It seemed to have in it a whole history of the country. He grew excited as he spoke, and walked about the room pulling his great white moustache. One thing he said which I shall put down as nearly as I can, for it tells in its way the story of his race.

"We Szekelys have a right to be proud, for in our veins flows the blood of many brave races who fought as the lion fights, for lordship." He held up his arms. "Is it a wonder that we were a conquering race, that we were proud, that when the Magyar, the Lombard, the Avar, the Bulgar, or the Turk poured his thousands on our frontiers, we drove them back? Was it not this Dracula, indeed, who inspired that other of his race who in a later age again and again brought his forces over the great river into Turkeyland, who, when he was beaten back, came again, and again, though he had to come alone from the bloody field where his troops were being slaughtered, since he knew that he alone could ultimately triumph! Bah! What good are peasants without a leader? Where ends the war without a brain and heart to conduct it? Ah, young sir, the Szekelys, and the Dracula as their heart's blood, their brains, and their swords, can boast a record that mushroom growths like the Hapsburgs and the Romanoffs can never reach. The warlike days are over. Blood is too precious a thing in these days of dishonourable peace, and the glories of the great races are as a tale that is told."

It was by this time close on morning, and we went to bed. (Mem., this diary seems horribly like the beginning of the "Arabian Nights," for everything has to break off at cockcrow, or like the ghost of Hamlet's father.)

12 May.--Let me begin with facts. I must not confuse them with experiences which will have to rest on my own observation, or my memory of them. Last evening when the Count came from his room he began by asking me questions on legal matters and on the doing of certain kinds of business. There was a certain method in the Count's inquiries, so I shall try to put them down in sequence. The knowledge may somehow or some time be useful to me.

First, he asked if a man in England might have two solicitors or more. I told him he might have a dozen if he wished. I asked to explain more fully.

"I shall illustrate. Now, suppose I, who have much of affairs, wish to ship goods, say, to Newcastle, or Durham, or Harwich, or Dover, might it not be that it could with more ease be done by consigning to one in these ports?"

I answered that certainly it would be most easy, but that we solicitors had a system of agency one for the other, so that local work could be done locally on instruction from any solicitor, so that the client, simply placing himself in the hands of one man, could have his wishes carried out by him without further trouble.

"But," said he, "I could be at liberty to direct myself. Is it not so?"

"Of course," I replied, and "Such is often done by men of business, who do not like the whole of their affairs to be known by any one person."

"Good!" he said, and then went on to ask about the means of making consignments and the forms to be gone through. I explained all these things to him to the best of my ability, and he certainly left me under the impression that he would have made a wonderful solicitor, for there was nothing that he did not think of or foresee. His knowledge and acumen were wonderful. When he had satisfied himself on these points of which he had spoken, and I had verified all as well as I could by the books available, he suddenly stood up and said, "Have you written since your first letter to our friend Mr. Peter Hawkins, or to any other?"

I answered that I had not, that as yet I had not seen any opportunity of sending letters to anybody.

"Then write now, my young friend," he said, laying a heavy hand on my shoulder, "write to our friend and to any other, and say, if it will please you, that you shall stay with me until a month from now."

"Do you wish me to stay so long?" I asked, for my heart grew cold at the thought.

"I desire it much, nay I will take no refusal."

What could I do but bow acceptance? It was Mr. Hawkins' interest and besides, while Count Dracula was speaking, there was that in his eyes and in his bearing which made me remember that I was a prisoner, and that if I wished it I could have no choice. The Count saw his victory in my bow, and his mastery in the trouble of my face, for he began at once to use them, but in his own smooth, resistless way.

"I pray you, my good young friend, that you will not discourse of things other than business in your letters. It will doubtless please your friends to know that you are well, and that you look forward to getting home to them. Is it not so?" As he spoke he handed me three sheets of note paper and three envelopes. They were all of the thinnest foreign post, and looking at them, then at him, and noticing his quiet smile, with the sharp, canine teeth lying over the red underlip, I understood as well as if he had spoken that I should be more careful what I wrote, for he would be able to read it. So I determined to write only formal notes now, but to write fully to Mr. Hawkins in secret, and also to Mina, for to her I could write shorthand, which would puzzle the Count, if he did see it. When I had written my two letters the Count wrote several notes. Then he took up my two and placed them with his own, and put by his writing materials, after which, the instant the door had closed behind him, I leaned over and looked at the letters, which were face down on the table. I felt no compunction in doing so for under the circumstances I felt that I should protect myself in every way I could.

One of the letters was directed to Samuel F. Billington, No. 7, The Crescent, Whitby, another to Herr Leutner, Varna. The third was to Coutts & Co., London, and the fourth to Herren Klopstock & Billreuth, bankers, Buda Pesth. The second and fourth were unsealed. I was just about to look at them when I saw the door handle move. I sank back in my seat, having just had time to resume my book before the Count, holding still another letter in his hand, entered the room. He took up the letters on the table and stamped them carefully, and then turning to me, said,

"I trust you will forgive me, but I have much work to do in private this evening. You will, I hope, find all things as you wish." At the door he turned, and after a moment's pause said, "Let me advise you, my dear young friend. Nay, let me warn you with all seriousness, that should you leave these rooms you will not by any chance go to sleep in any other part of the castle. It is old, and has many memories, and there are bad dreams for those who sleep unwisely. Be warned! But if you be not careful in this respect, then," He finished his speech in a gruesome way, for he motioned with his hands as if he were washing them. I quite understood. My only doubt was as to whether any dream could be more terrible than the unnatural, horrible net of gloom and mystery which seemed closing around me.

Later.--I endorse the last words written, but this time there is no doubt in question. I shall not fear to sleep in any place where he is not. I have placed the crucifix over the head of my bed, I imagine that my rest is thus freer from dreams, and there it shall remain.

When he left me I went to my room. After a little while, not hearing any sound, I came out and went up the stone stair to where I could look out towards the South. There was some sense of freedom in the vast expanse, inaccessible though it was to me, as compared with the narrow darkness of the courtyard. Looking out on this, I felt that I was indeed in prison, and I seemed to want a breath of fresh air, though it were of the night. I am beginning to feel this nocturnal existence tell on me. It is destroying my nerve. I start at my own shadow, and am full of all sorts of horrible imaginings. God knows that there is ground for my terrible fear in this accursed place! I looked out over the beautiful expanse, bathed in soft yellow moonlight till it was almost as light as day. In the soft light the distant hills became melted, and the shadows in the valleys and gorges of velvety blackness. The mere beauty seemed to cheer me. There was peace and comfort in every breath I drew. As I leaned from the window my eye was caught by something moving a storey below me, and somewhat to my left, where I imagined, from the order of the rooms, that the windows of the Count's own room would look out. The window at which I stood was tall and deep, stone-mullioned, and though weatherworn, was still complete. But it was evidently many a day since the case had been there. I drew back behind the stonework, and looked carefully out.

What I saw was the Count's head coming out from the window. I did not see the face, but I knew the man by the neck and the movement of his back and arms. In any case I could not mistake the hands which I had had some many opportunities of studying. I was at first interested and somewhat amused. But my very feelings changed to repulsion and terror when I saw the whole man slowly emerge from the window and begin to crawl down the castle wall over the dreadful abyss, face down with his cloak spreading out around him like great wings. At first I could not believe my eyes. I thought it was some trick of the moonlight, some weird effect of shadow, but I kept looking, and it could be no delusion. I saw the fingers and toes grasp the corners of the stones, worn clear of the mortar by the stress of years, and by thus using every projection and inequality move downwards with considerable speed, just as a lizard moves along a wall.

What manner of man is this, or what manner of creature, is it in the semblance of man? I feel the dread of this horrible place overpowering me. I am in fear, in awful fear, and there is no escape for me. I am encompassed about with terrors that I dare not think of.

15 May.--Once more I have seen the count go out in his lizard fashion. He moved downwards in a sidelong way, some hundred feet down, and a good deal to the left. He vanished into some hole or window. When his head had disappeared, I leaned out to try and see more, but without avail. I knew he had left the castle now, and thought to use the opportunity to explore. I went back to the room, and taking a lamp, tried all the doors. They were all locked, as I had expected, and the locks were comparatively new. But I went down the stone stairs to the hall where I had entered originally. I found I could pull back the bolts

easily enough and unhook the great chains. But the door was locked, and the key was gone! That key must be in the Count's room. I must watch should his door be unlocked, so that I may get it and escape. I went on to make a thorough examination of the various stairs and passages, and to try the doors that opened from them. One or two small rooms near the hall were open, but there was nothing to see in them except old furniture, dusty with age and moth-eaten. At last, however, I found one door at the top of the stairway which, though it seemed locked, gave a little under pressure. I exerted myself, and with many efforts forced it back so that I could enter. I was now in a wing of the castle further to the right than the rooms I knew and a storey lower down. The castle was built on the corner of a great rock, so that on three sides it was quite impregnable, and great windows were placed here where sling, or bow, or culverin could not reach, and consequently light and comfort, were secured. To the west was a great valley, and great jagged mountain fastnesses. This was evidently the portion of the castle occupied by the ladies in bygone days, for the furniture had more an air of comfort than any I had seen.

The windows were curtainless, and the yellow moonlight, flooding in through the diamond panes, enabled one to see the wealth of dust which lay over all and disguised in some measure the ravages of time and moth. My lamp seemed to be of little effect in the brilliant moonlight, but I was glad to have it with me, for there was a dread loneliness in the place which chilled my heart and made my nerves tremble. Still, it was better than living alone in the rooms which I had come to hate from the presence of the Count, and after trying a little to school my nerves, I found a soft quietude come over me. Here I am, sitting at a little oak table where in old times possibly some fair lady sat to pen, and writing in my diary in shorthand all that has happened since I closed it last. It is the nineteenth century up-to-date with a vengeance. And yet, unless my senses deceive me, the old centuries had, and have, powers of their own which mere "modernity" cannot kill.

Later: The morning of 16 May.--God preserve my sanity, for to this I am reduced. Whilst I live on here there is but one thing to hope for, that I may not go mad, if, indeed, I be not mad already. If I be sane, then surely it is maddening to think that of all the foul things that lurk in this hateful place the Count is the least dreadful to me, that to him alone I can look for safety, even though this be only whilst I can serve his purpose. Great God! I begin to get new lights on certain things which have puzzled me.

The Count's mysterious warning frightened me at the time.

When I had written in my diary and had fortunately replaced the book and pen in my pocket I felt sleepy. The Count's warning came into my mind, but I took pleasure in disobeying it. The sense of sleep was upon me. I determined not to return tonight to the gloom-haunted rooms, but to sleep here, where, of old, ladies had sat and sung and lived sweet lives whilst their gentle breasts were sad for their menfolk away in the midst of remorseless wars. I drew a great couch out of its place near the corner. I suppose I must have fallen asleep. I hope so, but I fear, for all that followed was startlingly real, so real that now sitting here in the broad, full sunlight of the morning, I cannot in the least believe that it was all sleep.

I was not alone. The room was the same, unchanged in any way since I came into it. I could see along the floor, in the brilliant moonlight, my own footsteps marked where I had disturbed the long accumulation of dust. In the moonlight opposite me were three young women, ladies by their dress and manner. I thought at the time that I must be dreaming when I saw them, they threw no shadow on the floor. They came close to me, and looked at me for some time, and then whispered together. Two were dark, and had high aquiline noses, like the Count, and great dark, piercing eyes, that seemed to be almost red when contrasted with the pale yellow moon. The other was fair, as fair as can be, with great masses of golden hair and eyes like pale sapphires. I seemed somehow to know her face, and to know it in connection with some dreamy fear, but I could not recollect at the moment how or where. All three had brilliant white teeth that shone like pearls against the ruby of their voluptuous lips. There was something about them that made me uneasy, some longing and at the same time some deadly fear. I felt in my heart a wicked, burning desire that they would kiss me with those red lips. It is not good to note this down, lest some day it should meet Mina's eyes and cause her pain, but it is the truth. They whispered together, and then they all three laughed, such a silvery, musical laugh, but as hard as though the sound never could have come through the softness of human lips. It was like the intolerable, tingling sweetness of waterglasses when played on by a cunning hand. The fair girl shook her head coquettishly, and the other two urged her on.

One said, "Go on! You are first, and we shall follow. Yours' is the right to begin."

The other added, "He is young and strong. There are kisses for us all."

I lay quiet, looking out from under my eyelashes in an agony of delightful anticipation. The fair girl advanced and bent over me till I could feel the movement of her breath upon me. Sweet it was in one sense, honey-sweet, and sent the same tingling through the nerves as her voice, but with a bitter underlying the sweet, a bitter offensiveness, as one smells in blood.

I was afraid to raise my eyelids, but looked out and saw perfectly under the lashes. The girl went on her knees, and bent over me, simply gloating. There was a deliberate voluptuousness which was both thrilling and repulsive, and as she arched her neck she actually licked her lips like an animal, till I could see in the moonlight the moisture shining on the scarlet lips and on the red tongue as it lapped the white sharp teeth. Lower and lower went her head as the lips went below the range of my mouth and chin and seemed to fasten on my throat. Then she paused, and I could hear the churning sound of her tongue as it licked her teeth and lips, and I could feel the hot breath on my neck. Then the skin of my throat began to tingle. I could feel the soft, shivering touch of the lips on the super sensitive skin of my throat, and the hard dents of two sharp teeth, just touching and pausing there. I closed my eyes in languorous ecstasy and waited, waited with beating heart.

But at that instant, another sensation swept through me as quick as lightning. I was conscious of the presence of the Count, and of his being as if lapped in a storm of fury. As my eyes opened involuntarily I saw his strong hand grasp the slender neck of the fair woman and with giant's power draw it back, the blue eyes transformed with fury, the white teeth champing with rage, and the fair cheeks blazing red with passion. But the Count! Never did I imagine such wrath and fury, even to the demons of the pit. His eyes were positively blazing. The red light in them was lurid, as if the flames of hell fire blazed behind them. His face was deathly pale, and the lines of it were hard like drawn wires. The thick eyebrows that met over the nose now seemed like a heaving bar of white-hot metal. With a fierce sweep of his arm, he hurled the woman from him, and then motioned to the others, as though he were beating them back. It was the same imperious gesture that I had seen used to the wolves. In a voice which, though low and almost in a whisper seemed to cut through the air and then ring in the room he said,

"How dare you touch him, any of you? How dare you cast eyes on him when I had forbidden it? Back, I tell you all! This man belongs to me!"

The fair girl, with a laugh of ribald coquetry, turned to answer him. "You yourself never loved! You never love!" On this the other women joined, and such a mirthless, hard, soulless laughter rang through the room that it almost made me faint to hear. It seemed like the pleasure of fiends.

Then the Count turned, after looking at my face attentively, and said in a soft whisper, "Yes, I too can love. You yourselves can tell it from the past. Is it not so? Well, now I promise you that when I am done with him you shall kiss him at your will. Now go! Go! I must awaken him, for there is work to be done."

"Are we to have nothing tonight?" said one of them, with a low laugh, as she pointed to the bag which he had thrown upon the floor, and which moved as though there were some living thing within it. For answer he nodded his head. One of the women jumped forward and opened it. If my ears did not deceive me there was a gasp and a low wail, as of a half smothered child. The women closed round, whilst I was aghast with horror. But as I looked, they disappeared, and with them the dreadful bag. There was no door near them, and they could not have passed me without my noticing. They simply seemed to fade into the rays of the moonlight and pass out through the window, for I could see outside the dim, shadowy forms for a moment before they entirely faded away.

Then the horror overcame me, and I sank down unconscious.

Jonathan Harker's Journal Continued

I awoke in my own bed. If it be that I had not dreamt, the Count must have carried me here. My clothes were folded and laid by in a manner which was not my habit. My watch was still unwound. But these things are no proof, for they may have been evidences that my mind was not as usual, and I had certainly been much upset. I must watch for proof. Of one thing I am glad. If it was that the Count carried me here and undressed me, he must have been hurried in his task, for my pockets are intact. I am sure this diary would have been a mystery to him which he would not have brooked. He would have taken or destroyed it. As I look around this room, it is now a sort of sanctuary, for nothing can be more dreadful than those awful women, who were, who are, waiting to suck my blood.

18 May.--I have been down to look at that room again in daylight, for I must know the truth. When I got to the doorway at the top of the stairs I found it closed. It had been so forcibly driven against the jamb that part of the woodwork was splintered. I could see that the bolt of the lock had not been shot, but the door is fastened from the inside. I fear it was no dream.

19 May.--Last night the Count asked me in the sauvest tones to write three letters, one saying that my work here was nearly done, and that I should start for home within a few days, another that I was starting on the next morning from the time of the letter, and the third that I had left the castle and arrived at Bistritz. I would fain have rebelled, but felt that in the present state of things it would be madness to quarrel openly with the Count whilst I am so absolutely in his power. And to refuse would be to excite his suspicion and to arouse his anger. He knows that I know too much, and that I must not live, lest I be dangerous to him. My only chance is to prolong my opportunities. Something may occur which will give me a chance to escape. I saw in his eyes something of that gathering wrath which was manifest when he hurled that fair woman from him. He explained to me that posts were few and uncertain, and that my writing now would ensure ease of mind to my friends. To oppose him would have been to create new suspicion. I therefore pretended to fall in with his views, and asked him what dates I should put on the letters.

He calculated a minute, and then said, "The first should be June 12,the second June 19,and the third June 29."

I know now the span of my life. God help me!

28 May.--There is a chance of escape, or at any rate of being able to send word home. A band of Szgany have come to the castle, and are encamped in the courtyard. These are gipsies. They are peculiar to this part of the world, though allied to the ordinary gipsies all the world over. There are thousands of them in Hungary and Transylvania, who are almost outside all law. They attach themselves as a rule to some great noble or boyar, and call themselves by his name. They are fearless and without religion, save superstition, and they talk only their own varieties of the Romany tongue.

I shall write some letters home, and shall try to get them to have them posted. I have already spoken to them through my window to begin acquaintanceship. They took their hats off and made obeisance and many signs, which however, I could not understand any more than I could their spoken language . . .

I have written the letters. Mina's is in shorthand, and I simply ask Mr. Hawkins to communicate with her. To her I have explained my situation, but without the horrors which I may only surmise. It would shock and frighten her to death were I to expose my heart to her. Should the letters not carry, then the Count shall not yet know my secret or the extent of my knowledge . . .

I have given the letters. I threw them through the bars of my window with a gold piece, and made what signs I could to have them posted. The man who took them pressed them to his heart and bowed, and then put them in his cap.

The Count has come. He sat down beside me, and said in his smoothest voice as he opened two letters, "The Szgany has given me these, of which, though I know not whence they come, I shall, of course, take care. See!"--He must have looked at it.--"One is from you, and to my friend Peter Hawkins. The other,"--here he caught sight of the strange symbols as he opened the envelope, and the dark look came into his face, and his eyes blazed wickedly,--"The other is a vile thing, an outrage upon friendship and hospitality! It is not signed. Well! So it cannot matter to us." And he calmly held letter and envelope in the flame of the lamp till they were consumed.

Then he went on, "The letter to Hawkins, that I shall, of course send on, since it is yours. Your letters are sacred to me. Your pardon, my friend, that unknowingly I did break the seal. Will you not cover it again?" He held out the letter to me, and with a courteous bow handed me a clean envelope.

I could only redirect it and hand it to him in silence. When he went out of the room I could hear the key turn softly. A minute later I went over and tried it, and the door was locked.

When, an hour or two after, the Count came quietly into the room, his coming awakened me, for I had gone to sleep on the sofa. He was very courteous and very cheery in his manner, and seeing that I had been sleeping, he said, "So, my friend, you are tired? Get to bed. I may not have the pleasure of talk tonight, since there are many labours to me, but you will sleep, I pray."

I passed to my room and went to bed, and, strange to say, slept without dreaming. Despair has its own calms.

31 May.--This morning when I woke I thought I would provide myself with some papers and envelopes from my bag and keep them in my pocket, so that I might write in case I should get an opportunity, but again a surprise, again a shock!

Every scrap of paper was gone, and with it all my notes, my memoranda, relating to railways and travel, my letter of credit, in fact all that might be useful to me were I once outside the castle. I sat and pondered awhile, and then I made search of the wardrobe where I had placed my clothes.

The suit in which I had travelled was gone, and also my overcoat and rug. I could find no trace of them anywhere. This looked like some new scheme of villainy . . .

17 June.--This morning, as I was sitting on the edge of my bed cudgelling my brains, I heard without a crackling of whips and pounding and scraping of horses' feet up the rocky path beyond the courtyard. With joy I hurried to the window, and saw drive into the yard two great leiter-wagons, each drawn by eight sturdy horses, and at the head of each pair a Slovak, with his wide hat, great nail-studded belt, dirty sheepskin, and high boots. They had also their long staves in hand. I ran to the door, intending to descend and try and join them. Again a shock, my door was fastened on the outside.

Then I ran to the window and cried to them. They looked up at me stupidly and pointed, but just then the "hetman" of the Szgany came out, and seeing them pointing to my window, said something, at which they laughed.

Henceforth no effort of mine, no piteous cry or agonized entreaty, would make them even look at me. They resolutely turned away. The leiter-wagons contained great, square, empty, boxes, with handles of thick rope.

When they were all unloaded and packed in a great heap in one corner of the yard, the Slovaks were given some money by the Szgany, and spitting on it for luck, lazily went each to his horse's head. Shortly afterwards, I heard the crackling of their whips die away in the distance.

24 June.--Last night the Count left me early, and locked himself into his own room. As soon as I dared I ran up the winding stair, and looked out of the window, which opened South. I thought I would watch for the Count, for there is something going on. The Szgany are quartered somewhere in the castle and are doing work of some kind. I hear a far-away muffled sound as of mattock and spade, and, whatever it is, it must be the end of some ruthless villainy.

I had been at the window somewhat less than half an hour, when I saw something coming out of the Count's window. I drew back and watched carefully, and saw the whole man emerge. It was a new shock to me to find that he had on the suit of clothes which I had worn whilst travelling here, and slung over his shoulder the terrible bag which I had seen the women take away. This, then, is his new scheme of evil, that he will allow others to see me, as they think, so that he may both leave evidence that I have been seen in the towns or villages posting my own letters, and that any wickedness which he may do shall by the local people be attributed to me.

It makes me rage to think that this can go on.

I thought I would watch for the Count's return, and for a long time sat doggedly at the window. Then I began to notice that there were some quaint little specks floating in the rays of the moonlight. They were like the tiniest grains of dust, and they whirled round and gathered in clusters in a nebulous sort of way. I watched them with a sense of soothing, and a sort of calm stole over me. I leaned back in the embrasure in a more comfortable position, so that I could enjoy more fully the aerial gambolling.

Something made me start up, a low, piteous howling of dogs somewhere far below in the valley, which was hidden from my sight. Louder it seemed to ring in my ears, and the floating moats of dust to take new shapes to the sound as they danced in the moonlight. I felt myself struggling to awake to some call of my instincts. Nay, my very soul was struggling, and my half-remembered sensibilities were striving to answer the call. I was becoming hypnotised!

Quicker and quicker danced the dust. The moonbeams seemed to quiver as they went by me into the mass of gloom beyond. More and more they gathered till they seemed to take dim phantom shapes. And then I started, broad awake and in full possession of my senses, and ran screaming from the place.

The phantom shapes, which were becoming gradually materialised from the moonbeams, were those three ghostly women to whom I was doomed.

I fled, and felt somewhat safer in my own room, where there was no moonlight, and where the lamp was burning brightly.

When a couple of hours had passed I heard something stirring in the Count's room, something like a sharp wail quickly suppressed. And then there was silence, deep, awful silence, which chilled me. With a beating heart, I tried the door, but I was locked in my prison, and could do nothing. I sat down and simply cried.

As I sat I heard a sound in the courtyard, the agonised cry of a woman. I rushed to the window, and throwing it up, peered between the bars.

There, indeed, was a woman with dishevelled hair, holding her hands over her heart as one distressed with running. She was leaning against the corner of the gateway. When she saw my face at the window she threw herself forward, and shouted in a voice laden with menace, "Monster, give me my child!"

She threw herself on her knees, and raising up her hands, cried the same words in tones which wrung my heart. Then she tore her hair and beat her breast, and abandoned herself to all the violences of extravagant emotion. Finally, she threw herself forward, and though I could not see her, I could hear the beating of her naked hands against the door.

Somewhere high overhead, probably on the tower, I heard the voice of the Count calling in his harsh, metallic whisper. His call seemed to be answered from far and wide by the howling of wolves. Before many minutes had passed a pack of them poured, like a pent-up dam when liberated, through the wide entrance into the courtyard.

There was no cry from the woman, and the howling of the wolves was but short. Before long they streamed away singly, licking their lips.

I could not pity her, for I knew now what had become of her child, and she was better dead.

What shall I do? What can I do? How can I escape from this dreadful thing of night, gloom, and fear?

25 June.--No man knows till he has suffered from the night how sweet and dear to his heart and eye the morning can be. My fear fell from me as if it had been a vaporous garment which dissolved in the warmth.

I must take action of some sort whilst the courage of the day is upon me. Last night one of my post-dated letters went to post, the first of that fatal series which is to blot out the very traces of my existence from the earth.

Let me not think of it. Action!

It has always been at night-time that I have been molested or threatened, or in some way in danger or in fear. I have not yet seen the Count in the daylight. Can it be that he sleeps when others wake, that he may be awake whilst they sleep? If I could only get into his room! But there is no possible way. The door is always locked, no way for me.

Yes, there is a way, if one dares to take it. I have seen him myself crawl from his window. Why should not I imitate him, and go in by his window? The chances are desperate, but my need is more desperate still. I shall risk it. At the worst it can only be death, and a man's death is not a calf's, and the dreaded Hereafter may still be open to me. God help me in my task! Goodbye, Mina, if I fail. Goodbye, my faithful friend and second father. Goodbye, all, and last of all Mina!

Same day, later.--I have made the effort, and God helping me, have come safely back to this room. I went whilst my courage was fresh straight to the window on the south side, and at once got outside on this side. The stones are big and roughly cut, and the mortar has by process of time been washed away between them. I took off my boots, and ventured out on the desperate way. I looked down once, so as to make sure that a sudden glimpse of the awful depth would not overcome me, but after that kept my eyes away from it. I know pretty well the direction and distance of the Count's window. I did not feel dizzy, I suppose I was too excited, and the time seemed ridiculously short till I found myself standing on the window sill and trying to raise up the sash. I was filled with agitation, however, when I bent down and slid feet foremost in through the window. Then I looked around for the Count, but with surprise and gladness, made a discovery. The room was empty! It was barely furnished with odd things, which seemed to have never been used.

The furniture was something the same style as that in the south rooms, and was covered with dust. I looked for the key, but it was not in the lock, and I could not find it anywhere. The only thing I found was a great heap of gold in one corner, gold of all kinds, Roman, and British, and Austrian, and Hungarian, and Greek and Turkish money, covered with a film of dust, as though it had lain long in the ground. None of it that I noticed was less than three hundred years old. There were also chains and ornaments, some jewelled, but all of them old and stained.

At one corner of the room was a heavy door. It was open, and led through a stone passage to a circular stairway, which went steeply down.

I descended, minding carefully where I went for the stairs were dark, being only lit by loopholes in the heavy masonry. At the bottom there was a dark, tunnel-like passage, through which came a deathly, sickly odour, the odour of old earth newly turned. As I went through the passage the smell grew closer and heavier. At last I pulled open a heavy door which stood ajar, and found myself in an old ruined chapel, which had evidently been used as a graveyard. The roof was broken, and in two places were steps leading to vaults, but the ground had recently been dug over, and the earth placed in great wooden boxes, manifestly those which had been brought by the Slovaks.

There was nobody about, and I made a search over every inch of the ground. I went down even into the vaults, where the dim light struggled, although to do so was a dread to my very soul. Into two of these I went, but saw nothing except fragments of old coffins and piles of dust. In the third, however, I made a discovery.

There, in one of the great boxes, of which there were fifty in all, on a pile of newly dug earth, lay the Count! He was either dead or asleep. I could not say which, for eyes were open and stony, but without the glassiness of death, and the cheeks had the warmth of life through all their pallor. The lips were as red as ever. But there was no sign of movement, no pulse, no breath, no beating of the heart.

I bent over him, and tried to find any sign of life, but in vain. He could not have lain there long, for the earthy smell would have passed away in a few hours. By the side of the box was its cover, pierced with holes here and there. I thought he might have the keys on him, but when I went to search I saw the dead eyes, and in them dead though they were, such a look of hate, though unconscious of me or my presence, that I fled from the place, and leaving the Count's room by the window, crawled again up the castle wall. Regaining my room, I threw myself panting upon the bed and tried to think.

29 June.--Today is the date of my last letter, and the Count has taken steps to prove that it was genuine, for again I saw him leave the castle by the same window, and in my clothes. As he went down the wall, lizard fashion, I wished I had a gun or some lethal weapon, that I might destroy him. But I fear that no weapon wrought along by man's hand would have any effect on him. I dared not wait to see him return, for I feared to see those weird sisters. I came back to the library, and read there till I fell asleep.

I was awakened by the Count, who looked at me as grimly as a man could look as he said, "Tomorrow, my friend, we must part. You return to your beautiful England, I to some work which may have such an end that we may never meet. Your letter home has been despatched. Tomorrow I shall not be here, but all shall be ready for your journey. In the morning come the Szgany, who have some labours of their own here, and also come some Slovaks. When they have gone, my carriage shall come for you, and shall bear you to the Borgo Pass to meet the diligence from Bukovina to Bistritz. But I am in hopes that I shall see more of you at Castle Dracula."

I suspected him, and determined to test his sincerity. Sincerity! It seems like a profanation of the word to write it in connection with such a monster, so I asked him pointblank, "Why may I not go tonight?"

"Because, dear sir, my coachman and horses are away on a mission."

"But I would walk with pleasure. I want to get away at once."

He smiled, such a soft, smooth, diabolical smile that I knew there was some trick behind his smoothness. He said, "And your baggage?"

"I do not care about it. I can send for it some other time."

The Count stood up, and said, with a sweet courtesy which made me rub my eyes, it seemed so real, "You English have a saying which is close to my heart, for its spirit is that which rules our boyars, `Welcome the coming, speed the parting guest.' Come with me, my dear young friend. Not an hour shall you wait in my house against your will, though sad am I at your going, and that you so suddenly desire it. Come!" With a stately gravity, he, with the lamp, preceded me down the stairs and along the hall. Suddenly he stopped. "Hark!"

Close at hand came the howling of many wolves. It was almost as if the sound sprang up at the rising of his hand, just as the music of a great orchestra seems to leap under the baton of the conductor. After a pause of a moment, he proceeded, in his stately way, to the door, drew back the ponderous bolts, unhooked the heavy chains, and began to draw it open.

To my intense astonishment I saw that it was unlocked. Suspiciously, I looked all round, but could see no key of any kind.

As the door began to open, the howling of the wolves without grew louder and angrier. Their red jaws, with champing teeth, and their blunt-clawed feet as they leaped, came in through the opening door. I knew than that to struggle at the moment against the Count was useless. With such allies as these at his command, I could do nothing.

But still the door continued slowly to open, and only the Count's body stood in the gap. Suddenly it struck me that this might be the moment and means of my doom. I was to be given to the wolves, and at my own instigation. There was a diabolical wickedness in the idea great enough for the Count, and as the last chance I cried out, "Shut the door! I shall wait till morning." And I covered my face with my hands to hide my tears of bitter disappointment.

With one sweep of his powerful arm, the Count threw the door shut, and the great bolts clanged and echoed through the hall as they shot back into their places.

In silence we returned to the library, and after a minute or two I went to my own room. The last I saw of Count Dracula was his kissing his hand to me, with a red light of triumph in his eyes, and with a smile that Judas in hell might be proud of.

When I was in my room and about to lie down, I thought I heard a whispering at my door. I went to it softly and listened. Unless my ears deceived me, I heard the voice of the Count.

"Back! Back to your own place! Your time is not yet come. Wait! Have patience! Tonight is mine. Tomorrow night is yours!"

There was a low, sweet ripple of laughter, and in a rage I threw open the door, and saw without the three terrible women licking their lips. As I appeared, they all joined in a horrible laugh, and ran away.

I came back to my room and threw myself on my knees. It is then so near the end? Tomorrow! Tomorrow! Lord, help me, and those to whom I am dear!

30 June.--These may be the last words I ever write in this diary. I slept till just before the dawn, and when I woke threw myself on my knees, for I determined that if Death came he should find me ready.

At last I felt that subtle change in the air, and knew that the morning had come. Then came the welcome cock-crow, and I felt that I was safe. With a glad heart, I opened the door and ran down the hall. I had seen that the door was unlocked, and now escape was before me. With hands that trembled with eagerness, I unhooked the chains and threw back the massive bolts.

But the door would not move. Despair seized me. I pulled and pulled at the door, and shook it till, massive as it was, it rattled in its casement. I could see the bolt shot. It had been locked after I left the Count.

Then a wild desire took me to obtain the key at any risk, and I determined then and there to scale the wall again, and gain the Count's room. He might kill me, but death now seemed the happier choice of evils. Without a pause I rushed up to the east window, and scrambled down the wall, as before, into the Count's room. It was empty, but that was as I expected. I could not see a key anywhere, but the heap of gold remained. I went through the door in the corner and down the winding stair and along the dark passage to the old chapel. I knew now well enough where to find the monster I sought.

The great box was in the same place, close against the wall, but the lid was laid on it, not fastened down, but with the nails ready in their places to be hammered home.

I knew I must reach the body for the key, so I raised the lid, and laid it back against the wall. And then I saw something which filled my very soul with horror. There lay the Count, but looking as if his youth had been half restored. For the white hair and moustache were changed to dark irongrey. The cheeks were fuller, and the white skin seemed ruby-red underneath. The mouth was redder than ever, for on the lips were gouts of fresh blood, which trickled from the corners of the mouth and ran down over the chin and neck. Even the deep, burning eyes seemed set amongst swollen flesh, for the lids and pouches underneath were bloated. It seemed as if the whole awful creature were simply gorged with blood. He lay like a filthy leech, exhausted with his repletion.

I shuddered as I bent over to touch him, and every sense in me revolted at the contact, but I had to search, or I was lost. The coming night might see my own body a banquet in a similar war to those horrid three. I felt all over the body, but no sign could I find of the key. Then I stopped and looked at the Count. There was a mocking smile on the bloated face which seemed to drive me mad. This was the being I was helping to transfer to London, where, perhaps, for centuries to come he might, amongst its teeming millions, satiate his lust for blood, and create a new and ever-widening circle of semi-demons to batten on the helpless.

The very thought drove me mad. A terrible desire came upon me to rid the world of such a monster. There was no lethal weapon at hand, but I seized a shovel which the workmen had been using to fill the cases, and lifting it high, struck, with the edge downward, at the hateful face. But as I did so the head turned, and the eyes fell upon me, with all their blaze of basilisk horror. The sight seemed to paralyze me, and the shovel turned in my hand and glanced from the face, merely making a deep gash above the forehead. The shovel fell from my hand across the box, and as I pulled it away the flange of the blade caught the edge of the lid which fell over again, and hid the horrid thing from my sight. The last glimpse I had was of the bloated face, blood-stained and fixed with a grin of malice which would have held its own in the nethermost hell. I thought and thought what should be my next move, but my brain seemed on fire, and I waited with a despairing feeling growing over me. As I waited I heard in the distance a gipsy song sung by merry voices coming closer, and through their song the rolling of heavy wheels and the cracking of whips. The Szgany and the Slovaks of whom the Count had spoken were coming. With a last look around and at the box which contained the vile body, I ran from the place and gained the Count's room, determined to rush out at the moment the door should be opened. With strained ears, I listened, and heard downstairs the grinding of the key in the great lock and the falling back of the heavy door. There must have been some other means of entry, or some one had a key for one of the locked doors.

Then there came the sound of many feet tramping and dying away in some passage which sent up a clanging echo. I turned to run down again towards the vault, where I might find the new entrance, but at the moment there seemed to come a violent puff of wind, and the door to the winding stair blew to with a shock that set the dust from the lintels flying. When I ran to push it open, I found that it was hopelessly fast. I was again a prisoner, and the net of doom was closing round me more closely.

As I write there is in the passage below a sound of many tramping feet and the crash of weights being set down heavily, doubtless the boxes, with their freight of earth. There was a sound of hammering. It is the box being nailed down. Now I can hear the heavy feet tramping again along the hall, with many other idle feet coming behind them.

The door is shut, the chains rattle. There is a grinding of the key in the lock. I can hear the key withdrawn, then another door opens and shuts. I hear the creaking of lock and bolt.

Hark! In the courtyard and down the rocky way the roll of heavy wheels, the crack of whips, and the chorus of the Szgany as they pass into the distance.

I am alone in the castle with those horrible women. Faugh! Mina is a woman, and there is nought in common. They are devils of the Pit!

I shall not remain alone with them. I shall try to scale the castle wall farther than I have yet attempted. I shall take some of the gold with me, lest I want it later. I may find a way from this dreadful place.

And then away for home! Away to the quickest and nearest train! Away from the cursed spot, from this cursed land, where the devil and his children still walk with earthly feet!

At least God's mercy is better than that of those monsters, and the precipice is steep and high. At its foot a man may sleep, as a man. Goodbye, all. Mina!

Letter From Miss Mina Murray To Miss Lucy Westenra, 9 May

My dearest Lucy,

Forgive my long delay in writing, but I have been simply overwhelmed with work. The life of an assistant schoolmistress is sometimes trying. I am longing to be with you, and by the sea, where we can talk together freely and build our castles in the air. I have been working very hard lately, because I want to keep up with Jonathan's studies. When we are married I shall be able to be useful to Jonathan, and if I can stenograph well enough I can take down what he wants to say in this way and write it out for him on the typewriter, at which also I am practicing very hard.

When I am with you I shall keep a diary. I shall try to do what I see lady journalists do. I am told that, with a little practice, one can remember all that goes on or that one hears said during a day.

However, we shall see. I have just had a few hurried lines from Jonathan from Transylvania. He is well, and will be returning in about a week. It must be nice to see strange countries. I wonder if we, I mean Jonathan and I, shall ever see them together. There is the ten o'clock bell ringing. Goodbye. Your loving Mina

You have not told me anything for a long time. I hear rumours, and especially of a tall, handsome, curly-haired man.???

LETTER, LUCY WESTENRA TO MINA MURRAY

17, Chatham Street

Wednesday

My dearest Mina,

I must say you tax me very unfairly with being a bad correspondent. I wrote you twice since we parted, and your last letter was only your second. Besides, I have nothing to tell you.

As to the tall, curly-haired man, I suppose it was the one who was with me at the last Pop. Someone has evidently been telling tales.

That was Mr. Holmwood. He often comes to see us, and he and Mamma get on very well together.

We met some time ago a man that would just do for you, if you were not already engaged to Jonathan. He is an excellant parti, being handsome, well off, and of good birth. He is a doctor and really clever. Just fancy! He is only nine-and twenty, and he has an immense lunatic asylum all under his own care. Mr. Holmwood introduced him to me, and he called here to see us, and often comes now. I think he is one of the most resolute men I ever saw, and yet the most calm. He has a curious habit of looking one straight in the face, as if trying to read one's thoughts. He tries this on very much with me.

Do you ever try to read your own face? I do, and I can tell you it is not a bad study.

I do not, as you know, take sufficient interest in dress to be able to describe the new fashions. Dress is a bore. That is slang again, but never mind. Arthur says that every day.

There, it is all out, Mina, we have told all our secrets to each other since we were children. We have slept together and eaten together, and laughed and cried together, and now, though I have spoken, I would like to speak more. Oh, Mina, couldn't you guess? I love him. I am blushing as I write, for although I think he loves me, he has not told me so in words. But, oh, Mina, I love him.

I wish I were with you, dear, sitting by the fire undressing, and I would try to tell you what I feel. I am afraid to stop, or I should tear up the letter. Let me hear from you at once, and tell me all that you think about it. Mina, pray for my happiness.

Lucy

P. S.--I need not tell you this is a secret. Goodnight again. L.

LETTER, LUCY WESTENRA TO MINA MURRAY
24 May
My dearest Mina,

Thanks, and thanks, and thanks again for your sweet letter. My dear, it never rains but it pours. Here am I, who shall be twenty in September, and yet I never had a proposal till today, not a real proposal, and today I had three. Just fancy! Three proposals in one day! Isn't it awful! I feel sorry for two of the poor fellows. Oh, Mina, I am so happy that I don't know what to do with myself. For goodness' sake, don't tell any of the girls, or they would be getting all sorts of extravagant ideas. Some girls are so vain! But you must keep it a secret, dear, from every one except, of course, Jonathan. A woman ought to tell her husband everything. Don't you think so, dear? And I must be fair. And women, I am afraid, are not always quite as fair as they should be.

Well, my dear, number One came just before lunch. I told you of him, Dr. John Seward, the lunatic asylum man, with the strong jaw and the good forehead. He was very cool outwardly, but was nervous all the same. He had evidently been schooling himself as to all sorts of little things, and remembered them, but he almost managed to sit down on his silk hat. He told me how dear I was to him. And then, Mina, I felt a sort of duty to tell him that there was some one.

Evening.

Arthur has just gone, so I can go on telling you about the day.

Well, my dear, number Two came after lunch. He is such a nice fellow, and American from Texas, and he looks so young and so fresh that it seems almost impossible that he has been to so many places and has such adventures.

Mr. Quincy P. Morris found me alone. It seems that a man always does find a girl alone.

He took my hand in his and began pouring out a perfect torrent of lovemaking, laying his very heart and soul at my feet. I suppose he saw something in my face which checked him, for he suddenly stopped, and said with a sort of manly fervour that I could have loved him for if I had been free...

I burst into tears, I am afraid, my dear, you will think this a very sloppy letter in more ways than one, and I really felt very badly.

Why can't they let a girl marry three men, or as many as want her, and save all this trouble? I was able to look into Mr. Morris' brave eyes, and I told him out straight . . .

"Yes, there is some one I love." I was right to speak to him so frankly, he put out both his hands and took mine, I think I put them into his, and said in a hearty way . . .

"Little girl, your honesty and pluck have made me a friend, and that's rarer than a lover, it's more selfish anyhow. Won't you give me one kiss?"

That quite won me, Mina, so I leant over and kissed him.

My dear, this quite upset me, and I feel I cannot write of happiness just at once, after telling you of it, and I don't wish to tell of the number Three until it can be all happy. Ever your loving . . . Lucy

P. S.--Oh, about number Three, I needn't tell you of number Three, need I? Besides, it was all so confused. It seemed only a moment from his coming into the room till both his arms were round me, and he was kissing me. I am very, very happy, and I don't know what I have done to deserve it. I must only try in the future to show that I am not ungrateful to God for all His goodness to me in sending to me such a lover, such a husband, and such a friend.

Goodbye.

DR. SEWARD'S DIARY (Kept in phonograph)

25 May.--Cannot eat, cannot rest, so diary instead. since my rebuff of yesterday I have a sort of empty feeling. Nothing in the world seems to be worth the doing. As I knew that the only cure for this sort of thing was work, I went amongst the patients. I picked out one who has afforded me a study of much interest. I am determined to understand

him as well as I can. Today I seemed to get nearer than ever before to the heart of his mystery.

I questioned him more fully than I had ever done, with a view to making myself master of the facts of his hallucination. In my manner of doing it there was, I now see, something of cruelty. I seemed to wish to keep him to the point of his madness, a thing which I avoid with the patients as I would the mouth of hell.

Hell has its price!

R. M, Renfield, age 59. Sanguine temperament, great physical strength, morbidly excitable, periods of gloom, ending in some fixed idea which I cannot make out. I presume that the sanguine temperament itself and the disturbing influence end in a mentally-accomplished finish, a possibly dangerous man.

LETTER, QUINCEY P. MORRIS TO HON. ARTHUR HOLMOOD
25 May.
My dear Art,

We've told yarns by the campfire in the prairies, and dressed one another's wounds after trying a landing at the Marquesas, and drunk healths on the shore of Titicaca. Won't you let this be at my campfire tomorrow night? I have no hesitation in asking you, as I know a certain lady is engaged to a certain dinner party, and that you are free. There will only be one other, our old pal at the Korea, Jack Seward. He's coming, too, and we both want to mingle our weeps over the wine cup, and to drink a health with all our hearts to the happiest man in all the wide world, who has won the noblest heart that God has made and best worth winning. We promise you a hearty welcome, and a loving greeting, and a health as true as your own right hand. Come!

Yours, as ever and always,
Quincey P. Morris

TELEGRAM FROM ARTHUR HOLMWOOD TO QUINCEY P. MORRIS
26 May

Count me in every time. I bear messages which will make both your ears tingle. Art

Mina Murray's Journal, 24 July

Whitby.--Lucy met me at the station, looking sweeter and lovlier than ever, and we drove up to the house at the Crescent in which they have rooms. This is a lovely place. The little river, the Esk, runs through a deep valley. Right over the town is the ruin of Whitby Abbey. It is a most noble ruin, of immense size, and full of beautiful and romantic bits. Between it and the town there is a big graveyard, all full of tombstones.

There are walks, with seats beside them, through the churchyard, and people go and sit there all day long looking at the beautiful view and enjoying the breeze.

I am writing now, with my book on my knee, and listening to the talk of three old men who are sitting beside me. They seem to do nothing all day but sit here and talk.

The harbour lies below me, with, on the far side, one long granite wall stretching out into the sea, with a curve outwards at the end of it, in the middle of which is a lighthouse.

They have a legend here that when a ship is lost bells are heard out at sea. I must ask the old man about this. He is coming this way . . .

He is a funny old man. His face is gnarled and twisted like the bark of a tree. He tells me that he is nearly a hundred, and that he was a sailor in the Greenland fishing fleet when Waterloo was fought. He is, I am afraid, a very sceptical person, for when I asked him about the bells at sea and the White Lady at the abbey he said very brusquely,

"I wouldn't fash masel' about them, miss. I wonder masel' who'd be bothered tellin' lies to them, even the newspapers, which is full of fool-talk."

I thought he would be a good person to learn interesting things from, so I asked him if he would mind telling me something about the whale fishing in the old days. He was just settling himself to begin when the clock struck six, whereupon he laboured to get up, and said,

"I must gang ageeanwards home now, miss. My granddaughter doesn't like to be kept waitin' when the tea is ready."

He hobbled away down the steps. They lead from the town to the church, there are hundreds of them. I shall go home too.

1 August.--I came up here an hour ago with Lucy, and we had a most interesting talk with my old friend and the two others who always come and join him. He is evidently the Sir Oracle of them.

If he can't out-argue them he bullies them, and then takes their silence for agreement with his views.

Lucy was looking sweetly pretty in her white lawn frock. She has got a beautiful colour since she has been here.

The old men did not lose any time in coming and sitting near her when we sat down. She is so sweet with old people, I think they all fell in love with her on the spot. Even my old man succumbed and did not contradict her, but gave me double share instead. I got him on the subject of the legends.

"It be all fool-talk. These bans an' wafts is only fit to set dizzy women a'belderin'. It makes me ireful to think o' them. Why, it's them that, not content with printin' lies on paper an' preachin' them ou t of pulpits, does want to be cuttin' them on the tombstones. Lies all of them, nothin' but lies of one kind or another!"

I could see the old fellow was "showing off," so I put in a word to keep him going.

"Oh, Mr. Swales, you can't be serious. Surely these tombstones are not all wrong?"

"Yabblins! You come here a stranger, an' you see this kirkgarth."

I nodded, for I thought it better to assent, though I did not quite understand his dialect. I knew it had something to do with the church.

He went on, "And you consate that all these steans be aboon folk that be haped here, snod an' snog?" I assented again. "Then that be just where the lie comes in. Why, there be scores of these laybeds that be toom as old Dun's `baccabox on Friday night."

He nudged one of his companions, and they all laughed. "And, my gog! How could they be otherwise? Look at that one, read it!"

I went over and read, "Edward Spencelagh, master mariner, murdered by pirates off the coast of Andres, April, 1854, age 30." When I came back Mr. Swales went on,

"Who brought him home, I wonder? Why, I could name ye a dozen whose bones lie in the Greenland seas above," he pointed northwards.

"But," I said, "You start on the assumption that all the poor people, or their spirits, will have to take their tombstones with them on the Day of Judgment. Do you think that will be really necessary?"

"Well, what else be they tombstones for? Answer me that, miss!"

"To please their relatives, I suppose."

"To please their relatives, you suppose!" This he said with intense scorn. "How will it pleasure their relatives to know that lies is wrote over them, and that everybody in the place knows that they be lies?"

" There's the clock, and'I must gang. My service to ye, ladies!" And off he hobbled.

Lucy and I sat awhile, and it was all so beautiful before us that we took hands as we sat, and she told me all over again about Arthur and their coming marriage. That made me just a little heart-sick, for I haven't heard from Jonathan for a whole month.

The same day. I came up here alone, for I am very sad. There was no letter for me. I hope there cannot be anything the matter with Jonathan.

DR. SEWARD'S DIARY

5 June.--The case of Renfield grows more interesting the more I get to understand the man. He has certain qualities very largely developed, selfishness, secrecy, and purpose.

He seems to have some settled scheme of his own, but what it is I do not know. His redeeming quality is a love of animals, though, indeed, he has such curious turns in it that I sometimes imagine he is only abnormally cruel. His pets are of odd sorts.

Just now his hobby is catching flies. He has at present such a quantity that I have had myself to expostulate. To my astonishment, he did not break out into a fury, as I expected, but took the matter in simple seriousness. He thought for a moment, and then said, "May I have three days? I shall clear them away." Of course, I said that would do. I must watch him.

18 June.--He has turned his mind now to spiders, and has got several very big fellows in a box. He keeps feeding them his flies, and the number of the latter is becoming sensibly diminished, although he has used half his food in attracting more flies from outside to his room.

1 July.--His spiders are now becoming as great a nuisance as his flies, and today I told him that he must get rid of them.

He looked very sad at this, and I gave him the same time as before for reduction.

A horrid blowfly, bloated with some carrion food, buzzed into the room, he caught it, held it exultantly for a few moments between his finger and thumb, and before I knew what he was going to do, put it in his mouth and ate it.

I scolded him for it, but he argued quietly that it was very good and very wholesome, that it was life, strong life, and gave life to him. This gave me an idea, or the rudiment of one. I must watch how he gets rid of his spiders.

He has evidently some deep problem in his mind, for he keeps a little notebook in which he is always jotting down something.

8 July.--There is a method in his madness, and the rudimentary idea in my mind is growing. Oh, unconscious cerebration.

Things remain as they were except that he has parted with some of his pets and got a new one.

He has managed to get a sparrow, and has already partially tamed it.

19 July--My friend has now a whole colony of sparrows, and his flies and spiders are almost obliterated. When I came in he ran to me and said he wanted to ask me a great favour, a very, very great favour. He fawned on me like a dog.

I asked him what it was, and he said, with a sort of rapture in his voice and bearing, "A kitten, a nice, little, sleek playful kitten, that I can play with, and teach, and feed, and feed, and feed!"

I had noticed how his pets went on increasing in size and vivacity, but I did not care that his pretty family of tame sparrows should be wiped out in the same manner as the flies and spiders. So I said I would see about it, and asked him if he would not rather have a cat than a kitten.

His eagerness betrayed him as he answered, "Oh, yes, I would like a cat!"

I shook my head, and said that at present I feared it would not be possible. His face fell, and I could see a warning of danger in it, for there was a sudden fierce, sidelong look which meant killing. The man is an undeveloped homicidal maniac.

10 pm.--I have visited him again and found him sitting in a corner brooding. When I came in he threw himself on his knees before me and implored me to let him have a cat, that his salvation depended upon it.

I told him that he could not have it, whereupon he went without a word, and sat down, gnawing his fingers, in the corner where I had found him.

20 July.--Visited Renfield very early, before attendant went his rounds. Found him up and humming a tune. He was spreading out his sugar, which he had saved, in the window, and was manifestly beginning his fly catching again.

I looked around for his birds, and not seeing them, asked him where they were. He replied, without turning round, that they had all flown away. There were a few feathers about the room and on his pillow a drop of blood. I said nothing.

11 am.--The attendant has just been to see me to say that Renfield has been very sick and has disgorged a whole lot of feathers. "My belief is, doctor," he said, "that he has eaten his birds, and that he just took and ate them raw!"

11 pm.--I gave Renfield a strong opiate tonight, enough to make even him sleep, and took away his pocketbook to look at it.

My homicidal maniac is of a peculiar kind. I shall have to invent a new classification for him, and call him a zoophagous (life-eating) maniac. What he desires is to absorb as many lives as he can, in a cumulative way. He gave many flies to one spider and many spiders to one bird, and then wanted a cat to eat the many birds. What would have been his later steps?

It would almost be worth while to complete the experiment.

Had I even the secret of one such mind, I might advance my own branch of science to a pitch compared with which Burdon-Sanderson's physiology or Ferrier's brain knowledge would be as nothing. I must not think too much of this, or I may be tempted.

I wonder at how many lives he values a man, or if at only one.

Oh, Lucy, Lucy, I cannot be angry with you, nor can I be angry with my friend whose happiness is yours, but I must only wait on hopeless and work. Work! Work!

MINA MURRAY'S JOURNAL

26 July.--I am unhappy about Lucy and about Jonathan. I had not heard from Jonathan for some time, but yesterday dear Mr. Hawkins, who is always so kind, sent me a letter from him. It is from Castle Dracula, and says that he is just starting for home. That is not like Jonathan.

Then, too, Lucy has lately taken to her old habit of walking in her sleep. Her mother has spoken to me about it, and we have decided that I am to lock the door of our room every night.

Mrs. Westenra has got an idea that sleep-walkers always go out on roofs of houses and along the edges of cliffs and then get suddenly wakened and fall.

Poor dear, she is naturally anxious about Lucy, and she tells me that her husband, Lucy's father, had the same habit.

Lucy is to be married in the autumn, and she is already planning out her dresses and how her house is to be arranged. I sympathise with her, for I do the same, only Jonathan and I will start in life in a very simple way, and shall have to try to make both ends meet.

Mr. Holmwood, he is the Hon. Arthur Holmwood, only son of Lord Godalming, is coming as soon as he can leave town, for his father is not very well, and I think dear Lucy is counting the moments till he comes.

27 July.--No news from Jonathan. I am getting quite uneasy about him.

Lucy walks more than ever. I am getting nervous and wakeful myself. Mr. Holmwood has been suddenly called to Ring to see his father, who has been taken seriously ill. Lucy frets at the postponement of seeing him.

3 August.--Another week gone by, and no news from Jonathan, not even to Mr. Hawkins, from whom I have heard. Oh, I do hope he is not ill. He surely would have written. I look at that last letter of his, but somehow it does not satisfy me. It does not read like him, and yet it is his writing. There is no mistake of that.

Lucy has not walked much in her sleep the last week, but even in her sleep she seems to be watching me. She tries the door, and finding it locked, goes about the room searching for the key.

6 August.--Another three days, and no news. If I only knew where to write to or where to go to.

Lucy is more excitable than ever, but is otherwise well. The fishermen say that we are in for a storm. I must try to watch it and learn the weather signs.

Today is a gray day. The fishing boats are racing for home, and rise and dip in the ground swell as they sweep into the harbour. Here comes old Mr. Swales. I can see, by the way he lifts his hat, that he wants to talk.

I have been quite touched by the change in the poor old man. When he sat down beside me, he said in a very gentle way, "I want to say something to you, miss."

I could see he was not at ease, so I took his poor old wrinkled hand in mine.

He said, "I'm afraid, my deary, that I must have shocked you by all the wicked things I've been sayin' about the dead, and such like, for weeks past, but I didn't mean them, and I want ye to remember that when I'm gone. Some day soon the Angel of Death will sound his trumpet for me. But don't ye dooal an' greet, my deary!"--for he saw that I was crying-- "Look! Look!" he cried suddenly. "There's something in that wind and in the hoast beyont that sounds, and looks, and tastes, and smells like death. It's in the air. I feel it comin'." He held up his arms devoutly, and raised his hat. His mouth moved as though he were praying. After a few minutes' silence, he said good-bye, and hobbled off. It all touched me, and upset me very much.

I was glad when the coastguard came along. He stopped to talk with me, as he always does, but all the time kept looking at a strange ship.

"I can't make her out," he said. "She's a Russian, by the look of her. But she's knocking about in the queerest way. She seems to see the storm coming, but can't decide whether to run up north in the open, or to put in here. Look there again! She is steered mighty strangely, for she doesn't mind the hand on the wheel, changes about with every puff of wind. We'll hear more of her before this time tomorrow."

Cutting From "The Dailygraph," 8 August

(PASTED IN MINA MURRAY'S JOURNAL)
From a correspondent.
Whitby.

One of the greatest and suddenest storms on record has just been experienced here, with results both strange and unique. The day was unusually fine till the afternoon.

The coastguard on duty at once made report the coming of a sudden storm. The sun was marked by myriad clouds of every sunset colour, with masses of absolute blackness, in all sorts of shapes, as well outlined as colossal silhouettes.

More than one captain made up his mind that his `cobble' or his `mule' would remain in the harbour till the storm had passed. At midnight there was a dead calm, a sultry heat, and that prevailing intensity which affects persons of a sensitive nature.

The only sail noticeable was a foreign schooner with all sails set, which was seemingly going westwards. The foolhardiness or ignorance of her officers was a prolific theme for comment, and efforts were made to signal her to reduce sail in the face of her danger.

A little after midnight came a strange sound from over the sea, and high overhead the air began to carry a strange, faint, hollow booming.

Then without warning the tempest broke. The waves rose in growing fury. The sea was like a roaring and devouring monster. Whitecrested waves beat madly on the level sands and rushed up the shelving cliffs.

Masses of sea-fog came drifting inland. White, wet clouds, swept by in ghostly fashion.

Before long the searchlight discovered some distance away the same vessel which had been noticed earlier in the evening. There was a shudder amongst the watchers on the cliff as they realized the terrible danger in which she now was.

The schooner, with all sails set, was rushing with such speed that, in the words of one old salt, "she must fetch up somewhere, if it was only in hell". Then came another rush of sea-fog.

The wind suddenly shifted to the northeast, and the remnant of the sea fog melted in the blast. And then, leaping from wave to wave, swept the strange schooner before the blast, with all sail set, and gained the safety of the harbour. The searchlight followed her, and a shudder ran through all who saw her, for lashed to the helm was a corpse, with drooping head, which swung horribly to and fro at each motion of the ship. No other form could be seen on the deck at all.

The ship had found the harbour, unsteered save by the hand of a dead man! The schooner rushing across the harbour, pitched herself on that accumulation of sand, known locally as Tate Hill Pier.

But, strangest of all, the very instant the shore was touched, an immense dog sprang up on deck from below, as if shot up by the concussion, and running forward, jumped from the bow on the sand.

Making straight for the steep cliff, it disappeared in the darkness.

The men working the searchlight turned the light on the derelict and kept it there. The coastguard ran aft, and when he came beside the wheel, recoiled at once as though under some sudden emotion.

By the courtesy of the chief boatman, I was, as your correspondent, permitted to climb on deck, and saw the dead seaman whilst actually lashed to the wheel.

The man was simply fastened by his hands, tied one over the other, to a spoke of the wheel. Between the inner hand and the wood was a crucifix. The cords with which he was tied had cut the flesh to the bone.

The man must have been dead for quite two days.

In his pocket was a bottle, carefully corked, empty save for a little roll of paper, which proved to be the addendum to the log.

The coastguard said the man must have tied up his own hands, fastening the knots with his teeth.

Already the sudden storm is passing, and its fierceness is abating. Crowds are scattering backward, and the sky is beginning to redden over the Yorkshire wolds.

I shall send, in time for your next issue, further details of the derelict ship which found her way so miraculously into harbour in the storm.

9 August.--The sequel to the strange arrival of the derelict in the storm last night is almost more startling than the thing itself. The schooner is Russian from Varna, and is called the Demeter. With only a small amount of cargo, a number of great wooden boxes filled with mould.

This cargo was consigned to a Whitby solicitor, Mr. S. F. Billington, of 7, The Crescent, who this morning went aboard and took formal possession of the goods consigned to him.

The Russian consul, too, acting for the charter-party, took formal possession of the ship, and paid all harbour dues, etc.

A good deal of interest was abroad concerning the dog which landed when the ship struck, and more than a few of the members of the S.P.C.A. have tried to befriend the animal. It seems to have disappeared entirely from the town.

Early this morning a large dog, a half-bred mastiff belonging to a coal merchant, was found dead in the roadway. It had been fighting, and manifestly had had a savage opponent, for its throat was torn away, and its belly was slit open as if with a savage claw.

Later.--By the kindness of the Board of Trade inspector, I have been permitted to look over the log book of the Demeter. The greatest interest, however, is with regard to the paper found in the bottle.

It almost seems as though the captain had been seized with some kind of mania before he had got well into blue water, and that this had developed persistently throughout the voyage. The Russian consul kindly translated for me.

LOG OF THE "DEMETER" Varna to Whitby
Written 18 July, things so strange happening, that I shall keep accurate note henceforth till we land.

On 6 July we finished taking in cargo, silver sand and boxes of earth. At noon set sail. East wind, fresh. Crew, five hands . . . two mates, cook, and myself, (captain).

On 11 July at dawn entered Bosphorus. Boarded by Turkish Customs officers. Backsheesh. All correct. Under way at 4 p. m.

On 12 July through Dardanelles. More Customs officers and flagboat of guarding squadron. Backsheesh again. Work of officers thorough, but quick. Want us off soon. At dark passed into Archipelago.

On 13 July passed Cape Matapan. Crew dissatisfied about something. Seemed scared, but would not speak out.

On 14 July was somewhat anxious about crew. Men all steady fellows, who sailed with me before. Mate could not make out what was wrong. They only told him there was SOME- THING, and crossed themselves. Mate lost temper with one of them that day and struck him. Expected fierce quarrel, but all was quiet.

On 16 July mate reported one of the crew, Petrofsky, was missing. Could not account for it. Took larboard watch eight bells last night, was relieved by Amramoff, but did not go to bunk. Men more downcast than ever. All said they expected something of the kind, but would not say more than there was SOMETHING aboard. Mate getting very impatient with them. Feared some trouble ahead.

On 17 July, yesterday, one of the men, Olgaren, confided to me that he thought there was a strange man aboard the ship. He said that in his watch he saw a tall, thin man, who was not like any of the crew, come up the companionway, and go along the deck forward and disappear. He was in a panic of superstitious fear, and I am afraid the panic may spread.

Later in the day I got together the whole crew, and told them, as they evidently thought there was some one in the ship, we would search from stem to stern. We left no corner unsearched. Men much relieved when search over, and went back to work cheerfully.

22 July.--Rough weather last three days, and all hands busy with sails, no time to be frightened. Mate cheerful again, and all on good terms. Praised men for work in bad weather. Passed Gibraltar and out through Straits. All well.

24 July.--There seems some doom over this ship. Already a hand short, and entering wild weather ahead, and yet last night another man lost, disappeared. Like the first, he came off his watch and was not seen again. Men all in a panic of fear, sent a round robin, asking to have double watch, as they fear to be alone. Mate angry. Fear there will be some trouble, as either he or the men will do some violence.

28 July.--Four days in hell, knocking about in a sort of malestrom, and the wind a tempest. No sleep for any one. Men all worn out. Hardly know how to set a watch, since no one fit to go on. Second mate volunteered to steer and watch, and let men snatch a few hours sleep. Wind abating, seas still terrific, but feel them less, as ship is steadier.

29 July.--Another tragedy. Had single watch tonight, as crew too tired to double. When morning watch came on deck could find no one except steersman. Raised outcry, and all came on deck. Thorough search, but no one found. Are now without second mate, and crew in a panic. Mate and I agreed to go armed henceforth and wait for any sign of cause.

30 July.--Last night. Rejoiced we are nearing England. Weather fine, all sails set. Retired worn out, slept soundly, awakened by mate telling me that both man of watch and steersman missing. Only self and mate and two hands left to work ship.

1 August.--Two days of fog, and not a sail sighted. Had hoped when in the English Channel to be able to signal for help. Not having power to work sails, have to run before wind. Dare not lower, as could not raise them again. We seem to be drifting to some terrible doom. Mate now more demoralised than either of men. His stronger nature seems to have worked inwardly against himself. Men are beyond fear, working stolidly and patiently, with minds made up to worst. They are Russian, he Roumanian.

2 August, midnight.--Woke up from few minutes sleep by hearing a cry, seemingly outside my port. Could see nothing in fog. Rushed on deck, and ran against mate. Tells me he heard cry and ran, but no sign of man on watch. One more gone. Lord, help us! Mate says we must be past Straits of Dover, as in a moment of fog lifting he saw North Foreland, just as he heard the man cry out. If so we are in the North Sea, and only God can guide us in the fog, which seems to move with us, and God seems to have deserted us.

3 August.--At midnight I went to relieve the man at the wheel and when I got to it found no one there. The wind was steady. I dared not leave it, so shouted for the mate. After a few seconds, he rushed up on deck in his flannels. He looked wild-eyed and haggard, and I greatly fear his reason has given way. He came close to me and whispered hoarsely, as though fearing the very air might hear. "It is here. I know it now. Last night I saw It, like a man, tall and thin, and ghastly pale. It was in the bows, and looking out. I crept behind It, and gave it my knife, but the knife went through It, empty as the air." And as he spoke he took the knife and drove it savagely into space. Then he went on, "It is in the hold, perhaps in one of those boxes. I'll unscrew them one by one and see. You work the helm." He went below. There was springing up a choppy wind, and I could not leave the helm. I saw him with a tool chest and lantern, and go down the forward hatchway. He is mad, stark, raving mad, and it's no use my trying to stop him. He can't hurt those big boxes, they are invoiced as clay. I can only trust in God and wait till the fog clears. Then signal for help . . .

It is nearly all over now. Just as I was beginning to hope that the mate would come out calmer, there came up the hatchway a sudden, startled scream, which made my blood run cold, and up on the deck he came as if shot from a gun, a raging madman, with his eyes rolling and his face convulsed with fear. "Save me! Save me!" he cried, and then looked round on the blanket of fog. His horror turned to despair, and in a steady voice he said, "You had better come too, captain, before it is too late. He is there! I know the secret now!" Before I could say a word, or move forward to seize him, he sprang on the bulwark and deliberately threw himself into the sea. I suppose I know the secret too, now. It was this madman who had got rid of the men one by one, and now he has followed them himself. God help me!

4 August.--Still fog, which the sunrise cannot pierce. I dared not leave the helm, so here all night I stayed, and I saw it, Him! The mate was right

to jump overboard. It was better to die like a man. But I am captain, and I must not leave my ship. But I shall baffle this fiend or monster, for I shall tie my hands to the wheel and along with them I shall tie that which He, It, dare not touch. And then, come good wind or foul, I shall save my soul, and my honour as a captain. The night is coming on. If He can look me in the face again, I may not have time to act. God and the Blessed Virgin and the Saints help a poor ignorant soul trying to do his duty . . .

The folk here hold almost universally that the captain is simply a hero, and he is to be given a public funeral. The owners of more than a hundred boats have already given in their names as wishing to follow him to the grave.

No trace has ever been found of the great dog. Tomorrow will see the funeral, and so will end this one more `mystery of the sea'.

MINA MURRAY'S JOURNAL

8 August.--Lucy was very restless all night, and I too, could not sleep. The storm was fearful, and as it boomed loudly it made me shudder. Strangely enough, Lucy did not wake, but she got up twice and dressed herself. It is a very strange thing, this sleep-walking.

Early in the morning we both got up and went down to the harbour to see if anything had happened in the night. There were very few people about, and the sun was bright, and the air clear and fresh. Somehow I felt glad that Jonathan was not on the sea last night. But, oh, is he on land or sea? Where is he, and how? I am getting fearfully anxious about him. If I only knew what to do, and could do anything!

10 August.--The funeral of the poor sea captain today was most touching. Lucy came with me. The poor fellow was laid to rest near our seat so that we stood on it, when the time came and saw everything.

Poor Lucy seemed much upset. She was restless and uneasy all the time. She will not admit to me that there is any cause for restlessness.

There is an additional cause in that poor Mr. Swales was found dead this morning on our seat, his neck being broken. He had evidently, as the doctor said, fallen back in the seat in some sort of fright, for there was a look of fear and horror on his face that the men said made them shudder. Poor dear old man!

One of the men who came up here often to look for the boats was followed by his dog. During the service the dog would not come to its master, but kept a few yards off, barking and howling. Its master spoke to it gently, and then harshly, and then angrily. But it would neither come nor cease to make a noise. It was in a fury, with its eyes savage, and all its hair bristling out.

Finally the man threw it on the tombstone. The moment it touched the stone the poor thing began to tremble. It did not try to get away, but crouched down, quivering and cowering, and was in such a pitiable state of terror that I tried, though without effect, to comfort it.

Mina Murray's Journal, Same Day

11 o'clock p. m..--We had a lovely walk. Lucy, after a while, was in gay spirits, owing, I think, to some dear cows who frightened the wits out of us. Then we walked home with some, or rather many, stoppages to rest.

Lucy is asleep and breathing softly. She has more color in her cheeks than usual, and looks, oh so sweet. If Mr. Holmwood fell in love with her seeing her only in the drawing room, I wonder what he would say if he saw her now. I should be quite happy if I only knew if Jonathan . . . God bless and keep him.

11 August.--We have had such an adventure, such an agonizing experience. I fell asleep as soon as I had closed my diary . . .Suddenly I became broad awake, and sat up, with a horrible sense of fear upon me, and of some feeling of emptiness. The room was dark. I stole across and felt for her. The bed was empty. The door was shut, but not locked, as I had left it. I feared to wake her mother, who has been more than usually ill lately. Dressing-gown and dress were both in their places. "Thank God," I said to myself, "she cannot be far, only in her nightdress."

I ran downstairs and looked in all the other rooms of the house. Not there! Finally, I came to the hall door and found it open. A vague over-mastering fear obscured all details.

I took a big, heavy shawl and ran out. There was not a soul in sight. I ran along the North Terrace. I looked across the harbour to the East Cliff, in the hope or fear of seeing Lucy in our favorite seat.

There was a bright full moon, with heavy black, driving clouds. As the cloud passed I could see the ruins of the abbey coming into view. There, on our favorite seat, the silver light of the moon struck a half-reclining figure, snowy white. It seemed to me as though something dark stood behind the seat where the white figure shone, and bent over it. What it was, whether man or beast, I could not tell.

I flew down the steep steps to the pier and along by the fish-market to the bridge. The town seemed as dead, for not a soul did I see. I rejoiced, for I wanted no witness of poor Lucy's condition. I toiled up the endless steps to the abbey. It seemed to me as if my feet were weighted with lead.

When I got almost to the top I could see the seat and the white figure. There was undoubtedly something, long and black, bending over the half-reclining white figure. I called in fright, "Lucy! Lucy!" and something raised a head, and I could see a white face and red, gleaming eyes.

Lucy did not answer, and I ran on to the entrance of the churchyard. I lost sight of her. When I came in view again the cloud had passed, and I could see Lucy half reclining with her head lying over the back of the seat. She was quite alone, and there was not a sign of any living thing about.

She was still asleep. Her lips were parted, and she was breathing in long, heavy gasps, as though striving to get her lungs full at every breath. She pulled the collar of her nightdress close around her, as though she felt the cold. I flung the warm shawl over her, and drew the edges tight around her neck. In order to have my hands free to help her, I fastened the shawl at her throat with a big safety pin. But I must have pinched or pricked her with it, for by-and-by, when her breathing became quieter, she put her hand to her throat again and moaned. When I had her carefully wrapped up I put my shoes on her feet, and then began very gently to wake her.

Gradually she became more and more uneasy in her sleep, moaning and sighing occasionally. I shook her forcibly, till finally she opened her eyes and awoke. She did not seem surprised to see me, as, of course, she did not realize all at once where she was.

Lucy always wakes prettily, and even at such a time she did not lose her grace. She trembled a little, and clung to me. When I told her to come at once with me home, she rose without a word, with the obedience of a child. As we passed along, the gravel hurt my feet.

Fortune favoured us, and we got home without meeting a soul. I was filled with anxiety about Lucy, not only for her health, but for her reputation in case the story should get wind. When we got in, and had washed our feet, and had said a prayer of thankfulness together, I tucked her into bed. Before falling asleep she asked, even implored, me not to say a word to anyone, even her mother, about her sleepwalking adventure.

On thinking of the state of her mother's health, and how the knowledge of such a thing would fret her, and think too, of how such a story might become distorted, nay, infallibly would, in case it should leak out, I thought it wiser to do so.

Same day, noon.--All goes well. Lucy slept till I woke her. The adventure of the night does not seem to have harmed her. I was sorry to notice that my clumsiness with the safety-pin hurt her. Indeed, the skin of her throat was pierced. I must have pinched up a piece of loose skin, for there are two little red points like pin-pricks. When I apologized, she laughed and petted me, and said she did not even feel it. Fortunately it cannot leave a scar, as it is so tiny.

Same day, night.--We passed a happy day. We took our lunch to Mulgrave Woods. I felt a little sad myself, for I could not but feel how absolutely happy it would have been had Jonathan been with me. Lucy seems more restful than she has been for some time, and fell asleep at once. I shall lock the door and secure the key the same as before, though I do not expect any trouble tonight.

12 August.--My expectations were wrong, for twice during the night I was wakened by Lucy trying to get out. I woke with the dawn. Lucy woke, too. She came and snuggled in beside me and told me all about Arthur. I told her how anxious I was about Jonathan, and then she tried to comfort me.

13 August.--Another quiet day, and to bed with the key on my wrist as before. Again I awoke in the night, and found Lucy sitting up in bed, still asleep, pointing to the window. I got up and looked out. It was brilliant moonlight. Between me and the moonlight flitted a great bat, coming and going in great whirling circles. Once or twice it came quite close, but was, I suppose, frightened at seeing me, and flitted away across the harbour towards the abbey. When I came back from the window Lucy had lain down again, and was sleeping peacefully. She did not stir again all night.

14 August.--On the East Cliff, reading and writing all day. Lucy seems to have become as much in love with the spot as I am. This afternoon she made a funny remark. We were coming home for dinner. The setting sun, low down in the sky, was just dropping behind Kettleness. The red light was thrown over on the East Cliff and the old abbey. Suddenly Lucy murmured as if to herself . . .

"His red eyes again! They are just the same." It quite startled me. Lucy was in a half dreamy state, so I said nothing, but followed her eyes. She appeared to be looking over at our own seat, whereon was a dark figure seated alone. I was quite a little startled myself, for it seemed for an instant as if the stranger had great eyes like burning flames, but a second look dispelled the illusion. She was thinking of that terrible night up there. We never refer to it, so I said nothing, and we went home to dinner. Lucy had a headache and went early to bed. I saw her asleep, and went out for a little stroll myself.

I walked along the cliffs to the westward, thinking of Jonathan. When coming home I threw a glance up at our window, and saw Lucy's head leaning out. I opened my handkerchief and waved it. She did not notice or make any movement whatever. Just then the light fell on the window. There distinctly was Lucy with her head lying up against the side of the window sill and her eyes shut. She was fast asleep, and by her, seated on the window sill, was something that looked like a good-sized bird. I was afraid she might get a chill, so I ran upstairs, but as I came into the room she was moving back to her bed, fast asleep, and breathing heavily. She was holding her hand to her throat, as though to protect it from the cold.

I did not wake her, but tucked her up warmly. I have taken care that the door is locked and the window securely fastened.

She looks so sweet as she sleeps, but she is paler, and there is a drawn, haggard look under her eyes.

15 August.--Lucy was languid and tired, and slept on after we had been called. Arthur's father is better, and wants the marriage to come off soon. Lucy is full of quiet joy, and her mother is glad and sorry at once. Poor dear, sweet lady! She confided to me that she has got her death warrant. She has not told Lucy, and made me promise secrecy. Her doctor told her that within a few months, at most, she must die, for her heart is weakening. At any time, even now, a sudden shock would be almost sure to kill her. Ah, we were wise to keep from her the affair of the dreadful night of Lucy's sleep-walking.

17 August.--Some sort of shadowy pall seems to be coming over our happiness. No news from Jonathan, and Lucy seems to be growing weaker, whilst her mother's hours are numbering to a close. I do not understand Lucy's fading away. She eats well and sleeps well, but she gets weaker and more languid day by day. At night I hear her gasping as if for air.

Last night I found her leaning out of the window when I woke up, and when I tried to wake her I could not.

She was in a faint. When I managed to restore her, she was weak as water, and cried silently between long, painful struggles for breath. When I asked her how she came to be at the window she shook her head and turned away.

I trust her feeling ill may not be from that unlucky prick of the safety-pin. I looked at her throat just now as she lay asleep, and the tiny wounds seem not to have healed. They are still open, and, if anything, larger than before, and the edges of them are faintly white. They are like little white dots with red centres. Unless they heal within a day or two, I shall insist on the doctor seeing about them.

LETTER, SAMUEL F. BILLINGTON & SON, SOLICITORS
WHITBY, TO MESSRS. CARTER, PATERSON & CO., LONDON.

17 August

"Dear Sirs, --

"Herewith please receive invoice of goods sent by Great Northern
Railway. Same are to be delivered at Carfax, near Purfleet, immediately on
receipt at goods station King's Cross. The house is at present empty, but
enclosed please find keys, all of which are labelled.

"You will please deposit the boxes, fifty in number, which form the
consignment, in the partially ruined building forming part of the house
and marked `A' on rough diagrams enclosed. It is the ancient chapel of
the mansion. We enclose cheque herewith for ten pounds, receipt of
which please acknowledge. You are to leave the keys on coming away in
the main hall of the house.

"We are, dear Sirs, "Faithfully yours, "SAMUEL F. BILLINGTON &
SON"

LETTER, MESSRS. CARTER, PATERSON & CO., LONDON,
TO MESSRS. BILLINGTON & SON, WHITBY.

21 August.

"Dear Sirs,--

"We beg to acknowledge 10 pounds received and to return cheque of
1 pound, 17s, 9d, amount of overplus, as shown in receipted account
herewith. Goods are delivered in exact accordance with instructions, and
keys left in parcel in main hall, as directed. "We are, dear Sirs, "Yours
respectfully, "Pro CARTER, PATERSON & CO."

MINA MURRAY'S JOURNAL.

18 August.--I am happy today, and write sitting on the seat in the
churchyard. Lucy is ever so much better. Last night she slept well all
night.

The roses seem coming back already to her cheeks, though she is still
sadly pale and wan-looking. All the morbid reticence seems to have
passed from her, and she has just reminded me, as if I needed any
reminding, of that night.

As she told me she tapped playfully with the heel of her boot on the
stone slab.

I asked her if she had dreamed at all that night.

Before she answered, that sweet, puckered look came into her
forehead, which Arthur says he loves. Then she went on in a half-
dreaming kind of way, as if trying to recall it to herself.

"I didn't quite dream, but it all seemed to be real. I only wanted to be here in this spot. I was afraid of something. I remember passing through the streets and over the bridge. A fish leaped as I went by. The whole town seemed as if it must be full of dogs all howling at once, as I went up the steps. Then I had a vague memory of something long and dark with red eyes, and something very sweet and very bitter all around me at once. And then I seemed sinking into deep green water, and there was a singing in my ears, as I have heard there is to drowning men, and then everything seemed passing away from me. My soul seemed to go out from my body and float about the air. I seem to remember that once the West Lighthouse was right under me, and then there was a sort of agonizing feeling, as if I were in an earthquake, and I came back and found you shaking my body. I saw you do it before I felt you."

Then she began to laugh. I did not quite like it, so we drifted on to another subject, and Lucy was like her old self again.

19 August.--At last, news of Jonathan! The dear fellow has been ill, that is why he did not write. I am to leave in the morning and go to Jonathan and bring him home. Mr. Hawkins says it would not be a bad thing if we were to be married out there. I have cried over the good Sister's letter till I can feel it wet against my bosom, where it lies. My journey is all mapped out, and my luggage ready. I am only taking one change of dress, for it may be that . . . I must write no more. I must keep it to say to Jonathan, my husband.

LETTER, SISTER AGATHA, HOSPITAL OF ST. JOSEPH AND STE. MARY BUDA-PESTH, TO MISS WILLHELMINA MURRAY

12 August,

"Dear Madam.

"I write by desire of Mr. Jonathan Harker, who is himself not strong enough to write, though progressing well, thanks to God and St. Joseph and Ste. Mary. He has been under our care for nearly six weeks, suffering from a violent brain fever. He wishes me to convey his love, with his dutiful respects, that he is sorry for his delay, and that all of his work is completed. He will require some few weeks' rest in our sanatorium. He wishes me to say that he has not sufficient money with him, and that he would like to pay for his staying here, so that others who need shall not be wanting for help.

Believe me,

Yours, with sympathy

and all blessings. Sister Agatha"

"P. S.--My patient being asleep, I open this to let you know something more. He has told me all about you, and that you are shortly to be his wife. All blessings to you both! He has had some fearful shock, so says our doctor, and in his delirium his ravings have been dreadful, of wolves and poison and blood, of ghosts and demons, and I fear to say of what. Be careful of him that there may be nothing to excite him of this kind for a long time to come. He came in the train from Klausenburg, and the guard was told by the station master there that he rushed into the station shouting for a ticket for home.

"Be assured that he is well cared for. He has won all hearts by his sweetness and gentleness. He is truly getting on well. But be careful of him for safety's sake."

DR. SEWARD'S DIARY

19 August.--Strange and sudden change in Renfield last night. About eight o'clock he began to get excited and sniff about as a dog.

All he would say was, "I don't want to talk to you. You don't count now. The master is at hand."

The attendant thinks it is some sudden form of religious mania. A strong man with homicidal and religious mania at once might be dangerous. The combination is a dreadful one.

At Nine o'clock I visited him myself. It looks like religious mania, and he will soon think that he himself is God.

How these madmen give themselves away! The real God taketh heed lest a sparrow fall. But the God created from human vanity sees no difference between an eagle and a sparrow. Oh, if men only knew!

For half an hour or more Renfield kept getting excited in greater and greater degree.

I tried to lead him to talk of his pets.

At first he made no reply, but at length said testily, "I don't care a pin about them."

"What" I said. "You don't mean to tell me you don't care about spiders?" (Spiders at present are his hobby and the notebook is filling up with columns of small figures.)

To this he answered enigmatically, "The Bride maidens rejoice the eyes that wait the coming of the bride. But when the bride draweth nigh, then the maidens shine not to the eyes that are filled."

He would not explain himself, but remained obstinately seated on his bed all the time I remained with him.

I am weary tonight and low in spirits. I cannot but think of Lucy, and how different things might have been. If I don't sleep at once, chloral, the modern Morpheus! I must be careful not to let it grow into a habit.

No, I shall take none tonight! I have thought of Lucy, and I shall not dishonour her by mixing the two.

Later.--Glad I made the resolution, gladder that I kept to it. The night watchman came to me to say that Renfield had escaped. My patient is too dangerous a person to be roaming about.

The attendant said he had looked through the observation trap in the door. His attention was called by the sound of the window being wrenched out. He ran back and saw his feet disappear through the window, and had at once sent up for me. He cannot be far off.

I am thin, so, with his aid, I got out, but feet foremost, and as we were only a few feet above ground landed unhurt.

I saw a white figure scale the high wall which separates our grounds from those of the deserted house.

I told the watchman to get three or four men immediately and follow me into the grounds of Carfax, in case our friend might be dangerous. I got a ladder myself, and crossing the wall, dropped down on the other side. I could see Renfield's figure just disappearing behind the angle of the house, so I ran after him. On the far side of the house I found him pressed close against the old ironbound oak door of the chapel.

He was talking, apparently to someone.

I could see that he did not take note of anything around him, and so ventured to draw nearer to him. I heard him say . . .

"I am here to do your bidding, Master. I am your slave, and you will reward me, for I shall be faithful. I have worshipped you long and afar off. Now that you are near, I await your commands."

When we closed in on him he fought like a tiger.

I never saw a naked lunatic in such a paroxysm of rage before, and I hope I shall not again.

He is safe now, at any rate. The strait waistcoat keeps him restrained, and he's chained to the wall in the padded room.

His cries are at times awful, but the silences that follow are more deadly still, for he means murder in every turn and movement.

Just now he spoke coherent words for the first time. "I shall be patient, Master. It is coming, coming, coming!"

Letter, Mina Harker To Lucy Westenra, Buda-Pesth, 24 August

"My dearest Lucy,

"I know you will be anxious to hear all that has happened since we parted at the railway station at Whitby.

"I found my dear one, oh, so thin and pale and weak looking. He is only a wreck of himself, and he does not remember anything. At least, he wants me to believe so.

"I fear it might tax his poor brain if he were to try to recall it. Sister Agatha tells me that he wanted her to tell me what they were, but she would only cross herself, and say she would never tell.

"She added, `It was not about anything which he has done wrong himself, and you, as his wife to be, have no cause to be concerned.'

"I felt a thrill of joy through me when I knew that no other woman was a cause for trouble. I am now sitting by his bedside. He is waking!

"When he woke he asked me for his coat.

"Then he said to me very solemnly, `Wilhelmina', he has never called me by that name since he asked me to marry him, `There should be no secret, no concealment. I had brain fever, and that is to be mad. The secret is here, and I do not want to know it. I want to take up my life here, with our marriage.' For, my dear, we had decided to be married as soon as the formalities are complete. `Are you willing, Wilhelmina, to share my ignorance? Here is the book. Read it if you will, but never let me know unless, indeed, some solemn duty should come upon me.' He fell back exhausted, and I put the book under his pillow, and kissed him. I have asked Sister Agatha to let our wedding be this afternoon, and am waiting her reply . . ."

"The Chaplain of the English mission church has been sent for. We are to be married in an hour."

"Jonathan woke a little after the hour, and all was ready, and he sat up in bed, propped up with pillows. He answered his `I will' firmly. My heart was so full that even those words seemed to choke me.

"I must tell you of my wedding present. I took the book from under his pillow, and wrapped it up in white paper, and tied it with pale blue ribbon which was round my neck, and sealed it over the knot with wax, and for my seal I used my wedding ring. Then I told him that I would keep it so.

"And, my dear, when he kissed me, and drew me to him with his poor weak hands, it was like a solemn pledge between us.

"I do hope you will be always as happy as I am now. Goodbye, my dear. I must attend my husband! "Your ever-loving "Mina Harker."

LETTER, LUCY WESTENRA TO MINA HARKER.
Whitby, 30 August.
"My dearest Mina,

"Oceans of love and millions of kisses. I wish you were coming home soon enough to stay with us here. The strong air would soon restore Jonathan. It has quite restored me. You will be glad to know that I have quite given up walking in my sleep. Arthur says I am getting fat. I forgot to tell you that Arthur is here. We have such walks and drives, and rides, and rowing, and tennis, and fishing together, and I love him more than ever. There he is, calling to me. From your loving, "Lucy.

"P. S.--Mother sends her love. She seems better, poor dear.

"P. P.S.--We are to be married on 28 September."

DR. SEWARDS DIARY

20 August.--The case of Renfield grows even more interesting. He has now so far quieted. For the first week after his attack he was perpetually violent. Then one night, just as the moon rose, he grew quiet, and kept murmuring to himself. "Now I can wait. Now I can wait."

Still in the strait waistcoat and padded room, but the suffused look had gone from his face, and his eyes had something of their old pleading. I directed him to be relieved. The attendants hesitated.

He said in a whisper, "They think I could hurt you! Fancy me hurting you! The fools!"

Tonight he will not speak. Even the offer of a kitten or even a full-grown cat will not tempt him.

He will only say, "I don't take any stock in cats. I have more to think of now, and I can wait. I can wait."

He was quiet until just before dawn, and then he began to get uneasy, and at length violent, until at last he fell into a paroxysm which exhausted him into a sort of coma.

. . . Three nights has the same thing happened, violent all day then quiet from moonrise to sunrise. Happy thought! We shall tonight play sane wits against mad ones. He escaped before without our help. Tonight he shall escape with it and we shall have the men ready to follow in case they are required.

23 August.--"The expected always happens." How well Disraeli knew life. Our bird when he found the cage open would not fly. We shall ease his bonds for a few hours each day. Hark! The unexpected again! I am called. The patient has once more escaped.

Later.--Another night adventure. Renfield artfully waited until the attendant was entering the room to inspect. Then he dashed out past him and flew down the passage. Again he went into the grounds of the deserted house, in the same place, pressed against the old chapel door. When he saw me he became furious, and had not the attendants seized him in time, he would have tried to kill me. As we were holding him a strange thing happened. He redoubled his efforts, and then as suddenly grew calm. I caught the patient's eye and followed it. A big bat was flapping its silent and ghostly way to the west. Bats usually wheel about, but this one seemed to go straight on, as if it knew where it was bound for or had some intention of its own.

The patient grew calmer, and said, "You needn't tie me. I shall go quietly!" Without trouble, we came back to the house. I feel there is something ominous in his calm.

LUCY WESTENRA'S DIARY
Hillingham,

24 August.--I feel so unhappy. Last night I seemed to be dreaming again just as I was at Whitby. It is all dark and horrid to me, for I can remember nothing. But I feel so weak and worn out. When Arthur came to lunch he looked quite grieved when he saw me, and I hadn't the spirit to try to be cheerful. I wonder if I could sleep in mother's room tonight. I shall make an excuse to try.

25 August.--Another bad night. Mother did not seem to take to my proposal. She seems not too well herself. I tried to keep awake, and succeeded for a while. Then the clock struck twelve. There was a sort of scratching or flapping at the window, but I did not mind it. I must have fallen asleep. More bad dreams. I wish I could remember them. This morning I am horribly weak. My face is ghastly pale, and my throat pains me. I shall try to cheer up when Arthur comes.

LETTER, ARTHUR TO DR. SEWARD
"Albemarle Hotel, 31 August "My dear Jack,

"I want you to do me a favour. Lucy is ill, she looks awful, and is getting worse every day. I not dare to ask her mother, for to disturb the poor lady's mind in her present state of health would be fatal. Mrs. Westenra has a disease of the heart. I told her I should ask you to see her. It will be a painful task for you, I know, old friend, but it is for her sake. You are to come to lunch at Hillingham tomorrow, two o'clock, so as not to arouse any suspicion in Mrs. Westenra, and after lunch Lucy will take an opportunity of being alone with you. I am filled with anxiety, and want to consult with you after you have seen her. Do not fail! "Arthur."

TELEGRAM, ARTHUR HOLMWOOD TO SEWARD
1 September
"Am summoned to see my father, who is worse. Write me fully by tonight's post to Ring. Wire me if necessary."

LETTER FROM DR. SEWARD TO ARTHUR HOLMWOOD
2 September
"My dear old fellow,

"With regard to Miss Westenra's health I hasten to let you know that in my opinion there is not any functal disturbance or any malady that I know of. At the same time, I am not satisfied with her appearance. Our very friendship makes a little difficulty which not even medical science or custom can bridge over.

"I found Miss Westenra in seemingly gay spirits. Her mother was present, and she was trying all she knew to mislead her mother.

"Then Mrs. Westenra went to lie down, and Lucy was left with me. We went into her boudoir.

"As soon as the door was closed, the mask fell from her face, and she sank down into a chair with a great sigh, and hid her eyes with her hand.

"She said to me very sweetly, `I loathe talking about myself.' I reminded her that a doctor's confidence was sacred, but that you were grievously anxious about her. She caught on to my meaning at once. `Tell Arthur everything you choose. I do not care for myself, but for him!' So I am quite free.

"I could easily see that she was somewhat bloodless, but I could not see the usual anemic signs, and by the chance, I was able to test the actual quality of her blood.

"The qualitative analysis give a quite normal condition. There is no need for anxiety, but as there must be a cause somewhere, it must be something mental.

"She complains of difficulty breathing satisfactorily at times, and of heavy, lethargic sleep, with dreams that frighten her, but regarding which she can remember nothing. She says that as a child, she used to walk in her sleep, and that when in Whitby the habit came back, and that once she walked out in the night and went to East Cliff, where Miss Murray found her. But she assures me that of late the habit has not returned.

"I am in doubt. I have written to my old friend and master, Professor Van Helsing, of Amsterdam, who knows as much about obscure diseases as any one in the world. I have asked him to come over, and as you told me that all things were to be at your charge, I have mentioned to him who you are and your relations to Miss Westenra. I am only too proud and happy to do anything I can for her.

"Van Helsing would, I know, do anything for me for a personal reason. He is a seemingly arbitrary man, this is because he knows what he is talking about better than anyone else. He is a philosopher and a metaphysician, and one of the most advanced scientists of his day. This, with an iron nerve, and toleration. I have asked him to come at once. I shall see Miss Westenra tomorrow again. She is to meet me at the Stores, so that I may not alarm her mother by too early a repetition of my call.

"Yours always."
John Seward

LETTER, ABRAHAM VAN HELSING, MD, DPh, D. LiT, ETC, ETC, TO DR. SEWARD
2 September.
"My good Friend,
"I am already coming to you. Till then goodbye, my friend John.
"Van Helsing."

LETTER, DR. SEWARD TO HON. ARTHUR HOLMWOOD
3 September
"My dear Art,
"Van Helsing has come and gone.
"Van Helsing made a very careful examination of the patient. He is, I fear, much concerned, but says he must think.

"Well, as to the visit, Lucy was more cheerful than on the day I first saw her, and certainly looked better. She had lost something of the ghastly look that so upset you, and her breathing was normal. She was very sweet to the Professor (as she always is), and tried to make him feel at ease, though I could see the poor girl was making a hard struggle for it.

"I believe Van Helsing saw it, too, and sauvely said,

"My dear young miss, I have the so great pleasure because you are so much beloved. They told me you were down in the spirit, and that you were of a ghastly pale. To them I say "Pouf!" ' And he snapped his fingers at me and went on. `But you and I shall show them how wrong they are. How can he', and he pointed at me with the same look and gesture as that with which he pointed me out in his class, `know anything of a young ladies? So, my dear, we will send him away, whiles you and I have little talk all to ourselves.' I took the hint, and strolled about, and presently the professor came to the window and called me in. He looked grave, but said, ` I have made careful examination, but there is no functional cause. I agree that there has been much blood lost. But the conditions of her are in no way anemic. And yet there is cause. There is always cause for everything. I must go back home and think. You must send me the telegram every day, and if there be cause I shall come again. She charm me, and for her, if not for you or disease, I come.'

"As I tell you, he would not say a word more. I shall keep stern watch. Do not be over-anxious unless you hear from me."

DR. SEWARD'S DIARY

4 September.--Zoophagous patient still keeps up our interest in him. He had only one outburst and that was yesterday at an unusual time. Just before the stroke of noon he began to grow restless. Fortunately the men were just in time, for at the stroke of noon he became so violent that it took all their strength to hold him. In about five minutes, however, he sank into a sort of melancholy, in which state he has remained up to now. His screams whilst in the paroxysm were really appalling. The sounds disturbed even me, though I was some distance away. Now my patient sits in a corner brooding, with a dull, sullen, woe-begone look in his face.

Later.--Another change in my patient. At five o'clock I looked in on him, and found him seemingly as happy and contented as he used to be. He was catching flies and eating them, and was keeping note of his capture by making nailmarks on the door. When he saw me, he apologized for his bad conduct, and asked me in a very humble, cringing way to be led back to his own room, and to have his notebook again. I thought it well to humour him, so he is back in his room with the window open. He has the sugar of his tea spread out on the window sill, and is reaping quite a harvest of flies. He is not now eating them, but putting them into a box, as of old, and is already examining the corners of his room to find a spider. I tried to get him to talk about the past few days, but he would not rise. He said in a sort of far away voice.

"All over! All over! He has deserted me. No hope for me now unless I do it myself!" Then suddenly turning to me in a resolute way, he said, "Doctor, won't you be very good to me and let me have a little more sugar? I think it would be very good for me."

"And the flies?" I said.

"Yes! The flies like it, too, and I like the flies, therefore I like it." And there are people who know so little as to think that madmen do not argue. I procured him a double supply, and left him as a happy man. I wish I could fathom his mind.

Midnight.--Another change in him. I had been to see Miss Westenra, whom I found much better, and had just returned, when once more I heard him yelling. It was a shock to me and my own desolate heart to endure it all. I reached him just as the sun was going down, and from his window saw the red disc sink. As it sank he became less and less frenzied, and just as it dipped he slid on the floor. What intellectual recuperative power lunatics have, for within a few minutes he stood up quite calmly and looked around him. I signalled to the attendants not to hold him. He went straight over to the window and brushed out the crumbs of sugar. Then he took his fly box, and emptied it outside, and threw away the box. Then he shut the window and sat down on his bed. All this surprised me, so I asked him, "Are you going to keep flies any more?"

"No," said he. "I am sick of all that rubbish!" He certainly is a wonderfully interesting study. I wish I could get some glimpse of his mind. There may be a clue if we can find why today his paroxysms came on at high noon and at sunset.

TELEGRAM. SEWARD, LONDON, TO VAN HELSING, AMSTERDAM

"4 September.--Patient better today."

TELEGRAM, SEWARD, LONDON, TO VAN HELSING, AMSTERDAM

"5 September.--Patient greatly improved. Good appetite, sleeps naturally, good spirits, color coming back."

TELEGRAM, SEWARD, LONDON, TO VAN HELSING, AMSTERDAM

"6 September.--Terrible change for the worse. Come at once.

Letter, Dr. Seward To Hon. Arthur Holmwood, 6 September

"My dear Art,

"Lucy this morning had gone back a bit. However, Mrs. Westenra has consulted me professionally about her. I told her that my old master, Van Helsing, the great specialist, would put her in his charge conjointly with myself. Now we can come and go without alarming her unduly, for a shock to her would mean sudden death, and this, in Lucy's weak condition, might be disastrous to her.

"Yours ever,"

John Seward

DR. SEWARD'S DIARY

7 September.--The first thing Van Helsing said was, "Have you said anything to our young friend, to lover of her?"

"No," I said. "I waited till I had seen you."

"Right, my friend," he said. "Quite right! You and I shall keep as yet what we know here, and here." He touched me on the heart and the forehead. "I have for myself thoughts at the present. Later I shall unfold to you."

"Why not now?" I asked.

He took my ear in his hand and pulled it playfully, as he used long ago to do at lectures, and said, "You do not dig up planted corn to see if he grow." He went on gravely, "You were always a careful student. And I trust that good habit have not fail. Let me tell you that this case may be of such interest to us and others. Take then good note of it. Nothing is too small. We learn from failure, not from success!"

When I described Lucy's symptoms, the same as before, but infinitely more marked, he looked very grave. He took with him a bag in which were many instruments and drugs, "the ghastly paraphernalia of our beneficial trade," as he once called the equipment of a professor of the healing craft.

When we were shown in, Mrs. Westenra met us.

I set down a rule that she should not be present with Lucy. Van Helsing and I were shown to Lucy's room. If I was shocked when I saw her yesterday, I was horrified when I saw her today.

She was ghastly, chalkily pale. The bones of her face stood out prominently. Her breathing was painful to see or hear. Van Helsing's face grew set as marble, and his eyebrows converged. Lucy lay motionless, and did not seem to have strength to speak. "My god!" Van Helsing said.

"This is dreadful. There is not time to be lost. She will die for sheer want of blood. There must be a transfusion of blood at once. Is it you or me?"

"I am younger and stronger, Professor. It must be me."

"Then get ready at once."

I went downstairs with him, and there was a knock at the hall door. When we reached the hall, the maid had just opened the door, and Arthur rushed up to me, saying in an eager whisper,

"Jack, I was so anxious. My dad was better, so I ran down here to see for myself. Is not that gentleman Dr. Van Helsing? I am so thankful to you, sir, for coming."

First the Professor had been angry at his interruption, but now, as he recognized the strong young manhood which seemed to emanate from him, his eyes gleamed. Without a pause he said,

"Sir, you have come in time. You are the lover of our dear miss. She is bad, very, very bad." Arthur suddenly grew pale and almost fainted. "You are to help her."

"What can I do?" asked Arthur hoarsely. "Tell me. My life is hers' and I would give the last drop of blood in my body for her."

"I do not ask so much as that!"

"What shall I do?" His open nostrils quivered with intent. Van Helsing slapped him on the shoulder.

"Come!" he said. "You are a man, and it is a man we want." Arthur looked bewildered.

"Young miss is bad, very bad. She wants blood, and blood she must have or die. We are about to perform what we call transfusion of blood, to transfer from full veins of one to the empty veins which pine for him. "

Arthur turned to him and said, "If you only knew how gladly I would die for her. . ." He stopped with a sort of choke in his voice.

"Good boy!" said Van Helsing. "Come now and be silent."

We all went up to Lucy's room. Arthur by direction remained outside. Lucy said nothing. She was too weak to make the effort. Her eyes spoke to us, that was all.

Van Helsing took some things from his bag and laid them on a little table out of sight. Then he mixed a narcotic and said cheerily, "Now, little miss, here is your medicine. Drink it off, like a good child." She had made the effort with success.

It astonished me how long the drug took to act. At last she fell into a deep sleep. The Professor called Arthur into the room, and bade him strip off his coat. Then he added, "You may take one little kiss whiles I bring over the table. Friend John, help to me!"

Van Helsing, turning to me, said, "He is so young and strong, and of blood so pure that we need not defibrinate it."

Then with absolute method, Van Helsing performed the operation. As the transfusion went on, something like life seemed to come back to poor Lucy's cheeks, and through Arthur's growing pallor the joy of his face seemed absolutely to shine. The loss of blood was telling on Arthur, strong man as he was. It gave me an idea of what a terrible strain Lucy's system must have undergone.

The Professor's face was set, with his eyes fixed now on the patient and on Arthur. I could hear my own heart beat. Presently, he said in a soft voice, "Do not stir an instant. It is enough. You attend him. I will look to her."

Arthur was weakened. I dressed the wound and took his arm to bring him away, when Van Helsing spoke without turning round, "The brave lover, I think, deserve another kiss." Van Helsing adjusted the pillow to the patient's head. As he did so the narrow black velvet band which she seems always to wear round her throat, buckled with an old diamond buckle which her lover had given her, was dragged a little up, and showed a red mark on her throat.

Arthur did not notice it, but I could hear the deep hiss of indrawn breath which is one of Van Helsing's ways of betraying emotion. He turned to me, saying, "Now take down our brave young lover, give him of the port wine, and let him lie down a while. He must then go home and rest, sleep much and eat much! You have saved her life. Goodbye."

When Arthur had gone I went back to the room. I asked the Professor in a whisper, "What do you make of that mark on her throat?"

"What do you make of it?"

"I have not examined it yet," I answered, and then and there proceeded to loose the band. Just over the external jugular vein there were two punctures, not large, but not wholesome looking. There was no sign of disease, but the edges were white and worn looking, as if by some trituration. It occurred to me that this wound might be the means of that manifest loss of blood. But such a thing could not be. The whole bed would have been drenched to a scarlet with the blood.

"Well?" said Van Helsing.

"Well," said I. "I can make nothing of it."

The Professor stood up. "I must go back to Amsterdam tonight," he said "There are books and things there which I want. You must not let your sight pass from her."

"Shall I have a nurse?" I asked.

"We are the best nurses. You keep watch all night. See that she is well fed, and that nothing disturbs her. You must not sleep all the night. I shall be back as soon as possible. And then we may begin."

"May begin?" I said. "What on earth do you mean?"

"We shall see!" he answered, as he hurried out. He came back a moment later and put his head inside the door and said with a warning finger held up, "Remember, she is your charge. If you leave her, and harm befall, you shall not sleep easy hereafter!"

DR. SEWARD'S DIARY--CONTINUED

8 September.--I sat up all night with Lucy. The opiate worked itself off towards dusk. When I told Mrs. Westenra that Dr. Van Helsing had directed that I should sit up with her, she almost pooh-poohed the idea, pointing out her daughter's renewed strength and excellent spirits. I was firm, however.

It was apparent that Lucy did not want to sleep, so I tackled the subject at once.

"You do not want to sleep?"

"No. I am afraid."

"Afraid to go to sleep! Why so? It is the boon we all crave for."

"Ah, not if you were like me, if sleep was to you a presage of horror!"

"What on earth do you mean?"

"I don't know. Oh, I don't know. And that is what is so terrible. All this weakness comes to me in sleep, until I dread the very thought."

"But, my dear girl. I am here watching you, and I can promise that nothing will happen."

"Ah, I can trust you!" she said.

I seized the opportunity, and said, "I promise that if I see any evidence of bad dreams I will wake you at once."

"You will? Oh, will you really? Then I will sleep!" And almost at the word she gave a deep sigh of relief, and sank back, asleep.

All night long I watched by her. She never stirred.

In the early morning her maid came, and I left her in her care and took myself back home. I sent a short wire to Van Helsing and to Arthur, telling them of the excellent result of the operation. My own work took me all day to clear off. It was dark when I was able to inquire about my zoophagous patient. The report was good. He had been quite quiet for the past day and night.

9 September.--I was pretty tired and worn out when I got to Hillingham. For two nights I had hardly had a wink of sleep, and my

brain was beginning to feel that numbness which marks cerebral exhaustion. Lucy was in cheerful spirits. She looked sharply in my face and said,

"No sitting up tonight for you. You are worn out. I am quite well again."

I would not argue the point, but went and had my supper. Lucy came with me, and, enlivened by her charming presence, I made an excellent meal, and had a couple of glasses of excellent port. Then Lucy took me upstairs, and showed me a room next her own, where a cozy fire was burning.

"Now," she said. "You must stay here. I shall leave this door open and my door too. I know that nothing would induce any of you doctors to go to bed whilst there is a patient above the horizon. If I want anything I shall call out, and you can come to me at once."

I could not but acquiesce. I lay on the sofa, and forgot all about everything.

LUCY WESTENRA'S DIARY

9 September.--I feel so happy tonight. Somehow Arthur feels very, very close to me. I know where my thoughts are. If only Arthur knew! Oh, the blissful rest of last night! How I slept, with that dear, good Dr. Seward watching me. Thank everybody for being so good to me. Thank God! Goodnight Arthur.

DR. SEWARD'S DIARY

10 September.--I was conscious of the Professor's hand on my head, and started awake all in a second.

"And how is our patient?"

"Well, when I left her, or rather when she left me," I answered.

"Come, let us see," he said. And together we went into the room.

Van Helsing stepped, with his soft, cat-like tread, over to the bed.

As I raised the blind, and the morning sunlight flooded the room, I heard the Professor's low hiss of inspiration, and a deadly fear shot through my heart. He exclaimed in horror, "Gott in Himmel!" I felt my knees begin to tremble.

There on the bed lay poor Lucy, more horribly white and wan-looking than ever. Even the lips were white, and the gums seemed to have shrunken back from the teeth, as in a corpse after a prolonged illness.

Van Helsing raised his foot to stamp in anger.

"Quick!" he said. "Bring the brandy."

I flew to the dining room, and returned with the decanter. He wetted the poor white lips with it, and together we rubbed palm and wrist and heart. He felt her heart and said,

"It is not too late but all our work is undone. I have to call on you yourself this time, friend John." As he spoke, he was dipping into his bag, and producing the instruments of transfusion. I had taken off my coat and rolled up my shirt sleeve. Without delay we began the operation.

The draining away of one's blood, no matter how willingly it be given, is a terrible feeling. "Do not stir," Van Helsing said. "I fear that with growing strength she may wake, and that would make danger, oh, so much danger. But I shall precaution take. I shall give hypodermic injection of morphia."

The effect on Lucy was not bad. No man knows, till he experiences it, what it is to feel his own lifeblood drawn away into the veins of the woman he loves.

The Professor watched me critically. "That will do," he said.

"Already?" I remonstrated.

When we stopped the operation, he attended to Lucy. I felt faint and a little sick. He bound up my wound, and sent me downstairs to get a glass of wine for myself. As I was leaving the room, he came after me, and half whispered.

"Mind, nothing must be said of this. If our young lover should turn up unexpected, as before, no word to him. It would at once frighten him and enjealous him, too."

When I came back he looked at me carefully, and then said, "You are not much the worse. Rest awhile, then have much breakfast and come here to me."

I followed out his orders. I felt very weak. I fell asleep on the sofa. Sleeping and waking my thoughts always came back to the little punctures in her throat.

Lucy slept well into the day, and when she woke she was fairly well and strong.

Lucy chatted with me freely, and seemed quite unconscious that anything had happened. When her mother came up to see her, she did not notice any change whatever, but said to me gratefully,

"We owe you so much, Dr. Seward. You are looking pale yourself. You want a wife to nurse and look after you a bit, that you do!" As she spoke, Lucy turned crimson, though it was only momentarily.

Van Helsing returned in a couple of hours, and presently said to me. "Now you go home, and eat much and drink enough. I stay here tonight. We must have none other to know. I have grave reasons. Goodnight."

11 September.--This afternoon I went over to Hillingham. Found Van Helsing in excellent spirits, and Lucy much better. A big parcel from abroad came for the Professor. He opened it and showed a great bundle of white flowers.

"These are for you, Miss Lucy," he said.

"For me? Oh, Dr. Van Helsing!"

"Yes, my dear, but not for you to play with. These are medicines." Here Lucy made a wry face. "Nay, you need not snub that so charming nose. This is medicinal, so you sleep well. Oh, yes!"

Lucy had been examining the flowers and smelling them. Now she threw them down saying, with half laughter, and half disgust,

"Oh, Professor, I believe you are putting a joke on me. Why, these flowers are only common garlic."

To my surprise, Van Helsing rose up and said with all his sternness, his iron jaw set and his bushy eyebrows meeting,

"No trifling with me! I never jest! There is grim purpose in what I do. Take care, for the sake of others if not for your own." Then seeing poor Lucy scared, he went on more gently, "Oh, little miss, my dear, do not fear me. I only do for your good. But hush! Friend John, you shall help me deck the room with my garlic, which is all the way from Haarlem."

We went into the room, taking the flowers with us. The Professor's actions were not to be found in any pharmacopeia that I ever heard of. First he fastened up the windows and latched them securely. Next, taking a handful of the flowers, he rubbed them all over the sashes. Then with the wisp he rubbed all over the jamb of the door, above, below, and at each side, and round the fireplace in the same way. I said, "Well, Professor, I know you always have a reason for what you do, but this certainly puzzles me. A sceptic would say that you were working some spell to keep out an evil spirit."

"Perhaps I am!" He answered quietly as he began to make the wreath which Lucy was to wear round her neck.

When she was in bed he fixed the wreath of garlic round her neck. The last words he said to her were,

"Take care you do not disturb it, and do not tonight open the window or the door."

"I promise," said Lucy.

As we left the house Van Helsing said, "Tonight I can sleep in peace!"

Lucy Westenra's Diary, 12 September

I quite love that dear Dr. Van Helsing. He was so anxious about these flowers. He positively frightened me. And yet, I feel comfort from them already. Somehow, I do not dread being alone tonight, and I can go to sleep without fear. I shall not mind any flapping outside the window. I never liked garlic before, but tonight it is delightful! There is peace in its smell. I feel sleep coming already. Goodnight, everybody.

DR. SEWARD'S DIARY

13 September.--Van Helsing and I arrived at Hillingham at eight o'clock. It was a lovely morning. We met Mrs. Westenra coming out of the morning room. She said,

"You will be glad to know that Lucy is better. The dear child is still asleep."

The Professor smiled, and looked quite jubilant. He rubbed his hands together, and said, "Aha! I thought I had diagnosed the case. My treatment is working."

To which she replied, "You must not take all the credit to yourself, doctor. Lucy's state this morning is due in part to me."

"How do you mean, ma'am?" asked the Professor.

"Well, I went into her room in the night. She was sleeping soundly. But the room was awfully stuffy. There were a lot of those horrible, strong-smelling flowers about everywhere, and she had actually a bunch of them round her neck. So I took them all away and opened a bit of the window. You will be pleased with her, I am sure."

As she had spoken, I watched the Professor's face, and saw it turn ashen gray. The instant she had disappeared he pulled me, suddenly and forcibly, into the dining room and closed the door.

Then, for the first time in my life, I saw Van Helsing break down. He sat down on a chair, and putting his hands before his face, began to sob, with loud, dry sobs that seemed to come from the very racking of his heart.

"What have we done? This poor mother does such thing as lose her daughter body and soul, and we must not even warn her, or she die, then both die. How are all the powers of the devils against us!"

Suddenly he jumped to his feet. "Come," he said. "Come, we must see and act. Devils or no devils, or all the devils at once, it matters not. We must fight him all the same." He went to the hall door for his bag, and together we went up to Lucy's room.

Once again I drew up the blind, whilst Van Helsing went towards the bed. He wore a look of stern sadness and infinite pity.

"As I expected," he murmured. Without a word he went and locked the door, and then began to set out on the little table the instruments for yet another operation of transfusion of blood. I had begun to take off my coat, but he stopped me with a warning hand. "No!" he said. "Today you must operate." As he spoke he took off his coat and rolled up his shirtsleeve.

Again the operation. Again the narcotic. Again some return of color, and the regular breathing of healthy sleep. This time I watched whilst Van Helsing recruited himself and rested.

Presently he took an opportunity of telling Mrs. Westenra that she must not remove anything from Lucy's room without consulting him. That the flowers were of medicinal value, and that the breathing of their odor was a part of the system of cure. Then he took over the care of the case himself, saying that he would watch this night and the next.

After another hour Lucy waked from her sleep, fresh and bright and seemingly not much the worse for her terrible ordeal.

What does it all mean? I am beginning to wonder if my long habit of life amongst the insane is beginning to tell upon my own brain.

LUCY WESTENRA'S DIARY

17 September.--Four days and nights of peace. I am getting so strong again that I hardly know myself. It is as if I had passed through some long nightmare. And then long spells of oblivion. Since, however, Dr. Van Helsing has been with me, all this bad dreaming seems to have passed away. The noises, the flapping against the windows, the distant voices which seemed so close to me, the harsh sounds that commanded me to do I know not what, have all ceased. I go to bed now without any fear of sleep. I have grown quite fond of the garlic, and a boxful arrives for me every day from Haarlem. Tonight Dr. Van Helsing is going away to Amsterdam. But I am well enough to be left alone.

Thank God for Mother's sake, and dear Arthur's, and for all our friends. Last night I did not fear to go to sleep again, although the boughs or bats or something flapped almost angrily against the window panes.

THE PALL MALL GAZETTE, 18 September.

THE ESCAPED WOLF PERILOUS ADVENTURE OF OUR INTERVIEWER

INTERVIEW WITH THE KEEPER IN THE ZOOLOGICAL GARDENS

After many inquiries and almost as many refusals, and perpetually using the words `PALL MALL GAZETTE' as a sort of talisman, I managed to find the keeper of the section of the Zoological Gardens in which the wold department is included. Thomas Bilder lives in one of the cottages in the enclosure behind the elephant house. Thomas and his wife are hospitable folk, elderly, and without children, and their lives must be pretty comfortable. He said,

"Now, Sir, you can go on and arsk me what you want. You'll excoose me refoosin' to talk of perfeshunal subjucts afore meals. Not even when you arsked me sarcastic like if I'd like you to arsk the Superintendent if you might arsk me questions. Without offence did I tell yer to go to `ell?"

"You did."

"An' when you said you'd report me for usin' obscene language that was `ittin' me over the `ead. But the `arfquid made that all right. I know what yer a-comin' at, that `ere escaped wolf."

"Exactly. I want you to give me your view of it."

"All right, guv'nor. This `ere is about the `ole story. That`ere wolf what we called Bersicker was one of three gray ones that came from Norway to Jamrach's, which we bought off him four years ago. He was a nice well-behaved wolf, that never gave no trouble to talk of. But, there, you can't trust wolves no more nor women."

"Don't you mind him, Sir!" broke in Mrs. Tom, with a cheery laugh. "`E's got mindin' the animiles so long that blest if he ain't like a old wolf `isself! But there ain't no `arm in `im."

"Well, Sir, it was about two hours after feedin' yesterday when I first hear my disturbance. I was makin' up a litter in the monkey house for a young puma which is ill. But when I heard the yelpin' and `owlin' I kem away straight. There was Bersicker a-tearin' like a mad thing at the bars as if he wanted to get out. There at hand was only one man, a tall, thin chap, with a `ook nose and a pointed beard, with a few white hairs runnin' through it. He had a `ard, cold look and red eyes, and I took a sort of mislike to him, for it seemed as if it was `im as they was hirritated at. He `ad white kid gloves on `is `ands, and he pointed out the animiles to me and says, `Keeper, these wolves seem upset at something.'

"`Maybe it's you,' says I, for I did not like the airs as he give `isself. He didn't get angry, as I `oped he would, but he smiled a kind of insolent smile, with a mouth full of white, sharp teeth. `Oh no, they wouldn't like me,' `e says.

" `Ow yes, they would,' says I, a-imitatin'of him.

"When I went over to Bersicker he let me stroke his ears same as ever. That there man kem over, and blessed but if he didn't put in his hand and stroke the old wolf's ears too!

" `Tyke care,' says I. `Bersicker is quick.'

" `Never mind,' he says. I'm used to `em!'

" `Are you in the business yourself?" I says, tyking off my `at, for a man what trades in wolves, anceterer, is a good friend to keepers.

" `Nom' says he, `not exactly in the business, but I `ave made pets of several.' and with that he lifts his `at as perlite as a lord, and walks away. Old Bersicker kep' a-lookin' arter `im till `e was out of sight, and then went and lay down in a corner and wouldn't come hout the `ole hevening. Well, larst night, so soon as the moon was hup, the wolves here all began a-`owling. There warn't nothing for them to `owl at. Just before twelve o'clock I just took a look round, but when I kem opposite to old Bersicker's cage I see the rails broken and twisted about and the cage empty. And that's all I know for certing."

"Now, Mr. Bilder, can you account in any way for the escape of the wolf?"

"Well then, Sir. It seems to me that `ere wolf escaped--simply because he wanted to get out."

From the hearty way that both Thomas and his wife laughed at the joke I could see that the whole explanation was simply an elaborate sell. I thought I knew a surer way to his heart, so I said, "Now, Mr. Bilder, we'll consider that first half-sovereign worked off, and this brother of his is waiting to be claimed when you've told me what you think will happen."

"Right y`are, Sir," he said briskly. "Ye`ll excoose me, I know, for a-chaffin' of ye, but the old woman her winked at me, which was as much as telling me to go on."

"Well, I never!" said the old lady.

"My opinion is this. That `ere wolf is a`idin' of, somewheres. My eye, won't some cook get a rum start when she sees his green eyes a-shinin' at her out of the dark! That's all."

I was handing him the half-sovereign, when something came bobbing up against the window, and Mr. Bilder's face doubled its natural length with surprise.

"God bless me!" he said. "If there ain't old Bersicker come back by `isself!"

He went to the door and opened it, a most unnecessary proceeding it seemed to me.

The animal itself was peaceful and well-behaved.

The wicked wolf that for a half a day had paralyzed London was petted like a sort of vulpine prodigal son. Old Bilder examined him all over and said,

"There, I knew the poor old chap would get into some kind of trouble. Here's his head all cut and full of broken glass. `E's been a-gettin' over some bloomin' wall or other. It's a shyme that people are allowed to top their walls with broken bottles. This `ere's what comes of it. Come along, Bersicker."

He took the wolf and locked him up in a cage, with a piece of meat, and went off to report.

I came off too, to report the only exclusive information that is given today regarding the strange escapade at the Zoo.

DR. SEWARD'S DIARY

17 September.--I was engaged after dinner in my study. Suddenly the door was burst open, and in rushed my patient, with his face distorted with passion. I was thunderstruck, for such a thing as a patient getting of his own accord into the Superintendent's study is almost unknown.

He made straight at me. He had a dinner knife in his hand, and as I saw he was dangerous, I tried to keep the table between us. He was too quick and too strong for me, however, for he struck at me and cut my left wrist rather severely.

Before he could strike again, however, I got in my right hand and he was sprawling on his back on the floor. My wrist bled freely, and quite a little pool trickled on to the carpet. I saw that my friend was not intent on further effort, and occupied myself binding up my wrist. When the attendants rushed in, and we turned our attention to him, his employment positively sickened me. He was lying on his belly on the floor licking up, like a dog, the blood which had fallen from my wounded wrist. He was easily secured, and to my surprise, went with the attendants quite placidly, simply repeating over and over again, "The blood is the life! The blood is the life!"

I have lost too much blood of late for my physical good, and then the prolonged strain of Lucy's illness is telling on me. I am over excited and weary, and I need rest, rest, rest. Happily Van Helsing has not summoned me, so I need not forego my sleep. Tonight I could not well do without it.

TELEGRAM, VAN HELSING, ANTWERP, TO SEWARD, CARFAX

(Sent to Carfax, Sussex, as no county given, delivered late by twenty-two hours.)

17 September.--Do not fail to be at Hilllingham tonight. See that flowers are as placed, very important, do not fail. Shall be with you as soon as possible after arrival.

DR. SEWARD'S DIARY

18 September.--Just off train to London. The arrival of Van Helsing's telegram filled me with dismay. Surely there is some horrible doom hanging over us that every possible accident should thwart us in all we try to do.

MEMORANDUM LEFT BY LUCY WESTENRA

17 September, Night.--I write this and leave it to be seen, so that no one may by any chance get into trouble through me. This is an exact record of what took place tonight. I feel I am dying of weakness, and have barely strength to write.

I went to bed as usual, taking care that the flowers were placed as Dr. Van Helsing directed, and soon fell asleep.

I was waked by the flapping at the window, which had begun after that sleep-walking on the cliff at Whitby when Mina saved me, and which now I know so well. I was not afraid. I tried to sleep. Then there came to me the old fear of sleep, and I determined to keep awake. I opened my door and called out. "Is there anybody there?" There was no answer. Then outside I heard a sort of howl like a dog's, but more fierce and deeper. I looked out, but could see nothing, except a big bat, which had evidently been buffeting its wings against the window. Presently the door opened, and mother looked in.

"I was uneasy about you, darling, and came in to see that you were all right."

I asked her to come in and sleep with me, so she came into bed, and lay down beside me. As she lay there in my arms, and I in hers the flapping and buffeting came to the window again. She was startled and a little frightened, and cried out, "What is that?"

I tried to pacify her. But I could hear her poor dear heart still beating terribly. After a while there was the howl again, and shortly after there was a crash at the window, and a lot of broken glass was hurled on the floor. The wind rushed in, and in the aperture of the broken panes there was the head of a great, gaunt gray wolf.

Mother cried out in a fright, and struggled up into a sitting posture, and clutched wildly at anything that would help her. Amongst other things, she clutched the wreath of flowers that Dr. Van Helsing insisted on my wearing round my neck, and tore it away from me. For a second or two she sat up, pointing at the wolf, and there was a strange and horrible gurgling in her throat. Then she fell over, as if struck with lightning, and her head hit my forehead.

The room and all round seemed to spin round. The wolf drew his head back, and a whole myriad of little specks seems to come blowing in through the broken window, and wheeling and circling round like a pillar of dust in the desert. I tried to stir, and dear Mother's poor body, which seemed to grow cold already, for her dear heart had ceased to beat, weighed me down, and I remembered no more for a while.

I recovered consciousness again. Somewhere near, a passing bell was tolling. The dogs all round the neighborhood were howling, and seemingly just outside, a nightingale was singing. I was dazed and stupid with pain and terror and weakness, but the sound of the nightingale seemed like the voice of my dead mother come back to comfort me. The sounds seemed to have awakened the maids, too, for I could hear their bare feet pattering outside my door. I called to them, and they came in, and when they saw what had happened they screamed out. The wind rushed in through the broken window, and the door slammed to. They lifted off the body of my dear mother, and laid her, covered up with a sheet, on the bed after I had got up. They were all so frightened and nervous that I directed them to go to the dining room and each have a glass of wine. The door flew open for an instant and closed again. The maids shrieked, and then went in a body to the dining room, and I laid what flowers I had on my dear mother's breast. When they were there I remembered what Dr. Van Helsing had told me, but I didn't like to remove them, and besides, I would have some of the servants to sit up with me now. I was surprised that the maids did not come back. I called them, but got no answer, so I went to the dining room to look for them.

My heart sank when I saw what had happened. They all four lay helpless on the floor, breathing heavily. The decanter of sherry was on the table half full, but there was a queer, acrid smell about. I was suspicious, and examined the decanter. It smelt of laudanum, and looking on the sideboard, I found that the bottle which Mother's doctor uses for her--oh! did use--was empty. What am I to do? What am I to do? I am back in the room with Mother. I cannot leave her, and I am alone, save for the sleeping servants, whom some one has drugged. Alone with the dead! I dare not go out, for I can hear the low howl of the wolf through the broken window.

The air seems full of specks, floating and circling in the draught from the window, and the lights burn blue and dim. What am I to do? God shield me from harm this night! I shall hide this paper in my breast, where they shall find it when they come to lay me out. My dear mother gone! It is time that I go too. Goodbye, dear Arthur, if I should not survive this night. God keep you, dear, and God help me!

Dr. Seward's Diary, 18 September

I drove at once to Hillingham. I knocked and rang as quietly as possible, for I hoped to only bring a servant to the door. After a while, finding no response, I knocked and rang again, still no answer. Hitherto I had blamed only the servants, but now a terrible fear began to assail me. Was it indeed a house of death to which I had come, too late? Every window and door was fastened and locked. I heard the rapid pit-pat of a swiftly driven horse's feet. I met Van Helsing running up the avenue. When he saw me, he gasped out, "How is she? Are we too late?"

I answered as quickly and coherently as I could. He paused and raised his hat as he said solemnly, "Then I fear we are too late. God's will be done!"

With his usual recuperative energy, he went on, "Come. If there be no way open to get in, we must make one."

We went round to the kitchen window. The Professor took a small surgical saw from his case, and handing it to me, pointed to the iron bars which guarded the window. I had very soon cut through three of them. Then with a long, thin knife we pushed back and opened the window. I helped the Professor in, and followed him. We tried all the rooms as we went along, and in the dining room found four servant women lying on the floor. Their stertorous breathing and the acrid smell of laudanum in the room left no doubt as to their condition.

Van Helsing said, "We can attend to them later." Then we ascended to Lucy's room. For an instant or two we paused at the door to listen, but there was no sound that we could hear. With white faces and trembling hands, we opened the door gently, and entered the room.

On the bed lay two women, Lucy and her mother. The latter lay farthest in, and she was covered with a white sheet, the edge of which had been blown back, showing the drawn, white, face, with a look of terror fixed upon it. By her side lay Lucy, with face white. The flowers which had been round her neck we found upon her mother's bosom, and her throat was bare, showing the two little wounds, but looking horribly white and mangled. Without a word the Professor bent over the bed, his head almost touching poor Lucy's breast. Then he cried out to me, "It is not yet too late! Quick! Quick! Bring the brandy!"

I flew downstairs and returned with it, taking care to smell and taste it. The maids were still breathing, but the narcotic was wearing off. I returned to Van Helsing. He rubbed the brandy on her lips and gums and on her wrists. He said to me, "I can do this. You go wake those maids. Make them get heat and fire and a warm bath. This poor soul is nearly as cold as that beside her. She will need be heated before we can do anything more."

I went at once, and found little difficulty in waking three of the women. The fourth was only a young girl, and the drug had evidently affected her more strongly so I lifted her on the sofa and let her sleep.

The others were dazed at first, but as remembrance came back to them they cried and sobbed in a hysterical manner. Sobbing and crying they went about their way, half clad as they were, and prepared fire and water. We got a bath and carried Lucy out as she was and placed her in it. There was a knock at the hall door. One of the maids returned and whispered to us that there was a gentleman who had come with a message from Mr. Holmwood. I bade her simply tell him that he must wait, for we could see no one now. She went away with the message, and, engrossed with our work, I clean forgot all about him.

I never saw Van Helsing work in such deadly earnest. It was a stand-up fight with death, and in a pause told him so. He answered me in a way that I did not understand.

"If that were all, I would stop here where we are now, and let her fade away into peace, for I see no light in life over her horizon." He went on with his work.

The heat was beginning to be of some effect. Lucy's heart beat a trifle more audibly to the stethoscope, and her lungs had a perceptible movement. Van Helsing's face almost beamed, and as we lifted her from the bath he said to me, "The first gain is ours! Check to the King!"

We took Lucy and laid her in bed and forced a few drops of brandy down her throat. Van Helsing tied a soft silk handkerchief round her throat. She was worse than we had ever seen her.

Van Helsing called in one of the women, and told her to stay with her and then beckoned me out of the room.

"We must consult," he said as we descended the stairs. In the hall he opened the dining room door, and we passed in, he closing the door carefully behind him. The shutters had been opened, but the blinds were already down, with that obedience to the etiquette of death which the British woman of the lower classes always rigidly observes. Van Helsing's sternness was somewhat relieved by a look of perplexity.

"We must have another transfusion of blood, and that soon, or that poor girl's life won't be worth an hour's purchase. You are exhausted already. I am exhausted too. I fear to trust those women. What are we to do for some one who will open his veins for her?"

"What's the matter with me, anyhow?"

The voice came from the sofa across the room, and its tones brought relief and joy to my heart, for they were those of Quincey Morris.

Van Helsing started angrily at the first sound, but his face softened and a glad look came into his eyes as I cried out, "Quincey Morris!" and rushed towards him with outstretched hands.

"What brought you her?" I cried as our hands met.

"I guess Art is the cause."

He handed me a telegram.-- 'Have not heard from Seward for three days, and am terribly anxious. Cannot leave. Father still in same condition. Send me word how Lucy is. Do not delay.--Holmwood.'

"I think I came just in the nick of time. You know you have only to tell me what to do."

Van Helsing strode forward, and took his hand, looking him straight in the eyes as he said, "Well, the devil may work against us, but God sends us men when we want them."

Once again we went through that ghastly operation. Lucy had got a terrible shock, and her body did not respond to the treatment as well as on the other occasions. Her struggle back into life was something frightful to see and hear. However, the action of both heart and lungs improved, and Van Helsing made a sub-cutaneous injection of morphia, as before, and with good effect. Her faint became a profound slumber.

I left Quincey lying down after having a glass of wine, and told the cook to get ready a good breakfast. Then a thought struck me, and I went back to the room where Lucy now was. When I came softly in, I found Van Helsing with a sheet or two of note paper in his hand. There was a look of grim satisfaction in his face, as of one who has had a doubt solved. He handed me the paper saying only, "It dropped from Lucy's breast when we carried her to the bath."

When I had read it I asked him, "In God's name, what does it all mean? Was she, or is she, mad, or what sort of horrible danger is it?" I was so bewildered. Van Helsing put out his hand and took the paper, saying,

"Forget it for the present. And now what is it that you came to me to say?" This brought me back to fact.

"I came to speak about the certificate of death. If we do not act properly and wisely, there may be an inquest. Mrs. Westenra had disease of the heart, and we can certify that she died of it. Let us fill up the certificate at once, and I shall take it myself to the registrar and go on to the undertaker."

"Good, oh my friend John! Well thought of!"

In the hall I met Quincey Morris, with a telegram for Arthur telling him that Mrs. Westenra was dead, that Lucy also had been ill, but was now going on better, and that Van Helsing and I were with her. I found no difficulty about the registration, and arranged with the local undertaker to come up in the evening to measure for the coffin and to make arrangements.

When I got back Quincey was waiting for me.

When we were alone, he said to me, "Jack Seward, I don't want to shove myself in anywhere where I've no right to be, but this is no common matter, and whatever it is, I have done my part. Is not that so?"

"That's so," I said, and he went on.

"I take it that both you and Van Helsing had done already what I did today. Is not that so?"

"That's so."

"And I guess Art was in it too. I was on the Pampas and had a mare that I was fond of go to grass all in a night. One of those big bats that they call vampires had got at her in the night, and what with his gorge and the vein left open, there wasn't enough blood in her to let her stand up, and I had to put a bullet through her as she lay. Jack, if you may tell me without betraying confidence, Arthur was the first, is not that so?"

As he spoke the poor fellow looked terribly anxious. He was in a torture of suspense regarding the woman he loved, and his utter ignorance of the terrible mystery which seemed to surround her intensified his pain.

"That's so."

"And how long has this been going on?"

"About ten days."

"Ten days! Then I guess, Jack Seward, that that poor pretty creature that we all love has had put into her veins within that time the blood of four strong men. Man alive, her whole body wouldn't hold it." Then coming close to me, he spoke in a fierce half-whisper. "What took it out?"

I shook my head. "That," I said, "is the crux. I can't even hazard a guess. Here we stay until all be well, or ill."

Quincey held out his hand. "Count me in," he said. "You and the Dutchman will tell me what to do, and I'll do it."

When she woke late in the afternoon, Lucy's first movement was to feel in her breast, and produced the paper which Van Helsing had given me to read. The careful Professor had replaced it where it had come from, lest on waking she should be alarmed. She gave a loud cry, and put her poor thin hands before her pale face.

She had realized to the full her mother's death. Towards dusk she fell into a doze. Whilst still asleep she took the paper from her breast and tore it in two. Van Helsing stepped over and took the pieces from her. She went on with the action of tearing, as though the material were still in her hands.

19 September.--All last night she slept fitfully, being always afraid to sleep. The Professor and I took in turns to watch, and we never left her for a moment unattended. Quincey Morris patrolled round and round the house.

When the day came, its searching light showed the ravages in poor Lucy's strength. Both Van Helsing and I noticed the difference in her, between sleeping and waking. Whilst asleep she looked stronger, although more haggard, and her breathing was softer. Her open mouth showed the pale gums drawn back from the teeth, which looked positively longer and sharper than usual. When she woke the softness of her eyes evidently changed the expression, for she looked her own self, although a dying one. In the afternoon she asked for Arthur, and we telegraphed for him.

When he arrived it was nearly six o'clock. When he saw her, Arthur was simply choking with emotion, and none of us could speak. Arthur's presence, however, seemed to act as a stimulant. She rallied a little, and spoke to him more brightly than she had done since we arrived.

I fear that tomorrow will end our watching, for the shock has been too great. The poor child cannot rally. God help us all.

LETTER MINA HARKER TO LUCY WESTENRA
(Unopened by her)
17 September
My dearest Lucy,

"It seems an age since I heard from you. Well, I got my husband back all right. When we arrived at Exeter there was a carriage, and in it, Mr. Hawkins. He took us to his house, where there were rooms for us all nice and comfortable, and we dined together. After dinner Mr. Hawkins said,

" `My dears, I know you both from children, and have, with love and pride, seen you grow up. Now I want you to make your home here with me. I have left to me neither chick nor child. All are gone, and in my will I have left you everything.' I cried, Lucy dear, as Jonathan and the old man clasped hands. Our evening was a very, very happy one.

"So here we are, installed in this beautiful old house. I am busy, I need not tell you, arranging things and housekeeping. Jonathan and Mr. Hawkins are busy all day, for now that Jonathan is a partner, Mr. Hawkins wants to tell him all about the clients.

"How is your dear mother getting on? Jonathan is beginning to put some flesh on his bones again, but he was terribly weakened by the long illness. And now I have told you my news, let me ask yours. When are you to be married? Jonathan asks me to send his `respectful duty', but I do not think that is good enough from the junior partner of the important firm Hawkins & Harker. And so, as you love me, and he loves me, and I love you with all the moods and tenses of the verb, I send you simply his `love' instead. Goodbye, my dearest Lucy, and blessings on you." Yours, Mina Harker

REPORT FROM PATRICK HENNESSEY, MD, MRCSLK, QCPI, ETC, ETC, TO JOHN SEWARD, MD

20 September

My dear Sir:

"In accordance with your wishes, I enclose report of the patient, Renfield. He has had another outbreak. This afternoon a carrier's cart with two men made a call at the empty house to which, you will remember, the patient twice ran away. The men stopped at our gate to ask the porter their way.

"I was myself looking out of the study window, having a smoke after dinner, and saw one of them come up to the house. As he passed the window of Renfield's room, the patient began to rate him from within, and called him all the foul names he could lay his tongue to. The man contented himself by telling him to `shut up for a foul-mouthed beggar', whereon our man accused him of robbing him and wanting to murder him and said that he would hinder him if he were to swing for it. I opened the window and signed to the man not to notice, so he contented himself by saying, `Lor' bless yer, sir, I wouldn't mind what was said to me in a bloomin' madhouse. I pity ye and the guv'nor for havin' to live in the house with a wild beast like that.'

"I told him where the gate of the empty house was. He went away followed by threats and curses and revilings from our man. I went down to see him and found him, to my astonishment, quite composed and most genial in his manner. I tried to get him to talk of the incident, but he blandly asked me questions as to what I meant, and led me to believe that he was completely oblivious of the affair. Within half an hour I heard of him again. This time he had broken out through the window of his room, and was running down the avenue. I ran after him. I saw the same cart which had passed before coming down the road, having on it some great wooden boxes. The men were wiping their foreheads, and were flushed in the face, as if with violent exercise. Before I could get up to him, the patient rushed at them, and pulling one of them off the cart, began to knock his head against the ground. If I had not seized him just at the moment, I believe he would have killed the man there and then. The other fellow jumped down and struck him over the head with the butt end of his heavy whip. It was a horrible blow, but he did not seem to mind it, but seized him also, and struggled with the three of us, pulling us to and fro as if we were kittens. You know I am no lightweight, and the others were both burly men. At first he was silent in his fighting, but as we began to master him, and the attendants were putting a strait waistcoat on him, he began to shout, `I'll frustrate them! They shan't rob me! They shan't murder me by inches! I'll fight for my Lord and Master!' and all sorts of similar incoherent ravings. It was with very considerable difficulty that they put him in the padded room. One of the attendants, Hardy, had a finger broken. However, I set it all right, and he is going on well.

"The two carriers said that if it had not been for the way their strength had been spent in carrying and raising the heavy boxes to the cart they would have made short work of him. I took their names and addresses, in case they might be needed. They are both in the employment of Harris & Sons, Moving and Shipment Company, Orange Master's Yard, Soho.

"I shall wire you at once if there is anything of importance.

"Believe me, dear Sir,

"Yours faithfully,

"Patrick Hennessey."

LETTER, MINA HARKER TO LUCY WESTENRA (Unopened by her)

18 September

"My dearest Lucy,

"Such a sad blow has befallen us. Mr. Hawkins has died very suddenly. I never knew either father or mother, so that the dear old man's death is a real blow to me. Jonathan is greatly distressed. He says the amount of responsibility which it puts upon him makes him nervous. He begins to doubt himself. Oh, it is too hard that a sweet, simple, noble, strong nature such as his, a nature which enabled him by our dear, good friend's aid to rise from clerk to master in a few years, should be so injured that the very essence of its strength is gone. Lucy dear, I must tell someone, for the strain of keeping up a brave and cheerful appearance to Jonathan tries me, and I have no one here that I can confide in. Forgive me for troubling you. With all blessings,

"Your loving

Mina Harker"

DR. SEWARD' DIARY

20 September.--I am too miserable, too low spirited, too sick of the world and all in it, including life itself, that I would not care if I heard this

moment the flapping of the wings of the angel of death. And he has been flapping those grim wings to some purpose of late, Lucy's mother and Arthur's father, and now . . .Let me get on with my work.

I duly relieved Van Helsing in his watch over Lucy. We wanted Arthur to go to rest also, but he refused at first.

Van Helsing was very kind to him. "Come, my child," he said. "Come with me. You are sick and weak."

Arthur went off with him, casting back a longing look on Lucy's face, which lay in her pillow, almost whiter than the lawn. She lay quite still. I could see the garlic. The whole of the window sashes reeked with it, and round Lucy's neck, over the silk handkerchief which Van Helsing made her keep on, was a rough chaplet of the same odorous flowers.

Lucy was breathing somewhat stertorously, and her face was at its worst, for the open mouth showed the pale gums. Her teeth seemed longer and sharper than they had been in the morning. In particular, the canine teeth looked longer and sharper than the rest.

I sat down beside her, and presently she moved uneasily. At the same moment there came a sort of dull flapping or buffeting at the window. I went over to the blind. There was a full moonlight, and I could see that the noise was made by a great bat, which wheeled around, doubtless attracted by the light, and every now and again struck the window with its wings. When I came back to my seat, I found that Lucy had moved slightly, and had torn away the garlic flowers from her throat. I replaced them as well as I could, and sat watching her.

It struck me as curious that whenever she got into that lethargic state, with the stertorous breathing, she put the flowers from her, but that when she waked she clutched them close.

At six o'clock Van Helsing came to relieve me. Arthur had then fallen into a doze, and he mercifully let him sleep on. When he saw Lucy's face I could hear the sissing indraw of breath, and he said to me in a sharp whisper. "Draw up the blind. I want light!" Then he bent down, and, with his face almost touching Lucy's, examined her carefully. He removed the flowers and lifted the silk handkerchief from her throat. As he did so he started back, "Mein Gott!" I looked, and as I noticed some queer chill came over me. The wounds on the throat had absolutely disappeared.

Van Helsing stood looking at her, with his face at its sternest. Then he said calmly, "She is dying. It will be much difference, mark me, whether she dies conscious or in her sleep. Wake that poor boy, and let him come and see the last."

I went to the dining room and waked him. I assured him that Lucy was still asleep, but told him I feared that the end was near. He covered his face with his hands, and slid down on his knees by the sofa. I took him by the hand and raised him up. "Come," I said, "my dear old fellow, summon all your fortitude."

When we came into Lucy's room I could see that Van Helsing had, with his usual forethought, been making everything look as pleasing as possible. He had even brushed Lucy's hair, so that it lay on the pillow in its usual sunny ripples. When we came into the room she opened her eyes, and seeing him, whispered softly, "Arthur! Oh, my love, I am so glad you have come!"

He was stooping to kiss her, when Van Helsing motioned him back. "No," he whispered, "not yet! Hold her hand, it will comfort her more."

So Arthur took her hand and knelt beside her, and she looked her best, with all the soft lines matching the angelic beauty of her eyes. Then gradually her eyes closed, and she sank to sleep. Her breast heaved softly, and her breath came and went like a tired child's.

And then insensibly there came the strange change which I had noticed in the night. Her breathing grew stertorous, the mouth opened, and the pale gums, drawn back, made the teeth look longer and sharper than ever. In a sort of sleepwaking, vague, unconscious way she opened her eyes, which were now dull and hard at once, and said in a soft, voluptuous voice, such as I had never heard from her lips, "Arthur! Oh, my love, I am so glad you have come! Kiss me!"

Arthur bent eagerly over to kiss her, but at that instant Van Helsing, who, like me, had been startled by her voice, swooped upon him, and catching him by the neck with both hands, dragged him back with a fury of strength which I never thought he could have possessed, and actually hurled him almost across the room. "Not on your life!" he said, and he stood between them like a lion at bay.

Arthur was so taken aback that he did not for a moment know what to do or say, and before any impulse of violence could seize him he realized the place and the occasion, and stood silent, waiting.

We saw a spasm as of rage flit like a shadow over Lucy's face. The sharp teeth clamped together. Then her eyes closed, and she breathed heavily.

Very shortly after she opened her eyes in all their softness, and putting out her poor, pale, thin hand, took Van Helsing's great brown one, drawing it close to her, she kissed it. "My true friend," she said, in a faint voice, but with untellable pathos, "My true friend, and his! Oh, guard him, and give me peace!"

"I swear it!" he said solemnly, kneeling beside her and holding up his hand, as one who registers an oath. Then he turned to Arthur, and said to him, "Come, my child, take her hand in yours, and kiss her on the forehead, and only once."

Their eyes met instead of their lips, and so they parted. Lucy's eyes closed, and Van Helsing, who had been watching closely, took Arthur's arm, and drew him away.

And then Lucy's breathing ceased.

"It is all over," said Van Helsing. "She is dead!"

I took Arthur by the arm, and led him away to the drawing room, where he sat down, and covered his face with his hands, sobbing in a way that nearly broke me down to see.

I went back to the room, and found Van Helsing looking at poor Lucy, and his face was sterner than ever. Some change had come over her body. Death had given back part of her beauty, for her brow and cheeks had recovered some of their flowing lines. Even the lips had lost their deadly pallor. It was as if the blood, no longer needed for the working of the heart, had gone to make the harshness of death as little rude as might be.

"We thought her dying whilst she slept, And sleeping when she died."

I stood beside Van Helsing, and said, "Ah well, poor girl, there is peace for her at last. It is the end!"

He said with grave solemnity, "Not so, alas! Not so. It is only the beginning!"

Dr. Seward's Diary --cont.

The funeral was arranged for the next succeeding day. I attended to all the ghastly formalities. The staff was afflicted, or blessed, with obsequious suavity. Even the woman who performed the last offices for the dead remarked to me, in a confidential way.

"She makes a very beautiful corpse, sir. It's quite a privilege to attend on her. She will do credit to our establishment!"

Van Helsing never kept far away. He insisted upon looking over Lucy's papers himself. I asked him why, for I feared that he, being a foreigner, might not be quite aware of English legal requirements.

He answered me, "I know, I know. You forget that I am a lawyer as well as a doctor. But this is not altogether for the law. You knew that, when you avoided the coroner. I have more than him to avoid. There may be papers more, such as this."

As he spoke he took from his pocket book the memorandum which had been in Lucy's breast, and which she had torn in her sleep.

"When you find anything of the solicitor who is for the late Mrs. Westenra, seal all her papers, and write him tonight. And I myself search for what may be. It is not well that her very thoughts go into the hands of strangers."

I found the name and address of Mrs. Westenra's solicitor and wrote to him. All the poor lady's papers were in order. I had hardly sealed the letter, when Van Helsing walked into the room, saying,

"Can I help you friend John?"

"Have you got what you looked for?" I asked.

To which he replied, "I did not look for any specific thing. I only hoped to find, and find I have, all that there was, only some letters and a few memoranda, and a diary new begun."

We finished the work in hand.

Before turning in we went to look at poor Lucy. The undertaker had certainly done his work well, for the room was turned into a small chapelle ardente. There was a wilderness of beautiful white flowers, and death was made as little repulsive as might be. The end of the winding sheet was laid over the face. All Lucy's loveliness had come back to her in death, and the hours that had passed, instead of leaving traces of `decay's effacing fingers', had but restored the beauty of life, till positively I could not believe my eyes that I was looking at a corpse.

The Professor looked sternly grave. He said to me, "Remain till I return," and left the room. He came back with a handful of wild garlic from the box waiting in the hall, and placed the flowers amongst the others on and around the bed. Then he took from his neck, inside his collar, a little gold crucifix, and placed it over the mouth. He restored the sheet to its place, and we came away.

I was undressing in my own room, when, with a premonitory tap at the door, he entered, and at once began to speak.

"Tomorrow I want you to bring me, before night, a set of post-mortem knives."

"Must we make an autopsy?" I asked.

"Yes and no. I want to cut off her head and take out her heart."

"The girl is dead. Why mutilate her poor body without need? And if there is no necessity for a post-mortem, why do it?"

For answer he put his hand on my shoulder, and said, with infinite tenderness, "Friend John, I pity your poor bleeding heart, and I love you the more because it does so bleed. Were you not amazed, nay horrified, when I would not let Arthur kiss his love, though she was dying? Yes! And yet you saw how she thanked me, and she kiss my rough old hand and bless me? Yes! And did you not hear me swear promise to her? Yes!

"Friend John, there are strange and terrible days before us. Will you not have faith in me?"

I took his hand, and promised him.

I must have slept long and soundly, for it was broad daylight when Van Helsing waked me by coming into my room. He came over to my bedside and said, "You need not trouble about the knives. We shall not do it."

"Why not?" I asked.

"Because," he said sternly, "it is too late, or too early. See!" Here he held up the little golden crucifix.

"This was stolen in the night."

"How stolen," I asked in wonder, "since you have it now?"

"Because I get it back from the worthless wretch who stole it. Now we must wait." He went away on the word, leaving me with a new mystery to think of, a new puzzle to grapple with.

At noon the solicitor came, Mr. Marquand, of Wholeman, Sons, Marquand & Lidderdale. He was very genial and took off our hands all cares as to details. He informed us that the whole estate, real and personal, was left absolutely to Arthur Holmwood.

He did not remain long. His coming, however, assured us that we should not have to dread hostile criticism as to any of our acts. Arthur was expected at five o'clock, so a little before that time we visited the death chamber. Both mother and daughter lay in it. The undertaker had made the best display he could of his goods, and there was a mortuary air about the place that lowered our spirits at once.

Van Helsing ordered the former arrangement to be adhered to, explaining that, as Lord Godalming was coming very soon, it would be less harrowing to his feelings to see all that was left of his fiancee quite alone.

Poor fellow! Arthur looked desperately sad and broken. I left him at the door of the room, but he took my arm and led me in, saying huskily,

"You loved her too, old fellow. She told me all about it, and there was no friend had a closer place in her heart than you. I don't know how to thank you for all you have done for her. I can't think yet . . ."

Here he suddenly broke down, and threw his arms round my shoulders and laid his head on my breast, crying, "Oh, Jack! Jack! What shall I do?"

I comforted him as well as I could. In such cases men do not need much expression. A grip of the hand, the tightening of an arm over the shoulder, a sob in unison, are expressions of sympathy dear to a man's heart. I stood still and silent till his sobs died away, and then I said softly to him, "Come and look at her."

Together we moved over to the bed, and I lifted the lawn from her face. God! How beautiful she was. Every hour seemed to be enhancing her loveliness. Arthur said to me in a faint whisper, "Jack, is she really dead?"

I assured him sadly that it was so. He took her dead hand in his and kissed it, and bent over and kissed her forehead. He came away, fondly looking back over his shoulder at her as he came.

I left him in the drawing room, and told Van Helsing of Arthur's question, and he replied, "I am not surprised. Just now I doubted for a moment myself!"

We all dined together, and I could see that poor Art was trying to make the best of things. Van Helsing had been silent all dinner time, but when we had lit our cigars he said, "Lord . . ., but Arthur interrupted him.

"No, no, not that, for God's sake! Not yet at any rate. Forgive me, sir. I did not mean to speak offensively."

The Professor answered very sweetly, "I only used that name because I was in doubt. I must not call you `Mr.' and I have grown to love you as Arthur."

Arthur held out his hand, and took the old man's warmly. "Call me what you will," he said. "I hope I may always have the title of a friend." He paused a moment, and went on, "And if I was rude or in any way wanting at that time you acted so, you remember,"-- the Professor nodded--"You must forgive me."

He answered with a grave kindness, "I know it was hard for you to quite trust me then. And there may be more times when I shall want you to trust when you cannot."

"And indeed, indeed, sir," said Arthur warmly. "I shall in all ways trust you. I know and believe you have a very noble heart, and you are Jack's friend, and you were hers. You shall do what you like."

The Professor cleared his throat a couple of times, as though about to speak, and finally said, "May I ask you something now?"

"Certainly."

"You know that Mrs. Westenra left you all her property?"

"No, poor dear. I never thought of it."

"I want you to give me permission to read all Miss Lucy's papers and letters. I have them all here. I took them before we knew that all was yours, so that no strange eye look through words into her soul. Even you may not see them yet, but I shall keep them safe. It is a hard thing that I ask, but you will do it, will you not, for Lucy's sake?"

Arthur spoke out heartily, like his old self, "Dr. Van Helsing, you may do what you will. My dear one would have approved."

The old Professor stood up as he said solemnly, "And you are right. There will be pain for us all, but it will not be all pain, nor will this pain be the last. We will have to pass through the bitter water before we reach the sweet. But we must be brave of heart and unselfish, and do our duty, and all will be well!"

I slept on a sofa in Arthur's room that night. Van Helsing did not go to bed at all. He went to and fro, as if patroling the house, and was never out of sight of the room where Lucy lay in her coffin, strewn with the wild garlic flowers, which sent through the odor of lily and rose, a heavy, overpowering smell into the night.

MINA HARKER'S JOURNAL

22 September.--In the train to Exeter. Jonathan sleeping. Jonathan a solicitor, a partner, rich, master of his business, Mr. Hawkins dead and buried, and Jonathan with another attack that may harm him. Some day he may ask me about it. Down it all goes.

The service was very simple and very solemn. There were only ourselves and the servants there. Jonathan and I stood hand in hand, and we felt that our best and dearest friend was gone from us.

We came back to town quietly and walked down Piccadilly. Jonathan was holding me by the arm, the way he used to in the old days before I went to school. I felt it very improper. But it was Jonathan, and he was my husband. I was looking at a very beautiful girl, in a big cart-wheel hat, sitting in a victoria outside Guiliano's, when I felt Jonathan clutch my arm so tight that he hurt me, and he said, "My God!"

I am always anxious about Jonathan, for I fear that some nervous fit may upset him again. So I asked him what it was that disturbed him.

He was very pale, and his eyes seemed bulging out as he gazed at a tall, thin man, with a beaky nose and black moustache and pointed beard, who was also observing the pretty girl. He was looking at her so hard that he did not see either of us, and so I had a good view of him. His face was not a good face. It was hard, and cruel, and sensual, and big white teeth, that looked all the whiter because his lips were so red, were pointed like an animal's. Jonathan kept staring at him, till I was afraid he would notice. I asked Jonathan why he was disturbed, and he answered, evidently thinking that I knew as much about it as he did, "Do you see who it is?"

"No, dear," I said. "Who is it?" His answer seemed to shock and thrill me. "It is the man himself!"

The poor dear was evidently terrified at something, very greatly terrified. The lady drove off. The dark man kept his eyes fixed on her, and when the carriage moved up Piccadilly he followed in the same direction, and hailed a hansom. Jonathan kept looking after him, and said, as if to himself,

"I believe it is the Count, but he has grown young. My God, if this be so! Oh, my God! If only I knew! If only I knew!" He was distressing himself, so I remained silent. I drew away quietly, and he, holding my arm, came easily. After a few minutes' staring at nothing, Jonathan's eyes closed, and he went quickly into a sleep, with his head on my shoulder. I did not disturb him. In about twenty minutes he woke up, and said to me quite cheerfully,

"Why, Mina, have I been asleep! Oh, do forgive me for being so rude. Come, and we'll have a cup of tea somewhere."

He had evidently forgotten all about the dark stranger, as in his illness he had forgotten all that this episode had reminded him of. I must somehow learn the facts of his journey abroad. The time is come, I fear, when I must open the parcel, and know what is written. Oh, Jonathan, you will, I know, forgive me if I do wrong, but it is for your own dear sake.

Later.--A sad home-coming in every way, the house empty of the dear soul who was so good to us. Jonathan still pale and dizzy under a slight relapse of his malady, and now a telegram from Van Helsing, whoever he may be. "You will be grieved to hear that Mrs. Westenra died five days ago, and that Lucy died the day before yesterday. They were both buried today."

Oh, what a wealth of sorrow in a few words! Poor Mrs. Westenra! Poor Lucy! Gone, gone, never to return to us! And poor, poor Arthur, to have lost such a sweetness out of his life! God help us all to bear our troubles.

DR. SEWARD'S DIARY-CONT.

22 September.--It is all over. Arthur has gone back to Ring, and has taken Quincey Morris with him. What a fine fellow is Quincey! If America can go on breeding men like that, she will be a power in the world indeed. Van Helsing goes to Amsterdam tonight, but says he returns tomorrow night. He says he has work to do in London. Poor old fellow! I fear that the strain of the past week has broken down even his iron strength. All the time of the burial he was, I could see, putting some terrible restraint on himself. When Arthur was speaking of his part in the operation where his blood had been transfused to his Lucy's veins I could see Van Helsing's face grow white and purple by turns. Arthur felt since then as if they two had been really married, and that she was his wife in the sight of God. None of us said a word of the other operations, and none of us ever shall. Arthur and Quincey went away together to the station, and Van Helsing and I came on here. The moment we were alone in the carriage he gave way to a regular fit of hysterics. He has denied to me since that it was hysterics, and insisted that it was only his sense of humor asserting itself under very terrible conditions. He laughed till he cried. And then he cried, till he laughed again, and laughed and cried together, just as a woman does. I tried to be stern with him, as one is to a woman under the circumstances, but it had no effect. Men and women are so different in manifestations of nervous strength or weakness! Then he said,

"Ah, friend John. Do not think that I am not sad, though I laugh. I give my blood for her. And my heart bleed for that poor boy.

"Oh, friend John, it is a strange world, a sad world. And yet when King Laugh come, he make them all dance to the tune he play."

"Well, for the life of me, Professor," I said, "I can't see anything to laugh at."

"Just so. Said Arthur not that the transfusion of his blood to her veins had made her truly his bride?"

"Yes, and it was a sweet and comforting idea for him."

"Quite so. But there was a difficulty, friend John. If so that, then what about the others? Ho, ho! Then this so sweet maid is a polyandrist, and me, with my poor wife dead to me, but alive by Church's law, even I am bigamist."

"I don't see where the joke comes in there either!" I said, and I did not feel particularly pleased with him for saying such things. He laid his hand on my arm, and said,

"Friend John, forgive me if I pain. If you could have looked into my heart then maybe you would perhaps pity me the most of all."

I was touched by the tenderness of his tone, and asked why.

"Because I know!"

THE WESTMINSTER GAZETTE, 25 SEPTEMBER A HAMPSTEAD MYSTERY

The neighborhood of Hampstead is known to the writers of headlines and "The Kensington Horror," or "The Stabbing Woman," or "The Woman in Black." During the past two or three days several cases have occurred of young children straying from home or neglecting to return from their playing on the Heath. In all these cases the children were too young to give any properly intelligible account of themselves, but the consensus of their excuses is that they had been with a "bloofer lady." It has always been late in the evening when they have been missed, and on two occasions the children have not been found until early in the following morning. As the first child missed gave as his reason for being away that a "bloofer lady" had asked him to come for a walk, the others had picked up the phrase and used it as occasion served.

Some of the children, indeed all who have been missed at night, have been slightly torn or wounded in the throat. The wounds might be made by a rat or a small dog, and although of not much importance individually, would tend to show that whatever animal inflicts them has a system or method of its own. The police are keeping a sharp lookout for straying children, especially when very young, in and around Hampstead Heath, and for any stray dog which may be about.

THE WESTMINSTER GAZETTE, 25 SEPTEMBER EXTRA SPECIAL

THE HAMPSTEAD HORROR
ANOTHER CHILD INJURED
THE "BLOOFER LADY"

Another child, missed last night, was only discovered late in the morning under a furze bush at the Shooter's Hill side of Hampstead Heath, which is perhaps, less frequented than the other parts. It has the same tiny wound in the throat as has been noticed in other cases. It was terribly weak, and looked quite emaciated. It too, when partially restored, had the common story to tell of being lured away by the "bloofer lady".

Mina Harker's Journal, 23 September

Jonathan is better after a bad night. He said he could not lunch at home. My household work is done, so I shall take his foreign journal, and read it.

24 September.--I hadn't the heart to write last night, that terrible record of Jonathan's upset me so. Poor dear! How he must have suffered. I wonder if there is any truth in it at all. Did he get his brain fever, and then write all those terrible things, or had he some cause for it all? And yet that man we saw yesterday! He seemed quite certain of him, poor fellow!

He believes it all himself. There seems to be through it all some thread of continuity. If ever Jonathan quite gets over the nervousness he may want to tell me of it all.

LETTER, VAN HELSING TO MRS. HARKER
24 September
(Confidence)
"Dear Madam,
"I pray you to pardon my writing to you the sad news of Miss Lucy Westenra's death. By the kindness of Lord Godalming, I am empowered to read her letters and papers, for I am deeply concerned about certain matters vitally important. In them I find some letters from you, which show how great friends you were and how you love her. I implore you, help me. May it be that I see you? You can trust me. I am friend of Dr. John Seward and of Lord Godalming (that was Arthur of Miss Lucy). I should come to Exeter to see you at once. I implore your pardon, Madam. I have read your letters to poor Lucy, and know how good you are and how your husband suffer. So I pray you, if it may be, enlighten him not, least it may harm. Again your pardon, and forgive me.
"VAN HELSING"

TELEGRAM, MRS. HARKER TO VAN HELSING
25 September.--Come today by quarter past ten train if you can catch it. Can see you any time you call. "WILHELMINA HARKER"

MINA HARKER'S JOURNAL
25 September.--I cannot help feeling terribly excited as the time draws near for the visit of Dr. Van Helsing, for somehow I expect that it will throw some light upon Jonathan's sad experience, as he attended poor dear Lucy in her last illness, he can tell me all about her. That is the

reason of his coming. Not about Jonathan. Then I shall never know the
real truth now! How silly I am. That awful journal gets hold of my
imagination and tinges everything with something of its own color. Of
course it is about Lucy. That awful night on the cliff must have made her
ill. I had almost forgotten in my own affairs how ill she was afterwards. I
hope I did right in not saying anything of it to Mrs. Westenra. I hope too,
Dr. Van Helsing will not blame me. I have had so much trouble and
anxiety of late that I feel I cannot bear more just at present.

I shall say nothing of Jonathan's journal unless he asks me. I am so
glad I have typewritten out my own journal, so that, in case he asks about
Lucy, I can hand it to him.

Later.--He has come and gone. Oh, what a strange meeting. I feel like
one in a dream. Can it be all possible, or even a part of it? If I had not
read Jonathan's journal first, I should never have accepted even a
possibility. Poor, poor, dear Jonathan! Dr. Van Helsing must be a good
man as well as a clever one if he is Arthur's friend and Dr. Seward's, and
if they brought him all the way from Holland to look after Lucy. I feel he
is good and kind and of a noble nature.

It was half-past two o'clock when the knock came. Mary opened the
door, and announced "Dr. Van Helsing".

I rose and bowed, and he came towards me, a man of medium
weight, strongly built, with his shoulders set back over a broad, deep
chest. The poise of the head strikes me at once as indicative of thought
and power. The face, clean-shaven. Big, dark blue eyes are set widely
apart. He said to me,

"Mrs. Harker, is it not?" I bowed assent.

"That was Miss Mina Murray?" Again I assented.

"Madam Mina, it is on account of the dead that I come."

"Sir," I said, "you could have no better claim on me than that you
were a friend and helper of Lucy Westenra."

I asked him what it was that he wanted to see me about, so he at once
began.

"I have read your letters to Miss Lucy. Forgive me, but I had to begin
to inquire somewhere. I know that you were with her at Whitby. She
sometimes kept a diary, an imitation of you, and in that diary she traces
by inference certain things to a sleep-walking in which you saved her."

"I can tell you, I think, Dr. Van Helsing, all about it."

"Ah, then you have good memory for facts, for details? It is not
always so with young ladies."

"No, doctor, but I wrote it all down at the time. I can show it to you
if you like."

"Oh, Madam Mina, I well be grateful."

So I took the typewritten copy from my work basket and handed it to him.

He took it and his eyes glistened. "You are so good," he said. "And may I read it now?"

"By all means," I said. "read it over whilst I order lunch, and then you can ask me questions whilst we eat."

He bowed and settled himself in a chair, and became absorbed in the papers. When I came back he rushed up to me and took me by both hands.

"Oh, Madam Mina," he said, "how can I say what I owe to you? This paper is as sunshine. It opens the gate to me. I am dazed, I am dazzled. Oh, but I am grateful to you, you so clever woman. Madame," he said this very solemnly, "if ever Abraham Van Helsing can do anything for you or yours, I trust you will let me know. There are darknesses in life, and there are lights. You are one of the lights."

"But, doctor, you praise me too much, and you do not know me."

"Oh, Madam Mina, good women tell all their lives. And your husband, tell me of him. Is he quite well? Is all that fever gone, and is he strong and hearty?"

I saw here an opening to ask him about Jonathan, so I said, "He was almost recovered, but he has been greatly upset by Mr. Hawkins death."

He interrupted, "Oh, yes. I know. I know. I have read your last two letters."

I went on, "I suppose this upset him, for Thursday last he had a sort of shock."

"A shock, and after brain fever so soon! That is not good. What kind of shock was it?"

"He thought he saw something which led to his brain fever." And here the whole thing seemed to overwhelm me in a rush. I suppose I was hysterical, for I threw myself on my knees and held up my hands to him, and implored him to make my husband well again. He held my hand in his, and said to me with, oh, such infinite sweetness,

"I promise you that I will gladly do all for him that I can. Therefore for his sake you must eat and smile."

After lunch, when we went back to the drawing room, he said to me, "And now tell me all about him."

"Dr. Van Helsing, what I have to tell you is so queer that you must not laugh at me or at my husband."

He said, "Oh, my dear, if you only know how strange is the matter regarding which I am here, it is you who would laugh."

"Thank you, thank you a thousand times! You have taken a weight off my mind. If you will let me, I shall give you a paper to read. It is long, but I have typewritten it out. It will tell you my trouble and Jonathan's. It is the copy of his journal when abroad, and all that happened. I dare not say anything of it. You will read for yourself and judge."

"I promise," he said as I gave him the papers. "I shall in the morning, as soon as I can, come to see you and your husband, if I may."

"Jonathan will be here at half-past eleven. You could catch the quick 3:34 train, which will leave you at Paddington before eight." He was surprised at my knowledge of the trains offhand. I have made up all the trains to and from Exeter, so that I may help Jonathan in case he is in a hurry.

So he took the papers with him and went away, and I sit here thinking, thinking I don't know what.

LETTER (by hand), VAN HELSING TO MRS. HARKER
25 September, 6 o'clock
"Dear Madam Mina,

"I have read your husband's so wonderful diary. You may sleep without doubt. Strange and terrible as it is, it is true! I will pledge my life on it. He is a noble fellow. His brain and his heart are all right, so be at rest. I shall have much to ask him. I am blessed that today I come to see you, for I have learn all at once so much that again I am dazzled, dazzled more than ever, and I must think.

"Yours the most faithful,
"Abraham Van Helsing."

LETTER, MRS. HARKER TO VAN HELSING
25 September, 6:30 p. m.
"My dear Dr. Van Helsing,

"A thousand thanks for your kind letter, which has taken a great weight off my mind. And yet, if it be true, what terrible things there are in the world, and what an awful thing if that man, that monster, be really in London! Will you, instead of lunching with us, please come to breakfast at eight o'clock? You can get away, if you are in a hurry, by the 10:30 train to Paddington by 2:35. Do not answer this, as I shall take it that, if I do not hear, you will come to breakfast.

"Your faithful and grateful friend,
"Mina Harker."

JONATHAN HARKER'S JOURNAL

26 September.--I thought never to write in this diary again, but the time has come. When I got home last night Mina had supper ready, and when we had supped she told me of Van Helsing's visit. She showed me in the doctor's letter that all I wrote down was true. It seems to have made a new man of me. It was the doubt as to the reality of the whole thing that knocked me over. I felt impotent, and in the dark, and distrustful. But, now that I know, I am not afraid, even of the Count. He has got younger, and how? Van Helsing is the man to unmask him and hunt him out, if he is anything like what Mina says. Mina is dressing, and I shall call at the hotel in a few minutes and bring him over.

When I came into the room where he was, and introduced myself, he took me by the shoulder, and turned my face round to the light, and said, after a sharp scrutiny,

"But Madam Mina told me you were ill, that you had had a shock."

It was so funny to hear my wife called `Madam Mina' by this kindly, strong-faced old man. I smiled, and said, "I was ill, but you have cured me already."

"And how?"

"By your letter to Mina last night. Doctor, you don't know what it is to doubt everything, even yourself. No, you don't, you couldn't with eyebrows like yours."

He seemed pleased, and laughed as he said, "So! You are a physiognomist. I learn more here with each hour. Oh, sir, you will pardon praise from an old man, but you are blessed in your wife."

I would listen to him go on praising Mina for a day.

"She is one of God's women, fashioned by His own hand. And you, sir. . . I have seen your true self since last night. You will give me your hand, will you not? And let us be friends for all our lives."

We shook hands, and he was so earnest and so kind that it made me quite choky.

"and now," he said, "may I ask you for some more help? Can you tell me what went before your going to Transylvania?"

"Look here, Sir," I said, "does what you have to do concern the Count?"

"It does," he said solemnly.

"Then I am with you heart and soul. I shall get the bundle of papers. You can take them with you and read them in the train."

After breakfast I saw him to the station. When we were parting he said, "Perhaps you will come to town if I send for you, and take Madam Mina too."

"We shall both come when you will," I said.

I had got him the morning papers and the London papers of the previous night, and while we were talking at the carriage window, waiting for the train to start, he was turning them over. His eyes suddenly seemed to catch something in one of them, "The Westminster Gazette", I knew it by the color, and he grew quite white. He read something intently, groaning to himself, "Mein Gott! Mein Gott! So soon! So soon!" Just then the whistle blew, and the train moved off. He leaned out of the window and waved his hand, calling out, "Love to Madam Mina. I shall write so soon as ever I can."

DR. SEWARD'S DIARY

26 September.--Renfield had become, to all intents, as sane as he ever was. He was already well ahead with his fly business, so he had not been of any trouble to me. I had a letter from Arthur, written on Sunday, he is bearing up wonderfully well. Quincey Morris is with him. As for myself, I was settling down to my work.

What is to be the end God only knows. Van Helsing went to Exeter yesterday, and stayed there all night. Today he came back, and almost bounded into the room at about half-past five o'clock, and thrust last night's "Westminster Gazette" into my hand.

"What do you think of that?" he asked as he stood back and folded his arms.

I looked over the paper, for I really did not know what he meant, but he took it from me and pointed out a paragraph about children being decoyed away at Hampstead. It did not convey much to me, until I reached a passage where it described small puncture wounds on their throats.

"Well?" he said.

"It is like poor Lucy's."

"And what do you make of it?"

"Whatever it was that injured her has injured them."

"That is true indirectly, but not directly."

"How do you mean, Professor?" I asked.

"Do you mean to tell me, friend John, that you have no suspicion as to what poor Lucy died of?"

"Of nervous prostration following a great loss or waste of blood."

"And how was the blood lost or wasted?" I shook my head.

He sat down beside me, and went on, "You are a clever man, friend John. You reason well, and your wit is bold, but you are too prejudiced. You do not let your eyes see nor your ears hear, and that which is outside your daily life is not of account to you. Do you not think that there are things which you cannot understand, and yet which are, that some people see things that others cannot? Ah, it is the fault of our science that it wants to explain all, and if it explain not, then it says there is nothing to explain. I suppose now you do not believe in corporeal transference. No? Nor in materialization. No? Nor in astral bodies. No? Nor in the reading of thought. No? Nor in hypnotism . . ."

"Yes," I said. "Charcot has proved that pretty well."

He smiled as he went on, "Then, friend John, am I to take it that you simply accept fact, and are satisfied to let from premise to conclusion be a blank? No? There are things done today in electrical science which would have been deemed unholy by the very man who discovered electricity, who would themselves not so long before been burned as wizards. There are always mysteries in life. Why was it that Methuselah lived nine hundred years, and yet that poor Lucy, with four men's blood in her poor veins, could not live even one day? Do you know all the mystery of life and death? Can you tell me why, when other spiders die small and soon, that one great spider lived for centuries in the tower of the old Spanish church and grew and grew, till, on descending, he could drink the oil of all the church lamps? Can you tell me why there are bats that come out at night and open the veins of cattle and horses and suck dry their veins, how in some islands of the Western seas there are bats which hang on the trees all day, like giant nuts or pods, and that when the sailors sleep on the deck, flit down on them and then, and then in the morning are found dead men, white as even Miss Lucy was?"

"Good God, Professor!" I said, starting up. "Do you mean Lucy was bitten by such a bat, and that such a thing is here in London in the nineteenth century?"

He waved his hand for silence, and went on, "Can you tell me why men believe in all ages and places that there are men and women who cannot die?"

Here I interrupted him. I was getting bewildered. I had a dim idea that he was teaching me some lesson, as long ago he used to do in his study at Amsterdam. I said,

"Tell me the thesis. I feel like a novice lumbering through a bog in a midst."

"That is a good image," he said. "Well, I shall tell you. My thesis is this, I want you to believe."

"To believe what?"

"To believe in things that you cannot. We shall have an open mind, and not let a little bit of truth check the rush of the big truth, like a small rock does a railway truck."

"Then you want me not to let some previous conviction inure the receptivity of my mind with regard to some strange matter."

"Ah, you are my favorite pupil still. You think then that those so small holes in the children's throats were made by the same that made the holes in Miss Lucy?"

"I suppose so."

He stood up and said solemnly, "Then you are wrong. No. It is worse, far, far worse."

"In God's name, Professor Van Helsing, what do you mean?" I cried.

He threw himself with a despairing gesture into a chair, covering his face with his hands as he spoke.

"They were made by Miss Lucy!"

Dr. Seward's Diary -cont.

For a while sheer anger mastered me. It was as if he had during her life struck Lucy on the face. I said to him, "Dr. Van Helsing, are you mad?"

"Would I were!" he said. "Madness were easy to bear compared with truth like this."

"Forgive me," said I.

He went on, "I do not expect you to believe. Tonight I go to prove it. Dare you come with me?"

This staggered me.

He saw my hesitation, and spoke, "The logic is simple. If it not be true, then proof will be relief. If it be true! Ah, there is the dread. First, we go off now and see that child in the hospital. Dr. Vincent, of the North Hospital, where the papers say the child is, is a friend of mine. And then . . ."

"And then?"

He took a key from his pocket. "And then we spend the night, you and I, in the churchyard where Lucy lies. This is the key that lock the tomb."

My heart sank, for I felt that there was some fearful ordeal before us.

We found the child awake. Dr, Vincent took the bandage from its throat, and showed us the punctures. There was no mistaking the similarity to Lucy's throat. They were smaller, and the edges looked fresher. We asked Vincent to what he attributed them, and he replied that it must have been a bite of some animal, perhaps a rat, or one of the bats which are so numerous on the northern heights of London. "Out of so many harmless ones," he said, "there may be some wild specimen. Some sailor may have brought one home, or one may have got loose. These things do occur, you, know. Only ten days ago a wolf got out, and traced up in this direction. For a week after, the children were playing nothing but Red Riding Hood until this `bloofer lady' scare came along. Even this poor little mite, when he woke up today, wanted to go to play with the `bloofer lady'."

"I hope," said Van Helsing, "you will caution its parents to keep strict watch over it. If the child were to remain out another night, it would probably be fatal."

We dined at `Jack Straw's Castle' along with a little crowd of bicyclists. About ten o'clock we started from the inn. It was very dark, and the scattered lamps made the darkness greater. The Professor went on unhesitatingly, but I was in quite a mixup as to locality. As we went further, we met fewer and fewer people. At last we reached the wall of the churchyard, which we climbed over. With some little difficulty we found the Westenra tomb. The Professor took the key, opened the creaky door, and standing back, politely, motioned me to precede him. There was a delicious irony in the offer on such a ghastly occasion. He fumbled in his bag, and taking out a matchbox and a piece of candle, proceeded to make a light. The tomb in the daytime had looked gruesome enough, but now, some days afterwards, when the flowers hung lank and dead, the effect was more miserable and sordid than could have been imagined.

Van Helsing went about his work systematically. Holding his candle so that he could read the coffin plates, he made assurance of Lucy's coffin. Another search in his bag, and he took out a turnscrew.

"What are you going to do?" I asked.

"To open the coffin. You shall yet be convinced."

Straightway he began taking out the screws, and finally lifted off the lid, showing the casing of lead beneath. The sight was almost too much for me. It seemed to be as much an affront to the dead as it would have been to have stripped off her clothing in her sleep whilst living. I actually took hold of his hand to stop him.

He only said, "You shall see," and again fumbling in his bag took out a tiny fret saw. Striking the turnscrew with a swift downward stab, which made me wince, he made a small hole. I had expected a rush of gas from the week-old corpse. Taking the edge of the loose flange, the Professor bent it back towards the foot of the coffin, and holding up the candle into the aperture, motioned to me to look.

I drew near and looked. The coffin was empty. It gave me a considerable shock, but Van Helsing was unmoved. He was now more sure than ever of his ground. "Are you satisfied now, friend John?" he asked.

I answered him, "That only proves one thing."

"And what is that, friend John?"

"That it is not there."

"That is good logic," he said, "so far as it goes. But how do you, account for it not being there?"

"Perhaps a body-snatcher," I suggested. It was the only real cause which I could suggest.

The Professor sighed. "Ah well!" he said," we must have more proof. Come with me."

He put on the coffin lid again, gathered up all his things and placed them in the bag. We went out. Behind us he closed the door and locked it. He handed me the key, saying, "Will you keep it? You had better be assured."

"A key is nothing," I said, "there are many duplicates, and lock picks."

He put the key in his pocket. Then he told me to watch at one side of the churchyard whilst he would watch at the other.

It was a lonely vigil. I heard a distant clock strike twelve, and in time came one and two. I was chilled and unnerved, and angry with the Professor for taking me on such an errand and with myself for coming. I was too cold and too sleepy to be keenly observant, and not sleepy enough to betray my trust, so altogether I had a dreary, miserable time.

Suddenly I saw something like a white streak, moving between two dark yew trees at the side of the churchyard farthest from the tomb. Then I moved, but I had to go round headstones and railed-off tombs, and I stumbled over graves. A little ways off a white dim figure flitted in the direction of the tomb. The tomb itself was hidden by trees, and I could not see where the figure had disappeared. I heard the rustle of actual movement, and coming over, found the Professor holding in his arms a tiny child. When he saw me he held it out to me, and said, "Are you satisfied now?"

"No," I said.

"Do you not see the child?"

"Yes, it is a child, but who brought it here? And is it wounded?"

"We shall see," said the Professor.

When we had got some little distance away, we struck a match, and looked at the child's throat. It was without a scratch or scar of any kind.

"Was I right?" I asked triumphantly.

"We were just in time," said the Professor thankfully.

At the edge of Hampstead Heath we heard a policeman's heavy tramp, and laying the child on the pathway, we waited and watched until he saw it. We heard his exclamation of astonishment, and then we went away silently.

I cannot sleep, so I make this entry. But I must try to get a few hours' sleep, as Van Helsing is to call for me at noon. He insists that I go with him on another expedition.

27 September.--It was two o'clock before we found a suitable opportunity for our attempt. The funeral held at noon was all completed. We knew that we were safe till morning. Again I felt that horrid sense, and I realized distinctly the perils of the law which we were incurring in our unhallowed work. I felt it was all so useless. Outrageous as it was to open a leaden coffin, to see if a woman dead nearly a week were really dead, it now seemed the height of folly to open the tomb again, when we knew, from our own eyesight, that the coffin was empty. Van Helsing had a way of going on his own road. He took the key, opened the vault, and again courteously motioned me to precede. The place was unutterably

mean looking when the sunshine streamed in. Van Helsing walked over
to Lucy's coffin, and I followed. He forced back the leaden flange, and a
shock of surprise and dismay shot through me.

There lay Lucy. She was, if possible, more radiantly beautiful than
ever, and I could not believe that she was dead. The lips were red, and on
the cheeks was a delicate bloom.

"Is this a juggle?" I said to him.

"Are you convinced now?" said the Professor, in response, and as he
spoke he pulled back the dead lips and showed the white teeth. "See," he
went on, "they are even sharper than before. With this," and he touched
one of the canine teeth, "the little children can be bitten. Are you of
belief now, friend John?"

I could not accept such an overwhelming idea as he suggested. I said,
"She may have been placed here since last night."

"Indeed? That is so, and by whom?"

"I do not know. Someone has done it."

"And yet she has been dead one week. Most peoples in that time
would not look so."

I had no answer for this, so was silent. Van Helsing was raising the
eyelids and looking at the eyes, and once more examining the teeth. Then
he turned to me and said,

"Here, there is one thing which is different from all recorded. She
was bitten by the vampire when she was in a trance, sleep-walking. And
in trance could he best come to take more blood. In trance she dies, and
in trance she is Un-Dead, too. So it is that she differ from all other.
Usually when the Un-Dead sleep at home," he made a comprehensive
sweep of his arm to designate what to a vampire was `home', "their face
show what they are, but this was when she not Un-Dead. There is no
malign there so it make hard that I must kill her in her sleep."

This turned my blood cold. But if she were really dead, what was
there of terror in the idea of killing her?

He said almost joyously, "Ah, you believe now?"

I answered, "How will you do this bloody work?"

"I shall cut off her head and fill her mouth with garlic, and I shall
drive a stake through her body."

It made me shudder to think of so mutilating the body of the
woman whom I had loved. And yet I was, in fact, beginning to shudder at
the presence of this being, this Un-Dead, as Van Helsing called it. Is it
possible that love is all subjective, or all objective?

I waited a considerable time for Van Helsing to begin, but he stood
as if wrapped in thought. Presently he closed the catch of his bag with a
snap, and said,

"I have been thinking, we may want Arthur, and how shall we tell him of this? I have done things that prevent him say goodbye as he ought, and he may think that in some more mistaken idea this woman was buried alive, and that in most mistake of all we have killed her. He, poor fellow, must have one hour that will make the very face of heaven grow black to him, then we can act for good all round and send him peace. I shall spend the night here in this churchyard in my own way. Tomorrow night you will come to me to the Berkeley Hotel at ten of the clock. I shall send for Arthur to come too, and also that so fine young man of America that gave his blood.

So we locked the tomb, and drove back to Piccadilly.

NOTE LEFT BY VAN HELSING IN HIS PORTMANTEAU, BERKELEY HOTEL DIRECTED TO JOHN SEWARD, M. D. (Not Delivered)

27 September

"Friend John,

"I write this in case anything should happen. I go alone to watch in that churchyard. It pleases me that the Un-Dead, Miss Lucy, shall not leave tonight, that so on the morrow night she may be more eager. Therefore I shall fix some things she like not, garlic and a crucifix, and so seal up the door of the tomb. She is young as Un-Dead, and will heed. I shall be at hand all the night from sunset till after sunrise, and if there be aught that may be learned I shall learn it. But that other Un-Dead, he have not the power to seek her tomb and find shelter. He is cunning. He have the strength of twenty men. Besides, he can summon his wolf and I know not what. So if it be that he came thither on this night he shall find me.

"Therefore I write this in case . . . Take the papers that are with this, the diaries of Harker and the rest, and read them, and then find this great Un-Dead, and cut off his head and burn his heart or drive a stake through it, so that the world may rest from him.

"If it be so, farewell.

"VAN HELSING."

DR. SEWARD'S DIARY

28 September.--It is wonderful what a good night's sleep will do for one. Yesterday I was almost willing to accept Van Helsing's monstrous ideas, but now they seem to me as outrages on common sense. Surely there must be some rational explanation. It would be almost as great a marvel as the other to find that Van Helsing was mad, but anyhow I shall watch him carefully. I may get some light on the mystery.

29 September.--Last night, at a little before ten o'clock, Arthur and Quincey came into Van Helsing's room. He began by saying that he hoped we would all come with him, "for," he said, "there is a grave duty to be done there. You were doubtless surprised at my letter?" This query was directly addressed to Lord Godalming.

"I was. It rather upset me for a bit. I have been curious, too, as to what you mean.

"Me too," said Quincey Morris laconically.

"Oh," said the Professor, "then you are nearer the beginning than friend John here."

Then, turning to the other two, he said with intense gravity,

"I want your permission to do what I think good this night. May I ask that you promise me."

"That's frank anyhow," broke in Quincey. "I don't quite see his drift, but I swear he's honest, and that's good enough for me."

"I thank you, Sir," said Van Helsing proudly. He held out a hand, which Quincey took.

Then Arthur spoke out, "Dr. Van Helsing, I don't quite like to `buy a pig in a poke', as they say in Scotland, and if it be anything in which my honour as a gentleman or my faith as a Christian is concerned, I cannot make such a promise."

"I accept your limitation," said Van Helsing, "and all I ask of you is that you will first consider it well and be satisfied that it does not violate your reservations."

"Agreed!" said Arthur. "May I ask what it is we are to do?"

"I want you to come with me, in secret, to the churchyard at Kingstead."

Arthur's face fell as he said in an amazed sort of way,

"Where poor Lucy is buried?"

The Professor bowed.

Arthur went on, "And when there?"

"To enter the tomb!"

"Professor, are you in earnest, or is it some monstrous joke?" There was silence until he asked again, "And when in the tomb?"

"To open the coffin."

"This is too much!" he said angrily. "I am willing to be patient in all things that are reasonable, but in this, this desecration of the grave, of one who . . ." He fairly choked with indignation.

The Professor looked pityingly at him. "If I could spare you," he said, "God knows I would. But this night our feet must tread in thorny paths, or later, and for ever, the feet you love must walk in paths of flame!"

Arthur looked up with set white face and said, "Take care, sir, take care!"

"Would it not be well to hear what I have to say?" said Van Helsing.

"That's fair enough," broke in Morris.

After a pause Van Helsing went on, evidently with an effort, "Miss Lucy is dead, is it not so? Yes! Then there can be no wrong to her. But if she be not dead. . ."

Arthur jumped to his feet, "Good God!" he cried. "What do you mean? Has there been any mistake, has she been buried alive?" He groaned in anguish.

"I did not say she was alive, my child. I go no further than to say that she might be Un-Dead."

"Un-Dead! Not alive! What do you mean?"

"May I cut off the head of dead Miss Lucy?"

"Heavens and earth, no!" cried Arthur in a storm of passion. "Not for the wide world will I consent to any mutilation of her dead body. I shall not give my consent to anything you do. I have a duty to do in protecting her grave from outrage, and by God, I shall do it!"

Van Helsing rose up from where he had all the time been seated, and said, gravely and sternly, "My Lord Godalming, I too, have a duty to do, and by God, I shall do it! All I ask you now is that you come with me, that you look and listen, and if when later I make the same request you do not be more eager for its fulfillment even than I am, then, I shall hold myself at your disposal to render an account to you, when and where you will." His voice broke a little, and he went on with a voice full of pity.

"Do not go forth in anger with me. I have never had so heavy a task as now. I gave her my nights and days, before death, after death, and if my death can do her good even now, when she is the dead Un-Dead, she shall have it freely."

He said this with a very grave, sweet pride, and Arthur was much affected by it.

He took the old man's hand and said in a broken voice, "I cannot understand, but at least I shall go with you and wait."

Dr. Seward's Diary -cont.

It was just a quarter before twelve o'clock when we got into the churchyard over the low wall. The night was dark with occasional gleams of moonlight between the dents of the heavy clouds. Van Helsing led the way. The Professor unlocked the vault door and entered first himself. The rest of us followed. He then lit a dark lantern and pointed to a coffin. Van Helsing said to me, "Was the body of Miss Lucy in that coffin yesterday?"

"It was."

The Professor turned to the rest saying, "You hear.'

He took his screwdriver and again took off the coffin lid. Arthur looked on, very pale but silent. When the lid was removed he stepped forward. Van Helsing forced back the leaden flange, and we all looked in and recoiled.

The coffin was empty!

For several minutes no one spoke a word. The silence was broken by Quincey Morris, "Professor, is this your doing?"

"I swear to you that I have not removed or touched her. Two nights ago my friend Seward and I opened that sealed coffin, and we found it as now, empty. We then saw something white come through the trees. The next day we came here in daytime and she lay there. Did she not, friend John?

"Yes."

"That night we were just in time. We found a small child unharmed amongst the graves. Yesterday I came here before sundown, for at sundown the Un-Dead can move. I waited here all night, but I saw nothing because I had laid over the clamps of those doors garlic, which the Un-Dead cannot bear, and other things which they shun. Tonight before sundown I took away my garlic and other things. And now this coffin is empty. Wait you with me outside, unseen and unheard, and things much stranger are yet to be. So," here he shut the slide of his his lantern, "now to the outside." We filed out, he coming last and locking the door behind him.

Oh! But it seemed fresh and pure in the night air after the terror of that vault. Each in his own way was solemn and overcome. Not being able to smoke, Quincey Morris cut himself a good-sized plug of tobacco and began to chew. As to Van Helsing, he took from his bag a wafer-like biscuit, which was carefully rolled up in a white napkin. Next he took out a double handful of some whitish stuff, like dough or putty. He crumbled the wafer up fine and worked it into the mass between his hands. He then, rolling it into thin strips, began to lay them into the crevices between the door and its setting in the tomb. I was somewhat puzzled at this, and being close, asked him what it was that he was doing.

He answered, "I am closing the tomb so that the Un-Dead may not enter."

"And is that stuff going to do it?"

"It Is."

"What is that?" Asked Arthur. Van Helsing reverently lifted his hat as he answered.

"The Host. I brought it from Amsterdam. I have an Indulgence."

It was an answer that appalled the most sceptical of us. Never did tombs look so ghastly white. Never did cypress seem the embodiment of funeral gloom. And never did the howling of dogs send such a woeful presage through the night.

There was a long spell of silence, aching, void, and then from the Professor a keen "S-s-s-s!" He pointed, and we saw a dim white figure advance, which held something dark at its breast. The figure stopped, and a ray of moonlight fell, and showed a dark-haired woman, dressed in the cerements of the grave. The face was bent down over a fair-haired child. There was a sharp little cry, such as a child gives in sleep. We were starting forward, but the Professor's warning hand kept us back. The white figure moved forwards again. My own heart grew cold as ice, and I could hear the gasp of Arthur, as we recognized the features of Lucy Westenra. Lucy Westenra, but changed. The sweetness was turned to adamantine, heartless cruelty, and the purity to voluptuous wantonness.

Van Helsing stepped out. The four of us ranged in a line before the door of the tomb. Van Helsing raised his lantern. We could see that Lucy's lips were crimson with fresh blood, and that the stream had trickled over her chin and stained the purity of her lawn death robe.

We shuddered with horror. I could see by the tremulous light that even Van Helsing's iron nerve had failed. If I had not seized Arthur's arm, he would have fallen.

When Lucy, I call it Lucy because it bore her shape, saw us she drew back with an angry snarl, such as a cat, then her eyes ranged over us. Lucy's eyes, unclean and full of hell fire, instead of the pure, gentle orbs we knew. At that moment the remnant of my love passed into hate and loathing. Had she then to be killed, I could have done it with savage delight. As she looked, her eyes blazed with unholy light, and the face became wreathed with a voluptuous smile. With a careless motion, she flung to the ground, callous as a devil, the child, growling over it as a dog growls over a bone. The child gave a sharp cry, and lay there moaning. When she advanced to Arthur with outstretched arms and a wanton smile he fell back and hid his face in his hands.

She still advanced, however, and with a languorous, voluptuous grace, said, "Come to me, Arthur. Leave these others and come to me. My arms are hungry for you. Come, and we can rest together. Come, my husband, come!"

There was something diabolically sweet in her tones, something of the tinkling of glass when struck, which rang through our brains.

Arthur seemed under a spell, moving his hands from his face, he opened wide his arms. She was leaping for them, when Van Helsing sprang forward and held between them his little golden crucifix. She recoiled from it, and, with a suddenly distorted face, full of rage, dashed past him as if to enter the tomb.

When within a foot of the door, however, she stopped, as if arrested by some irresistible force. Then she turned, and her face was shown in the moonlight. Never did I see such baffled malice on a face. The beautiful color became livid, the eyes seemed to throw out sparks of hell fire, the brows were wrinkled as though the folds of flesh were the coils of Medusa's snakes, and the lovely, blood-stained mouth grew to an open square, as in the passion masks of the Greeks and Japanese.

She remained between the lifted crucifix and the sacred closing of her means of entry.

Van Helsing broke the silence by asking Arthur, "Answer me, oh my friend! Am I to proceed in my work?"

"Do as you will, friend. Do as you will." And he groaned in spirit.

Coming close to the tomb, Van Helsing began to remove from the chinks some of the sacred emblem. We all looked on with horrified amazement when the woman, with a corporeal body as real as our own, pass through the interstice where scarce a knife blade could have gone. We all felt relief when we saw the Professor calmly restoring the strings of putty to the edges of the door.

When this was done, he lifted the child and said, "Come now, my friends. We can do no more till tomorrow. We shall leave this little one where the police will find him and then to home."

Coming close to Arthur, he said, "Forgive me."

29 September, night.--A little before twelve o'clock Arthur, Quincey Morris, and myself, called for the Professor. We got to the graveyard by half-past one. Van Helsing, instead of his little black bag, had with him a long leather one.

We silently followed the Professor to the tomb. He unlocked the door, and we entered, closing it behind us. Then he took from his bag the lantern, which he lit, and also two wax candles, which he stuck on other coffins. When he again lifted the lid off Lucy's coffin we all looked,

Arthur trembling like an aspen, and saw that the corpse lay there in all its death beauty. But there was no love in my own heart. I could see even Arthur's face grow hard as he looked. Presently he said to Van Helsing, "Is this really Lucy's body, or only a demon in her shape?"

"It is her body, and yet not it."

She seemed like a nightmare of Lucy as she lay there, the pointed teeth, the blood stained, voluptuous mouth, the whole carnal and unspirited appearance, seeming like a devilish mockery of Lucy's sweet purity. Van Helsing, with his usual methodicalness, began taking out the various contents from his bag, an oil lamp, then his operating knives, and last a round wooden stake, some three inches thick and about three feet long. One end of it was hardened by charring in the fire, and was sharpened to a fine point. With this stake came a heavy hammer, such as used in the coal cellar for breaking the lumps.

Van Helsing said, "It is out of the lore and experience of the ancients. When they become Un-dead, there comes the curse of immortality. They cannot die, but must go on age after age adding new victims and multiplying the evils of the world. For all that die from the Un-dead become themselves Un-dead, and prey on their kind. And so the circle goes on ever widening, like ripples in the water. Friend Arthur, if you had met that kiss before poor Lucy die, or again, last night, you would, when you had died, have become nosferatu, as they call it in Eastern europe, Un-Dead. Those children whose blood she sucked, if she lives on, Un-Dead, more and more they lose their blood and by her power over them they come to her, with that so wicked mouth. But if she die in truth, then all cease. The tiny wounds of the throats disappear, and they go back to their play. When this now Un-Dead be made to rest as true dead, then the soul of the poor lady whom we love shall again be free. Instead of working wickedness, she shall take her place with the other Angels. So it will be a blessed hand for her that shall strike the blow that sets her free. To this I am willing, but is there none amongst us who has a better right?"

We all looked at Arthur. He stepped forward and said bravely, though his hand trembled, "Tell me what I am to do!"

Van Helsing laid a hand on his shoulder, and said, "Brave lad! A moment's courage, and it is done. This stake must be driven through her."

"Go on," said Arthur hoarsely.

"Take this stake in your left hand, place the point over the heart, and the hammer in your right. Then when we begin our prayer for the dead, strike in God's name, that so the Un-Dead pass away." Arthur took the stake and the hammer. Van Helsing opened his missal and began to read, and Quincey and I followed as well as we could.

Arthur placed the point over the heart, and as I looked I could see its dint in the white flesh. Then he struck with all his might.

The thing in the coffin writhed, and a hideous, bloodcurdling screech came from the opened red lips. The body shook and quivered and twisted in wild contortions. The sharp white champed together till the lips were cut, and the mouth was smeared with a crimson foam. But Arthur never faltered. His untrembling arm rose and fell, driving deeper and deeper the mercybearing stake, whilst the blood spurted up around it. His face was set. Our voices seemed to ring through the little vault.

Finally it lay still. The terrible task was over.

The hammer fell from Arthur's hand. He reeled and would have fallen had we not caught him. Sweat sprang from his forehead, and his breath came in broken gasps. A murmur of startled surprise ran between us. We gazed towards the coffin so eagerly that Arthur rose, and looked too.

There, in the coffin lay no longer the foul Thing, but Lucy as we had seen her in life, with her face of unequalled sweetness and purity. There were the traces of care and pain and waste. But these marked her truth to what we knew.

Van Helsing laid his hand on Arthur's shoulder, and said, "And now, Arthur my friend, am I not forgiven?"

Arthur took the old man's hand and said, "Forgiven!"

Van Helsing then said to him, "And now, my child, you may kiss her."

Arthur bent and kissed her, and then we sent him and Quincey out of the tomb. The Professor and I sawed the top off the stake, leaving the point of it in the body. Then we cut off the head and filled the mouth with garlic. We soldered up the leaden coffin, screwed on the coffin lid, and came away. When the Professor locked the door he gave the key to Arthur.

Outside the air was sweet, and the sun shone. There was gladness and mirth and peace everywhere, for we were at rest ourselves on one account.

Van Helsing said, "Now, my friends, there remains a greater task, to find out the author of all this and to stamp him out. Shall you not all help me? And do we not promise to go on to the bitter end?"

Each in turn, we took his hand, and the promise was made.

Dr. Seward's Diary -cont

When we arrived at the Berkely Hotel, Van Helsing found a telegram waiting for him.

"Am coming up by train. Jonathan at Whitby. Important news. Mina Harker."

The Professor was delighted. "Ah, that wonderful Madam Mina," he said, "pearl among women! She arrive, but I cannot stay. Friend John, you must meet her at the station. Telegraph her en route."

Van Helsing told me of a diary kept by Jonathan Harker when abroad, and gave me a typewritten copy of it, and also of Mrs. Harker's diary at Whitby. "Take these," he said, "and study them well." He laid his hand heavily on the packet of papers. "We shall go through all these together when we meet." He then drove off. I took my way to Paddington, where I arrived about fifteen minutes before the train came in.

The crowd melted away, and a sweet-faced, dainty looking girl stepped up to me and said, "Dr. Seward, is it not?"

"And you are Mrs. Harker!" I answered.

"I knew you from the description of poor dear Lucy, but. . ." She stopped suddenly, and a quick blush overspread her face.

The blush that rose to my own cheeks somehow set us both at ease. I got her luggage, and we took the Underground to Fenchurch Street, after I had sent a wire to my housekeeper to have a sitting room and a bedroom prepared at once for Mrs. Harker.

In due time we arrived. She knew, of course, that the place was a lunatic asylum, but she was unable to repress a shudder.

She told me that she had much to say. So here I am finishing my entry in my phonograph diary whilst I await her. Here she is!

MINA HARKER'S JOURNAL

29 September.--After I had tidied myself, I went down to Dr. Seward's study. At the door I thought I heard him talking with some one.

To my intense surprise, there was no one with him. He was quite alone, and on the table opposite him was a phonograph. I had never seen one, and was much interested.

"I hope I did not keep you waiting," I said, "but I thought there was someone with you."

"Oh," he replied with a smile, "I was only entering my diary."

"Your diary?" I asked him in surprise.

"Yes," he answered. "I keep it in this." He laid his hand on the phonograph. I felt quite excited over it, and blurted out, "Why, this beats even shorthand! May I hear it say something?"

"Certainly," he replied with alacrity. Then he paused.

"The fact is," he began awkwardly. "I only keep my diary in it, and as it is about my cases it may be awkward, that is, I mean . . ." He stopped, and I tried to help him out of his embarrassment.

"You helped to attend dear Lucy at the end. Let me hear how she died. She was very, very dear to me."

He answered, with a horrorstruck look in his face, "Not for the wide world!"

"Why not?" I asked.

He stammered out, "You see, I do not know how to pick out any particular part of the diary. It never once struck me how I was going to find any particular part of it in case I wanted to look it up?"

By this time my mind was made up that the diary might have something to add to the sum of our knowledge of that terrible Being, and I said boldly, "Then, Dr. Seward, you had better let me copy it out for you on my typewriter."

He grew to a positively deathly pallor as he said, "No! No! No! For all the world. I wouldn't let you know that terrible story!"

Then it was terrible. My intuition was right!

"You do not know me," I said. "When you have read those papers, my own diary and my husband's also, which I have typed, you will. I must not expect you to trust me so far."

He is certainly a man of noble nature. Poor dear Lucy was right about him. He stood up and opened a large drawer, in which were arranged in order a number of hollow cylinders of metal covered with dark wax, and said,

"You are quite right. I did not trust you. I know that Lucy told you of me. She told me of you too. Take the cylinders and hear them. Then you will know me better. Dinner will by then be ready. In the meantime I shall read over some of these documents."

He carried the phonograph up to my sitting room. Now I shall learn something pleasant, I am sure. It will tell me a true love episode of which I know one side already.

DR. SEWARD'S DIARY

29 September.--I was so absorbed in that wonderful diary of Jonathan Harker and that of his wife that I let the time run on without thinking. I had just finished, when Mrs. Harker came in. She looked

sweetly pretty, but very sad, and her eyes were flushed with crying. So I said as gently as I could, "I greatly fear I have distressed you."

"Oh, no, not distressed me," she replied. "But I have been touched by your grief. That is a wonderful machine. It told me, in its very tones, the anguish of your heart. I have copied out the words on my typewriter, and none other need now hear your heart beat, as I did."

"No one need ever know," I said in a low voice.

She laid her hand on mine, "Ah, but they must!"

"Must! but why?" I asked.

"Because it is a part of the terrible story. We need have no secrets amongst us. Working together and with absolute trust, we can surely be stronger than if some of us were in the dark."

She looked at me so appealingly, that I gave in at once to her wishes. "You shall," I said, "do as you like in the matter. We have a cruel and dreadful task."

MINA HARKER'S JOURNAL

29 September.--After dinner I came with Dr. Seward to his study. He brought back the phonograph from my room, and arranged it so that I could touch it without getting up. Then he began to read. I put the forked metal to my ears and listened.

When the terrible story of Lucy's death was done, I lay back in my chair powerless. When Dr. Seward saw me he jumped up with a horrified exclamation, and gave me some brandy, which in a few minutes somewhat restored me. It is all so wild and mysterious; I didn't know what to believe. I took the cover off my typewriter, and said to Dr. Seward,

"Let me write this all out now. We must be ready for Dr. Van Helsing. "You tell me that Lord Godalming and Mr. Morris are coming too. Let us be able to tell them when they come."

Dr. Seward sat near me, reading, so that I did not feel too lonely whilst I worked. The world seems full of good men, even if there are monsters in it.

Seeing that Dr. Seward keeps his newspapers, I borrowed the files of `The Westminster Gazette' and `The Pall Mall Gazette' and took them to my room. I remember how much the `Dailygraph' and `The Whitby Gazette', of which I had made cuttings, had helped us to understand the terrible events at Whitby when Count Dracula landed, so I shall look through the evening papers since then, and perhaps I shall get some new light. I am not sleepy, and the work will help to keep me quiet.

DR. SEWARD'S DIARY

30 September.--Mr. Harker arrived at nine o'clock. He is uncommonly clever, if one can judge from his face, and full of energy. If this journal be true, and judging by one's own wonderful experiences, it must be, he is also a man of great nerve. That going down to the vault a second time was a remarkable piece of daring. After reading his account of it I was prepared to meet a good specimen of manhood, but hardly the quiet, business-like gentleman who came here today.

LATER.--After lunch Harker and his wife went back to their own room, and as I passed a while ago I heard the click of the typewriter. They are hard at it. Mrs. Harker says that knitting together in chronological order every scrap of evidence they have. Harker has got the letters between the consignee of the boxes at Whitby and the carriers in London who took charge of them. He is now reading his wife's transcript of my diary. I wonder what they make out of it. Here it is . . .

Strange that it never struck me that the very next house might be the Count's hiding place! Goodness knows that we had enough clues from the conduct of the patient Renfield! Oh, if we had only had them earlier we might have saved poor Lucy! Stop! That way madness lies! Harker says that by dinner time they will be able to show a whole connected narrative. He thinks that in the meantime I should see Renfield, as hitherto he has been a sort of index to the coming and going of the Count. What a good thing that Mrs. Harker put my cylinders into type! We never could have found the dates otherwise.

I found Renfield sitting placidly in his room with his hands folded, smiling benignly. I sat down and talked with him on a lot of subjects, all of which he treated naturally. He then spoke of going home, a subject he has never mentioned. I believe that, had I not had the chat with Harker, I should have been prepared to sign for him after a brief time of observation. As it is, I am darkly suspicious. All those outbreaks were in some way linked with the proximity of the Count. What then does this absolute content mean? Can it be that his instinct is satisfied as to the vampire's ultimate triumph? Outside the chapel door of the deserted house he always spoke of `master'. My friend is just a little too sane at present to make it safe to probe him with questions. He might begin to think, and then . . . So I came away.

JOHNATHAN HARKER'S JOURNAL

29 September, in train to London.--When I received Mr. Billington's courteous message that he would give me any information in his power I thought it best to go down to Whitby. It was now my object to trace that

horrid cargo of the Count's to its place in London. Mr. Billington had ready in his office all the papers concerning the consignment of boxes. It gave me almost a turn to see again one of the letters which I had seen on the Count's table. Everything had been carefully thought out, and done systematically and with precision. I saw the invoice, and took note of it. `Fifty cases of common earth, to be used for experimental purposes'. This was all the information Mr. Billington could give me, so I went down to the port and saw the coastguards, the Customs Officers and the harbor master, who kindly put me in communication with the men who had actually received the boxes. Their tally was exact with the list, and they had nothing to add.

30 September.--The station master was good enough to give me a line with the proper officials, and I saw that their tally was correct with the original invoice.

All those boxes which arrived at Whitby from Varna in the Demeter were safely deposited in the old chapel at Carfax. There should be fifty of them there, unless any have since been removed, as from Dr. Seward's diary I fear.

Later.--Mina and I have worked all day, and we have put all the papers into order.

MINA HARKER'S JOURNAL

30 September.--I saw Jonathan leave for Whitby with as brave a face as could, but I was sick with apprehension. He was never so resolute, never so strong, as at present. Professor Van Helsing said he is true grit, and he improves under strain that would kill a weaker nature. He came back full of life and hope and determination. We have got everything in order for tonight. I feel myself quite wild with excitement. I suppose one ought to pity anything so hunted as the Count. That is just it. This thing is not human, not even a beast. To read Dr. Seward's account of poor Lucy's death, and what followed, is enough to dry up the springs of pity in one's heart.

Later.--Lord Godalming and Mr. Morris arrived. Dr. Seward was out on business, and had taken Jonathan with him, so I had to see them. Poor fellows, neither of them is aware that I know all about the proposals they made to Lucy. So they had to keep on neutral subjects. However, I thought the best thing I could do would be to post them on affairs right up to date. I gave them each a copy to read in the library. When Lord

Godalming got his and turned it over, it does make a pretty good pile, he said, "Did you write all this, Mrs. Harker?"

I nodded, and he went on.

"I don't quite see the drift of it, but you people are all so good and kind so I will try to help you. Besides, I know you loved my Lucy . . ."

Here he turned away and covered his face with his hands. I could hear the tears in his voice. Mr. Morris just laid a hand for a moment on his shoulder, and then walked quietly out of the room. I suppose there is something in a woman's nature that makes a man free to break down before her without feeling it derogatory to his manhood. Lord Godalming sat down and gave way utterly and openly. I sat down beside him and took his hand. I hope he didn't think it forward of me. I said to him, "I loved dear Lucy, and I know what she was to you, and what you were to her. She and I were like sisters, and now she is gone, will you not let me be like a sister to you in your trouble?"

The poor dear fellow was overwhelmed with grief. It seemed to me that all that he had of late been suffering in silence found a vent at once. He grew quite hysterical, and raising his open hands, beat his palms together in a perfect agony of grief. I felt an infinite pity for him, and opened my arms unthinkingly. With a sob he laid his head on my shoulder and cried like a wearied child, whilst he shook with emotion.

I felt this big sorrowing man's head resting on me, and I stroked his hair as though he were my own child. I never thought at the time how strange it all was.

"I know now how I suffered," he said, as he dried his eyes. "You will let me be like a brother, for dear Lucy's sake?"

"For dear Lucy's sake," I said as we clasped hands.

"Ay, and for your own sake," he added. "If ever you need a man's help, promise me that you will let me know."

He was so earnest, so I said, "I promise."

As I came along the corridor I saw Mr. Morris looking out of a window. "How is Art?" he said. Then noticing my red eyes, he went on, "Ah, I see you have been comforting him. He needs it. No one but a woman can help a man when he is in trouble of the heart, and he had no one to comfort him."

He bore his own trouble so bravely that my heart bled for him. So I said to him, "I wish I could comfort all who suffer from the heart. Will you let me be your friend, and will you come to me for comfort if you need it? You will know later why I speak."

He saw that I was in earnest, and stooping, took my hand, and raising it to his lips, kissed it. Impulsively I bent over and kissed him. The tears rose in his eyes, and there was a momentary choking in his throat. He said quite calmly, "Little girl, you will never forget that true hearted kindness, so long as ever you live!" Then he went into the study to his friend.

"Little girl!" The very words he had used to Lucy, and, oh, but he proved himself a friend.

Dr. Seward's Diary, 30 September

I got home at five o'clock, and found that Godalming and Morris had not only arrived, but had already studied the transcript of the various diaries and letters. Harker had not yet returned. Mrs. Harker gave us a cup of tea, and for the first time, this old house seemed like home. When we had finished, Mrs. Harker said,

"Dr. Seward, may I ask a favor? I want to see your patient, Mr. Renfield. What you have said of him in your diary interests me so much!"

She looked so appealing and so pretty that I could not refuse her. I told Renfield that a lady would like to see him, to which he simply answered, "Why?"

"She is going through the house, and wants to see every one in it," I answered.

"Oh, very well," he said, "by all means, but just wait a minute till I tidy up the place."

His method of tidying was peculiar, he simply swallowed all the flies and spiders in the boxes before I could stop him. He then said cheerfully, "Let the lady come in," and sat down on the edge of his bed with his head down. For a moment I thought that he might have some homicidal intent. I remembered how quiet he had been just before he attacked me.

She came into the room with an easy gracefulness which would at once command the respect of any lunatic. She walked over to him, smiling pleasantly, and held out her hand.

"Good evening, Mr. Renfield," said she. "Dr. Seward has told me of you." He made no immediate reply, then to my intense astonishment he said, "You're not the girl the doctor wanted to marry, are you? You can't be, you know, for she's dead."

Mrs. Harker smiled sweetly as she replied, "Oh no! I have a husband of my own. I am Mrs. Harker."

"Then what are you doing here?"

"My husband and I are staying on a visit with Dr. Seward."

"Don't stay."

"But why not?"

"How did you know I wanted to marry anyone?" I asked.

His reply was simply contemptuous, "What an asinine question!"

"I don't see that at all, Mr. Renfield," said Mrs. Harker, at once championing me.

He replied to her with as much courtesy as he had shown contempt to me, "You will, of course, understand, Mrs. Harker, that when a man is so loved and honored as our host is, everything regarding him is of interest in our little community. Dr. Seward is loved not only by his household and his friends, but even by his patients. I cannot but notice that the sophistic tendencies of some of its inmates lean towards the errors of non causa and ignoratio elenche."

Here was my own pet lunatic talking elemental philosophy, and with the manner of a polished gentleman.

Mrs. Harker ventured, looking at me questioningly as she began, to lead him to his favorite topic.

"Why, I had a strange belief. Indeed, it was no wonder that my friends were alarmed, and insisted on my being put under control. I used to fancy that by consuming live things, no matter how low in the scale of creation, one might indefinitely prolong life. I actually tried to take human life. The doctor here will bear me out that on one occasion I tried to kill him for the purpose of strengthening my vital powers by the assimilation with my own body of his life through the medium of his blood, relying of course, upon the Scriptural phrase, `For the blood is the life.' Though, indeed, the vendor of a certain nostrum has vulgarized the truism to the very point of contempt. Isn't that true, doctor?"

I nodded assent, for I was so amazed that I hardly knew what to either think or say, it was hard to imagine that I had seen him eat up his spiders and flies not five minutes before. Looking at my watch, I saw that I should go to the station to meet Van Helsing, so I told Mrs. Harker that it was time to leave.

She came at once, after saying pleasantly to Mr. Renfield, "Goodbye, and I hope I may see you often, under auspices pleasanter to yourself."

To which, to my astonishment, he replied, "Goodbye, my dear. I pray God I may never see your sweet face again. May He bless and keep you!"

When I went to the station to meet Van Helsing I left the boys behind me.

Van Helsing stepped from the carriage with the eager nimbleness of a boy. "Ah, friend John, how goes all? I have much to tell."

As I drove to the house I told him of what had passed, and of how my own diary had come to be of some use through Mrs. Harker's suggestion, at which the Professor interrupted me.

"Ah, that wonderful Madam Mina! She has man's brain, and a woman's heart. We are determined to destroy this monster? But it is no part for a woman. She must consult with us, but tomorrow she say goodbye to this work, and we go alone."

I agreed heartily with him, and then I told him that the house which Dracula had bought was the very next one to my own. He was amazed, and a great concern seemed to come on him.

"Oh that we had known it before!" he said, "for then we might have reached him in time to save poor Lucy. However, `the milk that is spilt cries not out afterwards,' as you say." Then he fell into a silence.

And so now, up to this very hour, all the records we have are complete and in order. The Professor took away one copy to study after dinner, and before our meeting, which is fixed for nine o'clock.

MINA HARKER'S JOURNAL

30 September.--When we met in Dr. Seward's study two hours after dinner, which had been at six o'clock, we unconsciously formed a sort of board or committee. Professor Van Helsing took the head of the table, and asked me to act as secretary.

The Professor said, "I may, I suppose, take it that we are all acquainted with the facts that are in these papers." We all expressed assent, and he went on, "Then I tell you something of the kind of enemy with which we have to deal.

"There are such beings as vampires. I admit that at the first I was sceptic. But that is gone, and we must so work, that other poor souls perish not. The nosferatu do not die like the bee when he sting once. He is only stronger, and being stronger, have yet more power to work evil. This vampire which is amongst us is of himself so strong in person as twenty men, he is of cunning more than mortal, for his cunning be the growth of ages, he have still the aids of necromancy, which is the divination by the dead, and all the dead that he can come nigh to are for him at command, he is brute, and more than brute, he is devil in callous, he can, within his range, direct the elements, the storm, the fog, the thunder, he can command the rat, and the owl, and the bat, the moth, and the fox, and the wolf, he can grow and become small, and he can at times vanish and come unknown. It is a terrible task that we undertake. But to fail here, is not mere life or death. It is that we become as him, become foul things of the night like him, without heart or conscience, preying on the bodies and the souls of those we love best. To us forever are the gates of heaven shut. But we are face to face with duty, and in such case must we shrink? For me, I say no, but then I am old. You others are young. Some have seen sorrow, but there are fair days yet in store. What say you?"

Whilst he was speaking, Jonathan had taken my hand. He looked in my eyes, and I in his, there was no need for speaking between us.

"I answer for Mina and myself," he said.

"Count me in, Professor," said Mr. Quincey Morris, laconically as usual.

"I am with you," said Lord Godalming, "for Lucy's sake, if for no other reason."

Dr. Seward simply nodded.

The Professor stood up and, after laying his golden crucifix on the table, held out his hand on either side. So as we all took hands our solemn compact was made. I felt my heart icy cold.

"We too, are not without strength. We have on our side power of combination, a power denied to the vampire kind, we have sources of science, we are free to act and think, and the hours of the day and the night are ours equally. We have self devotion in a cause and an end to achieve which is not a selfish one. These things are much.

"Now, let us consider the limitations of the vampire in general.

"All we have to go upon are traditions and superstitions. Yet, tradition and superstition, are everything. A year ago which of us would have received such a possibility, in the midst of our scientific, sceptical, matter-of-fact nineteenth century? He is known everywhere that men have been. In old Greece, in old Rome, he flourish in Germany all over, in France, in India, even in the Chermosese, and in China, so far from us in all ways. He have follow the wake of the berserker Icelander, the devil-begotten Hun, the Slav, the Saxon, the Magyar.

"The vampire live on, and cannot die by mere passing of the time, he can flourish when that he can fatten on the blood of the living. Even more, we have seen amongst us that he can even grow younger, that his vital faculties grow strenuous.

"But he cannot flourish without this diet, he eat not as others. Even friend Jonathan, who lived with him for weeks, did never see him eat, never! He throws no shadow, he make in the mirror no reflect, as again Jonathan observe. He has the strength of many of his hand, witness again Jonathan when he shut the door against the wolves. He can transform himself to wolf, as we gather from the ship arrival in Whitby, when he tear open the dog, he can be as bat, as Madam Mina saw him on the window at Whitby.

"He can come in mist which he create, that noble ship's captain proved him of this, but, from what we know, it can only be round himself.

"He come on moonlight rays as elemental dust, as again Jonathan saw those sisters in the castle of Dracula. He become so small, we ourselves saw Miss Lucy slip through a hairbreadth space at the tomb door. He can, when once he find his way, come out from anything or into anything, no matter how close it be bound or even fused up with fire, solder you call it. He can see in the dark.

"He can do all these things, yet he is not free. Nay, he is even more prisoner than the madman in his cell. He has yet to obey some of nature's laws, why we know not. He may not enter anywhere at the first, unless there be some one of the household who bid him to come, though afterwards he can come as he please. His power ceases, as does that of all evil things, at the coming of the day.

"If he be not at the place whither he is bound, he can only change himself at noon or at exact sunrise or sunset. Thus, whereas he can do as he will within his limit, when he have his earth-home, his coffin-home, his hellhome, the place unhallowed, as we saw when he went to the grave of the suicide at Whitby, still at other time he can only change when the time come. It is said, too, that he can only pass running water at the slack or the flood of the tide. Then there are things which so afflict him that he has no power, as the garlic that we know of, and as for things sacred, as this symbol, my crucifix.

"The branch of wild rose on his coffin keep him that he move not from it, a sacred bullet fired into the coffin kill him so that he be true dead, and as for the stake through him or the cut off head that giveth rest. We have seen it with our eyes.

"Thus when we find the habitation of this man-that-was, we can confine him to his coffin and destroy him, if we obey what we know. But he is clever. I have asked my friend Arminius, of Buda-Pesth University and he tell me of what he has been. He must have been that Voivode Dracula who won his name against the Turk. If it be so, then was he no common man, for in that time, and for centuries after, he was spoken of as the cleverest and the most cunning, as well as the bravest of the sons of the `land beyond the forest.' That mighty brain and that iron resolution went with him to his grave, and are even now arrayed against us. The Draculas were a great and noble race, though now and again were scions who were held by their coevals to have had dealings with the Evil One. They learned his secrets in the Scholomance, amongst the mountains over Lake Hermanstadt, where the devil claims the tenth scholar as his due. In the records are such words as `stregoica' witch, `ordog' and `pokol' Satan and hell, and in one manuscript this very Dracula is spoken of as `wampyr,' which we all understand too well. For it is not the least of its terrors that this evil thing is rooted deep in all good, in soil barren of holy memories it cannot rest."

Whilst they were talking Mr. Morris was looking steadily at the window got up quietly, and went out of the room. The Professor went on.

"We have here much data, and we must proceed to lay out our campaign. We know from Jonathan that from the castle to Whitby came fifty boxes of earth, all of which were delivered at Carfax, we also know that at least some of these boxes have been removed. It seems to me, that our first step should be to ascertain whether all the rest remain in the house, or whether any more have been removed. If the latter, we must trace . . ."

Here we were interrupted in a very startling way. The sound of a pistol shot, and the glass of the window was shattered with a bullet. I am at heart a coward, for I shrieked out. The men all jumped to their feet, Lord Godalming flew over to the window and threw up the sash. As he did so we heard Mr. Morris' voice without, "Sorry!"

He came in and said, "I ask your pardon, Mrs. Harker, most sincerely. But the fact is that there came a big bat and sat on the window sill. I have got such a horror of the damned brutes, and I went out to have a shot."

"Did you hit it?" asked Dr. Van Helsing.

"I don't know." Without saying any more he took his seat, and the Professor began to resume his statement.

"We must trace each of these boxes, and capture or kill this monster in his lair, sterilize the earth, so that no more he can seek safety in it. Thus in the end we may find him in his form of man between the hours of noon and sunset, and so engage with him when he is at his most weak.

"And now for you, Madam Mina, this night is the end until all be well. You are too precious to us to have such risk. We are men and are able to bear, but you must be our star and our hope."

All the men, even Jonathan, seemed relieved, but it did not seem to me good that they should brave danger and, perhaps lessen their safety, strength being the best safety, through care of me, but their minds were made up, and though it was a bitter pill for me to swallow, I could say nothing, save to accept their chivalrous care of me.

Mr. Morris resumed the discussion, "I vote we have a look at his house right now."

I own that my heart began to fail me when the time for action came so close, but I did not say anything, for fear they might even leave me out of their counsels altogether. They have now gone off to Carfax, with means to get into the house.

Manlike, they had told me to go to bed and sleep, as if a woman can sleep when those she loves are in danger! I shall lie down, and pretend to sleep, lest Jonathan have added anxiety about me when he returns.

DR. SEWARD'S DIARY

1 October, 4 a. m.--Just as we were about to leave the house, an urgent message was brought to me from Renfield to know if I would see him at once, as he had something of the utmost importance to say to me.

The attendant added, "If you don't see him soon, he will have one of his violent fits." I said, "All right, I'll go now," and I asked the others to wait.

"Take me with you, friend John," said the Professor.

"May I come also?" asked Lord Godalming.

"Me too?" said Quincey Morris. "May I come?" said Harker. I nodded, and we all went down the passage together.

We found him in a state of considerable excitement, but far more rational in his speech and manner than I had ever seen him. We all five went into the room. His request was that I would at once release him from the asylum and send him home.

"I appeal to your friends," he said, "By the way, you have not introduced me."

I was so much astonished, that the oddness of introducing a madman in an asylum did not strike me at the moment, that I at once made the introduction, "Lord Godalming, Professor Van Helsing, Mr. Quincey Morris, of Texas, Mr. Jonathan Harker, Mr. Renfield."

He shook hands with each of them, saying in turn, "Lord Godalming, I had the honor of seconding your father at the Windham, I grieve to know, by your holding the title, that he is no more. He was a man loved and honored by all. Mr. Morris, you should be proud of your great state. Its reception into the Union was a precedent which may have far reaching effects hereafter. The power of Treaty may yet prove a vast engine of enlargement, when the Monroe doctrine takes its true place as a political fable. What shall any man say of his pleasure at meeting Van Helsing? Sir, I make no apology for dropping all forms of conventional prefix. When an individual has revolutionized therapeutics by his discovery of the continuous evolution of brain matter, conventional forms are unfitting. You, gentlemen, who by nationality, by heredity, or by the possession of natural gifts, are fitted to hold your respective places in the moving world, I take to witness that I am as sane as at least the majority of men who are in full possession of their liberties. And I am sure that you, Dr. Seward, humanitarian and medico-jurist as well as scientist, will deem it a moral duty to be considered as under exceptional circumstances." He made this last appeal with a courtly air of conviction which was not without its own charm.

I think we were all staggered. For my own part, I was under the conviction, that his reason had been restored. I thought it better to wait, however, for of old I knew the sudden changes to which this particular patient was liable. So I contented myself with making a general statement that I would have a longer chat with him in the morning.

He said quickly, "But I fear, Dr. Seward, that you hardly apprehend my wish. I desire to go at once, here, now, this very hour, this very moment, if I may. Time presses."

He went on, "Is it possible that I have erred in my supposition?"

"You have," I said frankly, but at the same time, as I felt, brutally.

There was a considerable pause, and then he said slowly, "Then for the sake of others, take it from me that my reasons are good ones, sound and unselfish, and spring from the highest sense of duty.

"Could you look, sir, into my heart, you would count me amongst the best and truest of your friends."

Again he looked at us all keenly. Van Helsing was gazing at him with a look of utmost intensity, his bushy eyebrows almost meeting with the fixed concentration of his look. He said to Renfield, "Can you not tell frankly your real reason for wishing to be free tonight?"

He shook his head sadly, and with a look of poignant regret on his face. The Professor went on, "You claim the privilege of reason in the highest degree. If you will not help us, how can we aid you to achieve your wish."

He still shook his head as he said, "Dr. Van Helsing, I have nothing to say. If I am refused, the responsibility does not rest with me."

I went towards the door, simply saying, "Come, my friends, we have work to do. Goodnight."

As I got near the door, a new change came over the patient. He moved towards me so quickly that for the moment I feared another homicidal attack.

He threw himself on his knees, and held up his hands, wringing them in plaintive supplication, with tears rolling down his cheeks, and his whole face and form expressive of the deepest emotion.

"Let me out of this house at once. Send keepers with me with whips and chains. Hear me! Let me go, let me go, let me go!"

I took him by the hand and raised him up.

"Come," I said sternly, "no more of this, we have had quite enough already. Get to your bed and try to behave more discreetly."

He suddenly stopped. Then, without a word, he sat down on the side of the bed.

When I was leaving the room he said to me in a quiet, well-bred voice, "I did what I could to convince you tonight."

Jonathan Harker's Journal, 1 October

5 a. m.--I am so glad that Mina consented to hold back and let us men do the work. It is due to her energy and brains that the whole story is put together. When we came away from Renfield's room we were silent till we got back to the study.

Then Mr. Morris said to Dr. Seward, "Say, Jack. It was pretty rough on him not to get a chance."

Lord Godalming and I were silent, but Dr. Van Helsing added, "Friend John, I fear that if it had been to me to decide I would before that last hysterical outburst have given him free."

Dr. Seward seemed to answer them both in a dreamy way, "I don't know but he seems so mixed up with the Count in an indexy kind of way. Besides, he called the Count `lord and master'. I suppose the Count isn't above trying to use a respectable lunatic. He certainly did seem earnest, though."

The Professor stepped over, and laying his hand on his shoulder, said in his grave, kindly way, "Friend John, what else have we to hope for, except the pity of the good God?"

Lord Godalming held up a little silver whistle, as he remarked, "That old place may be full of rats, and if so, I've got an antidote on call."

Having passed the wall, we took our way to the house, taking care to keep in the shadows. When we got to the porch the Professor opened his bag as he spoke.

"My friends, we are going into a terrible danger, and we need arms of many kinds. Keep this near your heart." He lifted a little silver crucifix and held it out to me, "put these flowers round your neck," he handed me a wreath of withered garlic blossoms, "for other enemies more mundane, this revolver and this knife, and for aid in all, these so small electric lamps, which you can fasten to your breast, and for all, and above all at the last, this."

This was a portion of Sacred Wafer, which he put in an envelope and handed to me. Each of the others was similarly equipped.

"Now," he said, "friend John, the skeleton keys?"

Dr. Seward tried one or two skeleton keys. After a little play back and forward the bolt yielded, and with a rusty clang, shot back. We pressed on the door, the rusty hinges creaked, and it slowly opened. It was startlingly like the image of the opening of Miss Westenra's tomb. The Professor was the first to move forward, and stepped into the open door.

"In manus tuas, Domine!" he said, crossing himself as he passed over the threshold. We closed the door behind us.

The light from the tiny lamps fell in all sorts of odd forms, as the rays crossed each other. I felt there was someone else amongst us. I suppose it was the recollection of that terrible experience in Transylvania. I noticed that the others kept looking over their shoulders at every sound and every new shadow, just as I felt myself doing.

The whole place was thick with dust. In the corners were masses of spider's webs. On a table in the hall was a great bunch of keys, with a timeyellowed label on each. They had been used several times, for on the table were several similar rents in the blanket of dust.

The Professor turned to me and said, "You know this place, Jonathan. Which is the way to the chapel?"

I led the way, and after a few wrong turnings found myself opposite a low, arched oaken door, ribbed with iron bands.

"This is the spot," said the Professor as he turned his lamp on a small map of the house. With a little trouble we found the key and opened the door. We were prepared for some unpleasantness, for as we were opening the door a faint, malodorous air seemed to exhale through the gaps. The air was stagnant and foul. It was composed of all the ills of mortality and with the pungent, acrid smell of blood, but it seemed as though corruption had become itself corrupt. Every breath exhaled by that monster seemed to have clung to the place and intensified its loathsomeness.

We made an accurate examination of the place, the Professor saying as we began, "The first thing is to see how many of the boxes are left, we must then examine every hole and corner and see if we cannot get some clue as to what has become of the rest."

There were only twenty-nine left out of the fifty! Once I got a fright, for, seeing Lord Godalming suddenly turn and look out of the vaulted door into the dark passage beyond, I looked too, and for an instant my heart stood still. Somewhere, looking out from the shadow, I seemed to see the high lights of the Count's evil face, the ridge of the nose, the red eyes, the red lips, the awful pallor. Lord Godalming said, "I thought I saw a face, but it was only the shadows," and resumed his inquiry, I turned my lamp in the direction, and stepped into the passage. There was no sign of anyone, only the solid walls of the passage.

A few minutes later I saw Morris step suddenly back from a corner, which he was examining. We saw a whole mass of phosphorescence, which twinkled like stars. We all instinctively drew back. The whole place was becoming alive with rats.

We stood appalled, all save Lord Godalming. Rushing over to the great iron-bound oaken door, he turned the key and swung the door open. Then, taking his little silver whistle from his pocket, he blew a low, shrill call. It was answered from behind Dr. Seward's house by the yelping of dogs, and after about a minute three terriers came dashing round the corner of the house. But even in the minute that had elapsed the number of the rats had vastly increased. They seemed to swarm over the place all at once, till the lamplight, shining on their moving dark bodies and glittering, baleful eyes, made the place look like a bank of earth set with fireflies. The dogs dashed on, but at the threshold suddenly stopped and snarled, and then, simultaneously lifting their noses, began to howl. The rats were multiplying in thousands, and we moved out.

Lord Godalming lifted one of the dogs, and carrying him in, placed him on the floor. The instant his feet touched the ground he seemed to recover his courage, and rushed at his natural enemies. They fled before him so fast that before he had shaken the life out of a score, the whole mass had vanished.

With their going it seemed as if some evil presence had departed, for the dogs frisked about and barked merrily as they made sudden darts at their prostrate foes, and turned them over and over and tossed them in the air with vicious shakes. Whether it was the purifying of the deadly atmosphere, or finding ourselves in the open I know not, but most certainly the shadow of dread seemed to slip from us like a robe. We closed the outer door, and bringing the dogs with us, began our search of the house. We found nothing throughout except dust in extraordinary proportions, and all untouched save for my own footsteps when I had made my first visit. Never once did the dogs exhibit any symptom of uneasiness.

The morning was quickening in the east when we emerged from the front. Dr. Van Helsing locked the door in orthodox fashion, putting the key into his pocket.

"So far," he said, "our night has been eminently successful. No harm has come to us and yet we have ascertained how many boxes are missing. One lesson, too, the brute beasts which are to the Count's command are yet themselves not amenable to his spiritual power, for look, they run pell-mell from the so little dogs of my friend Arthur. We have other matters before us, other dangers, other fears, and that monster . . . He has gone elsewhere. Good! Let us go home. The dawn is close at hand."

The house was silent when we got back, save for a low, moaning sound from Renfield's room. The poor wretch was doubtless torturing himself.

I came tiptoe into our own room, and found Mina asleep, breathing so softly that I had to put my ear down to hear it. She looks paler than usual. I hope the meeting tonight has not upset her. It is too great a strain for a woman to bear. Henceforth our work is to be a sealed book to her.

I daresay it will be difficult to begin to keep silence after such confidence as ours, but I must be resolute. I rest on the sofa, so as not to disturb her.

1 October, later.--I suppose it was natural that we should have all overslept. Even Mina must have felt its exhaustion, I had to call two or three times before she awoke. Indeed, she was so sound asleep that for a few seconds she did not recognize me, but looked at me with a sort of blank terror. She complained a little of being tired, and I let her rest till later in the day.

We now know of twenty-one boxes having been removed, we may be able to trace them all. I shall look up Thomas Snelling today.

DR. SEWARD'S DIARY

1 October.--It was towards noon when I was awakened by the Professor. He was more jolly and cheerful than usual.

He said, "Your patient interests me much. May it be that with you I visit him this morning? It is a new experience to me to find a lunatic who talk philosophy, and reason so sound."

I told him that if he would go alone I would be glad. I cautioned him against getting any false impression from my patient.

"But," he answered, "I want him to talk of himself and of his delusion as to consuming live things. Why do you smile, friend John?"

"Excuse me," I said, "but the answer is here." I laid my hand on the typewritten matter. "When our sane and learned lunatic made that very statement of how he used to consume life, his mouth was actually nauseous with the flies and spiders which he had eaten just before Mrs. Harker entered the room."

Van Helsing smiled in turn. "Good!" he said. " I should have remembered. Perhaps I may gain more knowledge out of the folly of this madman than I shall from the teaching of the most wise. Who knows?"

I went on with my work. It seemed that the time had been very short indeed, but there was Van Helsing back in the study.

"Do I interrupt?" he asked politely as he stood at the door.

"Not at all," I answered. "Come in. My work is finished, and I am free. I can go with you now, if you like."

"It is needless, I have seen him!"

"Well?"

"Our interview was short. When I entered his room he was sitting on a stool, with his elbows on his knees, and his face was the picture of sullen discontent. I spoke to him. He made no reply whatever. 'Don't you know me?' I asked. His answer was not reassuring. "You are the old fool Van Helsing. I wish you would take yourself and your idiotic brain theories somewhere else. Damn all thick-headed Dutchmen!' Not a word more would he say. I shall go and cheer myself with a few happy words with that sweet soul Madam Mina. Friend John, it does rejoice me unspeakable that she is no more to be pained, no more to be worried with our terrible things. Though we shall much miss her help, it is better so."

"I agree with you with all my heart," I answered earnestly, for I did not want him to weaken in this matter. "Mrs. Harker is better out of it. Things are quite bad enough for us, all men of the world, but it is no place for a woman, it would in time infallibly have wrecked her."

MINA HARKER'S JOURNAL

1 October.--It is strange to me to be kept in the dark, after Jonathan's full confidence for so many years. This morning I slept late after the fatigues of yesterday. He spoke to me before he went out, never more sweetly, but he never mentioned a word of what had happened in the Count's house. They all agreed that it was best. But to think that he keeps anything from me! And now I am crying like a silly fool.

I feel strangely sad and low-spirited today. I suppose it is the reaction from the terrible excitement.

Last night I went to bed when the men had gone, simply because they told me to. I didn't feel sleepy, and I did feel full of devouring anxiety. There now, crying again! I wonder what has come over me today. I must hide it from Jonathan, for if he knew. . . I suppose it is just one of the lessons that we poor women have to learn . . .

I can't quite remember how I fell asleep last night. I remember hearing the sudden barking of the dogs and a lot of queer sounds, like praying, from Mr. Renfield's room, which is somewhere under this. And then there was silence, and I got up and looked out of the window. All was dark and silent. Not a thing seemed to be stirring, but all to be grim and fixed as death or fate, so that a thin streak of white mist, that crept with almost imperceptible slowness across the grass towards the house, seemed to have a sentience and a vitality of its own. When I got back to bed I found a lethargy creeping over me. I lay a while, but could not quite sleep, so I got out and looked out of the window again. The mist was spreading, and was now close up to the house, so that I could see it lying thick against the wall, as though it were stealing up to the windows. Renfield was more loud than ever. Then there was the sound of a struggle, and I knew that the attendants were dealing with him. I was so frightened that I crept into bed, and pulled the clothes over my head. I do not remember anything until the morning, when Jonathan woke me. I think that it took me an effort and a little time to realize where I was, and that it was Jonathan who was bending over me. My dream was very peculiar, and was almost typical of the way that waking thoughts become merged in, or continued in, dreams.

I thought that I was asleep, and waiting for Jonathan to come back. I was powerless to act, nothing could proceed at the usual pace. And so I slept uneasily and thought. Then it began to dawn upon me that the air was heavy, and dank, and cold. All was dim around. The gaslight which I had left lit for Jonathan came only like a tiny red spark through the fog. Then it occurred to me that I had shut the window before I had come to bed. Some leaden lethargy seemed to chain my limbs and even my will. I lay still and endured. I closed my eyes, but could still see through my eyelids. (It is wonderful what tricks our dreams play us.) The mist grew thicker and thicker and I could see now how it came in, for I could see it like smoke, or with the white energy of boiling water, pouring in, not through the window, but through the joinings of the door. It got thicker and thicker, till it seemed as if it became concentrated into a sort of pillar of cloud in the room, through the top of which I could see the light of the gas shining like a red eye. Things began to whirl through my brain just as the cloudy column was now whirling in the room. The fire divided, and seemed to shine on me through the fog like two red eyes, such as Lucy told me of when, on the cliff, the dying sunlight struck the windows of St. Mary's Church. Suddenly the horror burst upon me that it was thus that Jonathan had seen those awful women growing into reality through the moonlight, and in my dream I must have fainted, for all became black darkness. The last conscious effort which imagination made was to show me a livid white face bending over me out of the mist.

I must be careful of such dreams. I would get Dr. Van Helsing or Dr. Seward to prescribe something for me which would make me sleep, only that I fear to alarm them. Tonight I shall strive hard to sleep naturally. If I do not, I shall tomorrow night get them to give me a dose of chloral and it will give me a good night's sleep.

2 October 10 p. m.--Last night I slept, but did not dream. I was not waked by Jonathan coming to bed, but the sleep has not refreshed me, for today I feel terribly weak and spiritless. In the afternoon, Mr. Renfield asked if he might see me. Poor man, he was very gentle, and when I came away he kissed my hand and bade God bless me. I am crying when I think of him. This is a new weakness. Jonathan would be miserable if he knew I had been crying. He and the others were out till dinner time, and they all came in tired. I did what I could to brighten them up, and I suppose that the effort did me good. After dinner they sent me to bed, and all went off to smoke together, as they said, but I knew that they

wanted to tell each other of what had occurred to each during the day. Dr. Seward very kindly made me up a sleeping draught, it was very mild . . . I have taken it, and am waiting for sleep. As sleep begins to flirt with me, a new fear comes, that I may have been foolish in thus depriving myself of the power of waking. I might want it. Here comes sleep. Goodnight.

Jonathan Harker's Journal, 1 October

evening.--I found Thomas Snelling in his house at Bethnal Green, but unhappily he was not in a condition to remember anything. I learned, however, from his wife that he was only the assistant of Smollet. So off I drove to Walworth, and found Mr. Joseph Smollet at home. He remembered all about the incident of the boxes, and from a wonderful dog-eared notebook he gave me the destinations of the boxes. There were, he said, six in the cartload which he took from Carfax and left at 197 Chicksand Street, Mile End New Town, and another six which he deposited at Jamaica Lane, Bermondsey. The Count meant to scatter these ghastly refuges of his over London. I went back to Smollet, and asked him if he could tell us if any other boxes had been taken from Carfax.

He replied, "I'm thinkin' that maybe Sam Bloxam could tell ye summut."

I asked if he could tell me where to find him.

He said, "Look 'ere, guv'nor. If you can give me a envelope with a stamp on it, and put yer address on it, I'll find out where Sam is to be found and post it ye tonight."

This was all practical. We're on the track anyhow. Mina is fast asleep, and looks a little too pale. Her eyes look as though she had been crying. Poor dear, I've no doubt it frets her to be kept in the dark. The doctors were quite right to insist on her being kept out of this dreadful business. I must be firm and not ever enter on the subject with her.

2 October, evening--By the first post I got my directed envelope with a dirty scrap of paper enclosed, on which was written with a carpenter's pencil in a sprawling hand, "Sam Bloxam, Korkrans, 4 Poters Cort, Bartel Street, Walworth. Arsk for the depite."

Mina looked heavy and sleepy and pale, and far from well. I would arrange for her going back to Exeter. I drove to Walworth and found, with some difficulty, Potter's Court.

Mr. Bloxam told me that he had made two journeys between Carfax and a house in Piccadilly, and had taken nine great boxes, "main heavy ones," with a horse and cart hired by him for this purpose.

I asked the number of the house in Piccadilly, to which he replied, "Well, guv'nor, I forgits the number, but it was only a few door from a big white church. It was a dusty old 'ouse, too."

"How did you get in?"

"There was the old party what engaged me a waitin' in the 'ouse at Purfleet. He 'elped me to lift the boxes. Curse me, but he was the strongest chap I ever struck, an' him a old feller, with a white moustache, one that thin you would think he couldn't throw a shadder."

How this phrase thrilled through me!

"Why, 'e took up 'is end o' the boxes like they was pounds of tea, and me a puffin' an' a blowin' afore I could upend mine anyhow, an' I'm no chicken, neither."

"How did you get into the house in Piccadilly?" I asked.

"He was there too. He must 'a started off and got there afore me, for when I rung of the bell he kem an' opened the door 'isself an' 'elped me carry the boxes into the 'all."

"The whole nine?" I asked.

"Yus. It was main dry work, an' I don't so well remember 'ow I got 'ome."

I interrupted him, "Were the boxes left in the hall?"

"Yus, it was a big 'all, an' there was nothin' else in it."

"And you can't remember the number of the house?"

"No, sir. But ye needn't have no difficulty about that. It's a 'igh 'un with a stone front with a bow on it, an' 'igh steps up to the door. I know them steps, 'avin' 'ad to carry the boxes."

I thought that with this description I could find the house, so having paid my friend for his information, I started off for Piccadilly. The Count could handle the earth boxes himself. Time was precious, for now that he had achieved a certain amount of distribution, he could complete the task unobserved. At Piccadilly Circus I came across the house described. The house looked as though it had been long untenanted. The shutters were up. All the framework was black with time. It was evident that up to lately there had been a large notice board in front of the balcony. It had, however, been roughly torn away.

I asked one of the helpers if they could tell me anything about the empty house. He told me that up to very lately there had been a notice board of "For Sale" up, and that perhaps Mitchell, Sons, & Candy the house agents could tell me something. I was soon at their office in Sackville Street.

The gentleman who saw me was particularly suave in manner. Having once told me that the Piccadilly house, which he called a "mansion," was sold, he considered my business as concluded. When I asked who had purchased it, he opened his eyes a thought wider, before replying, "It is sold, sir."

"Pardon me," I said, with equal politeness, "but I have a special reason."

"It is sold, sir," was again his laconic reply.

"Surely," I said, "you do not mind letting me know so much."

"But I do mind," he answered. "The affairs of their clients are absolutely safe in the hands of Mitchell, Sons,& Candy."

There was no use arguing with him, "I am myself a professional man."

Here I handed him my card. "I act on the part of Lord Godalming, who wishes to know something of the property which was, he understood, lately for sale."

These words put a different complexion on affairs. He said, "If you will let me have his lordship's address I will consult the House and communicate with his lordship by tonight's post. It will be a pleasure if we can so far deviate from our rules as to give the required information to his lordship."

I thanked him, gave the address at Dr. Seward's and came away.

I found all the others at home. Mina was looking tired and pale, but she made a gallant effort to be bright and cheerful. It wrung my heart to think that I had had to keep anything from her and so caused her inquietude.

After dinner, followed by a little music to save appearances, I took Mina to her room and left her to go to bed. The dear girl was more affectionate with me than ever. Thank God, the ceasing of telling things has made no difference between us.

When I came down again I found the others all gathered round the fire in the study. In the train I had written my diary so far, and simply read it off to them.

Van Helsing said, "This has been a great day's work, friend Jonathan. We must search until we find the missing boxes. Then shall we make our final coup, and hunt the wretch to his real death."

Mr. Morris spoke, "Say! How are we going to get into that house?"

"We got into the other," answered Lord Godalming quickly.

"But, Art, this is different. We broke house at Carfax, but we had night and a walled park to protect us. It will be a mighty different thing to commit burglary in Piccadilly, either by day or night. I confess I don't see how we are going to get in."

Lord Godalming's brows contracted. "Quincey's head is level. This burglary business is getting serious. We got off once all right, but we have now a rare job on hand. Unless we can find the Count's key basket."

We decided not to take any active step before breakfast time. For a good while we sat and smoked, discussing the matter. I am very sleepy and shall go to bed . . .

Mina sleeps soundly and her breathing is regular. Her forehead is puckered up, as though she thinks even in her sleep. She is still too pale, but does not look so haggard as she did this morning. She will be herself at home in Exeter. Oh, but I am sleepy!

DR. SEWARD'S DIARY

1 October.--I am puzzled afresh about Renfield. His moods change so rapidly. This morning, when I went to see him after his repulse of Van Helsing, his manner was that of a man commanding destiny. He was in the clouds and looked down on all the weaknesses and wants of us poor mortals.

I asked him, "What about the flies these times?"

In quite a superior sort of way, he answered me, "The fly, my dear sir, has one striking feature. It's wings are typical of the aerial powers of the psychic faculties. The ancients did well when they typified the soul as a butterfly!"

I said quickly, "Oh, it is a soul you are after now, is it?"

His madness foiled his reason, and a puzzled look spread over his face.

He said, "Oh, no, oh no! I want no souls. Life is all I want." Here he brightened up. "I have all I want."

This puzzled me a little, so I drew him on. "Then you command life. You are a god, I suppose?"

He smiled. "Oh no! Far be it from me to arrogate to myself the attributes of the Deity. I am, so far as concerns things purely terrestrial, somewhat in the position which Enoch occupied spiritually!"

"And why with Enoch?"

"Because he walked with God."

I could not see the analogy, but did not like to admit it. "So you don't care about life and you don't want souls. Why not?"

Bent low before me, he replied. "They would be no manner of use to me. I couldn't eat them or . . ."

He suddenly stopped and the old cunning look spread over his face.

"And doctor, as to life, what is it after all? I have friends, good friends, like you, Dr. Seward." This was said with a leer of inexpressible cunning. "I know that I shall never lack the means of life!"

He at once fell back on the last refuge of a dogged silence. He was sulky, and so I came away.

Later in the day he sent for me.

I found him sitting in the middle of the floor on his stool, a pose which is generally indicative of some mental energy on his part. When I came in, he said at once. "What about souls?"

It was evident then that my surmise had been correct. Unconscious cerebration was doing its work, even with the lunatic. I determined to have the matter out.

"I don't want any souls!" He said in a feeble, apologetic way. The matter seemed preying on his mind, so I said, "You like life, and you want life?"

"Oh yes! But that is all right. You needn't worry about that!"

"But," I asked, "how are we to get the life without getting the soul also?"

This seemed to puzzle him, so I followed it up, "A nice time you'll have with the souls of thousands of flies and spiders and birds and cats buzzing and twittering and moaning all around you. You've got their lives, you know, and you must put up with their souls!"

Something seemed to affect his imagination, for he put his fingers to his ears and shut his eyes, just as a small boy does when his face is being soaped. There was something pathetic in it that touched me. I thought I would enter into his mind as well as I could and go with him

I asked him, speaking pretty loud so that he would hear me through his closed ears, "Would you like some sugar to get your flies around again?"

He seemed to wake up all at once, and shook his head. With a laugh he replied, "Not much! Flies are poor things, after all!" After a pause he added, "But I don't want their souls buzzing round me, all the same."

"Or spiders?" I went on.

"Blow spiders! What's the use of spiders? There isn't anything in them to eat or . . ." He stopped suddenly as though reminded of a forbidden topic.

"So, so!" I thought to myself, "this is the second time he has suddenly stopped at the word 'drink'. What does it mean?"

Renfield seemed himself aware of having made a lapse, for he hurried on, as though to distract my attention from it, "I don't take any stock at all in such matters. 'Rats and mice and such small deer,' as Shakespeare has it. I'm past all that sort of nonsense. You might as well ask a man to eat molecules with chopsticks."

"I see," I said. "You want big things that you can make your teeth meet in? How would you like to breakfast on an elephant?"

"What ridiculous nonsense you are talking?" He was getting too wide awake, so I thought I would press him hard.

"I wonder," I said reflectively, "what an elephant's soul is like!"

"I don't want an elephant's soul, or any soul at all!" he said. For a few moments he sat despondently. Suddenly he jumped to his feet, with his eyes blazing and all the signs of intense cerebral excitement. "To hell with you and your souls!" he shouted. "Why do you plague me about souls? Haven't I got enough to worry, and pain, to distract me already, without thinking of souls?"

He looked so hostile that I thought he was in for another homicidal fit, so I blew my whistle.

The instant, however, that I did so he became calm, and said apologetically, "Forgive me, Doctor. I forgot myself. You do not need any help. I am so worried in my mind. If you only knew the problem I have to face, you would pity, and tolerate, and pardon me. Pray do not put me in a strait waistcoat."

When the attendants came I told them not to mind, and they withdrew. Renfield watched them go. When the door was closed he said, "Dr. Seward, you have been very considerate towards me. Believe me that I am very, very grateful to you!"

I thought it well to leave him in this mood, and so I came away. There is certainly something to ponder over in this man's state. If one could only get them in proper order. Here they are:

Will not mention "drinking."

Fears the thought of being burdened with the "soul" of anything.

Has no dread of wanting "life" in the future.

Despises the meaner forms of life altogether, though he dreads being haunted by their souls.

He has assurance of some kind that he will acquire some higher life.

He dreads the consequence, the burden of a soul. Then it is a human life he looks to!

And the assurance . . . ?

Merciful God! The Count has been to him, and there is some new scheme of terror afoot!

Later.--I went to Van Helsing and told him my suspicion. He grew very grave and asked me to take him to Renfield. I did so. As we came to the door we heard the lunatic within singing gaily.

When we entered we saw with amazement that he had spread out his sugar as of old. The flies were beginning to buzz into the room. We tried to make him talk, but he would not attend. He went on with his singing, just as though we had not been present. He had got a scrap of paper and was folding it into a notebook. We had to come away as ignorant as we went in.

His is a curious case indeed. We must watch him tonight.

LETTER, MITCHELL, SONS & CANDY TO LORD GODALMING.

"1 October. "My Lord,

"We are at all times only too happy to meet your wishes. The following information concerns the sale and purchase of No. 347,Piccadilly. The original vendors are the executors of the late Mr. Archibald Winter-Suffield. The purchaser is a foreign nobleman, Count de Ville, who effected the purchase himself paying the purchase money in notes `over the counter,' if your Lordship will pardon us using so vulgar an expression. Beyond this we know nothing whatever of him.

"We are, my Lord,

"Your Lordship's humble servants,

"MITCHELL, SONS & CANDY."

DR. SEWARD'S DIARY

2 October.--I placed a man in the corridor near Renfield's room, and gave him instructions that if there should be anything strange he was to call me. After dinner, Mrs. Harker having gone to bed, we discussed the attempts and discoveries of the day. Harker was the only one who had any result, and we are in great hopes that his clue may be an important one.

Before going to bed I went round to the patient's room and looked in through the observation trap. He was sleeping soundly.

This morning the man on duty reported to me that a little after midnight he was restless and kept saying his prayers somewhat loudly. There was something about his manner, so suspicious that I asked him point blank if he had been asleep. He denied sleep, but admitted to having "dozed" for a while. It is too bad that men cannot be trusted unless they are watched.

Today Harker is out following up his clue, and Art and Quincey are looking after horses. We must sterilize all the imported earth between sunrise and sunset. We shall thus catch the Count at his weakest, and without a refuge to fly to. Van Helsing is off to the British Museum looking up some authorities on ancient medicine. The Professor is searching for witch and demon cures which may be useful to us later.

I sometimes think we must be all mad and that we shall wake to sanity in strait waistcoats.

Later.--We have met again. We seem at last to be on the track, and our work of tomorrow may be the beginning of the end. I wonder if Renfield's quiet has anything to do with this. His moods have so followed the doings of the Count, that the coming destruction of the monster may be carried to him some subtle way. If we could only get some hint as to what passed in his mind, between the time of my argument with him today and his resumption of fly-catching, it might afford us a valuable clue. He is now seemingly quiet for a spell . . . Is he? That wild yell seemed to come from his room . . .

The attendant came bursting into my room and told me that Renfield had somehow met with some accident. He had heard him yell, and when he went to him found him lying on his face on the floor, all covered with blood. I must go at once . . .

Dr. Seward's Diary, 3 October

I found Renfield lying on the floor in a glittering pool of blood. I went to move him. As the face was exposed I could see that it was horribly bruised, as though it had been beaten against the floor.

The attendant who was kneeling beside the body said to me as we turned him over, "I think his back is broken. I can't understand the two things. He could mark his face like that by beating his own head on the floor. I saw a young woman do it once at the Eversfield Asylum. He might have broken his neck by falling out of bed. But for the life of me I can't imagine how the two things occurred. If his back was broke, he couldn't beat his head, and if his face was like that before the fall out of bed, there would be marks of it."

I said to him, "Go to Dr. Van Helsing, and ask him to kindly come here at once."

The man ran off, and within a few minutes the Professor, in his dressing gown and slippers, appeared. When he saw Renfield on the ground, he looked keenly at him a moment, and then turned to me. He said very quietly, "Ah, a sad accident! I shall first dress myself. If you will remain I shall in a few minutes join you."

Van Helsing returned with a surgical case. He whispered to me, "Send the attendant away. We must be alone with him when he becomes conscious, after the operation."

I said, "I think that will do now, Simmons. We have done all that we can at present. Dr. Van Helsing will operate."

The man withdrew, and we went into a strict examination of the patient. The wounds of the face were superficial. The real injury was a depressed fracture of the skull, extending right up through the motor area.

The Professor said, "We must reduce the pressure and get back to normal conditions, as far as can be. The rapidity of the suffusion shows the terrible nature of his injury. The whole motor area seems affected. The suffusion of the brain will increase quickly, so we must trephine at once."

As he was speaking there was a soft tapping at the door. I found Arthur and Quincey in pajamas and slippers, the former spoke, "May we come in?"

I nodded, and held the door open. Quincey said softly, "My God! What has happened to him? Poor, poor devil!"

I told him briefly. He went at once and sat down on the edge of the bed, with Godalming beside him. We all watched in patience.

"We shall wait," said Van Helsing, "just long enough to fix the best spot for trephining, so that we may remove the blood clot, for it is evident that the haemorrhage is increasing."

The minutes passed with fearful slowness. I had a horrible sinking in my heart, and from Van Helsing's face I gathered that he felt some fear. I dreaded the words Renfield might speak. The poor man's breathing came in uncertain gasps. I could almost hear the beating of my own heart, and the blood surging through my temples sounded like blows from a hammer. The silence finally became agonizing. I looked at my companions and saw they were enduring equal torture.

The patient was sinking fast. He might die at any moment. I looked up at the Professor. His face was sternly set as he spoke, "There is no time to lose. His words may be worth many lives. We shall operate just above the ear."

Without another word he made the operation. Then there came a breath so prolonged that it seemed as though it would tear open his chest. Suddenly his eyes opened, in a wild, helpless stare. Then it was softened into a glad surprise, and from his lips came a sigh of relief. He moved convulsively, and as he did so, said, "I'll be quiet, Doctor. Take off the strait waistcoat. I have had a terrible dream, I cannot move. What's wrong with my face? It feels all swollen, and it smarts dreadfully."

He tried to turn his head, but his eyes seemed to grow glassy again. Then Van Helsing said, "Tell us your dream, Mr. Renfield."

His face brightened, through its mutilation, and he said, "That is Dr. Van Helsing. How good it is of you to be here. Give me some water, my lips are dry, and I shall try to tell you. I dreamed" . . .

He stopped and seemed fainting. I called quietly to Quincey, "The brandy, it is in my study, quick!" He flew and returned with a glass, the decanter of brandy and a carafe of water. We moistened the parched lips, and the patient quickly revived.

He looked at me piercingly with an agonized confusion which I shall never forget, and said, "It was no dream." Then his eyes roved round the room.

For an instant his eyes closed as though he were bringing all his faculties to bear. When he opened them he said, hurriedly, and with more energy than he had yet displayed, "It was that night after you left me, when I implored you to let me go away. I couldn't speak then. But I was as sane then, except in that way, as I am now. I was in an agony of despair. Then there came a sudden peace to me. I realized where I was. I heard the dogs bark behind our house, but not where He was!"

As he spoke, Van Helsing's eyes never blinked. He said, "Go on," in a low voice.

Renfield proceeded. "He came up to the window in the mist, as I had seen him often before, but he was solid then, not a ghost, and his eyes were fierce like a man's when angry. He was laughing with his red mouth, the sharp white teeth glinted in the moonlight when he turned to look back over the belt of trees, to where the dogs were barking. I wouldn't ask him to come in at first, though I knew he wanted to, just as he had wanted all along. Then he began promising me things, not in words but by doing them."

He was interrupted by the Professor, "How?"

"By making them happen. Just as he used to send in the flies. Great big fat ones with steel and sapphire on their wings. And big moths, in the night, with skull and cross-bones on their backs."

Van Helsing whispered, "The Acherontia Atropos of the Sphinges, what you call the `Death's-head Moth'?"

The patient went on without stopping, "Then he began to whisper. `Rats, rats, rats! Hundreds, thousands, millions of them, and every one a life. And dogs to eat them, and cats too. All lives! All red blood, with years of life in it!' I laughed at him, for I wanted to see what he could do. Then the dogs howled, in His house. He beckoned me to the window. I got up and looked out, and He raised his hands. A dark mass spread over the grass, like a flame of fire. And then He moved the mist to the right and left, and I could see that there were thousands of rats with their eyes blazing red, like His only smaller. He held up his hand, and they all stopped, and I thought he seemed to be saying, `All these lives will I give you, ay, and many more and greater, through countless ages, if you will fall down and worship me!' And then a red cloud, like the color of blood, seemed to close over my eyes, and I found myself opening the sash and saying to Him, `Come in, Lord and Master!' The rats were all gone, but He slid into the room through the sash, though it was only open an inch wide, just as the Moon through the tiniest crack."

His voice was weaker, so I moistened his lips with the brandy again. Van Helsing whispered to me, "Let him go on. Do not interrupt him."

He proceeded, "All day I waited to hear from him, but he did not send me anything, not even a blowfly, and when the moon got up I was pretty angry with him. When he did slide in through the window, though it was shut, and did not even knock, I got mad with him. He sneered at me, and his white face looked out of the mist with his red eyes gleaming, and he went on as though he owned the whole place, and I was no one. He didn't even smell the same as he went by me. I couldn't hold him. I thought that, somehow, Mrs. Harker had come into the room."

The two men sitting on the bed stood up. The Professor started and quivered. Renfield went on without noticing, "When Mrs. Harker came in to see me this afternoon she wasn't the same. It was like tea after the teapot has been watered." Here we all moved, but no one said a word.

He went on, "I didn't know that she was here till she spoke, and she didn't look the same. I don't care for the pale people. I like them with lots of blood in them, and hers all seemed to have run out. It made me mad to know that He had been taking the life out of her." I could feel that the rest quivered, as I did. "So when He came tonight I was ready for Him. I saw the mist stealing in, and I grabbed it tight. Ay, and He felt it too, for He had to come out of the mist to struggle with me. I held tight, and I thought I was going to win, for I didn't mean Him to take any more of her life, till I saw His eyes. They burned into me, and my strength became like water. He slipped through it, and when I tried to cling to Him, He raised me up and flung me down. There was a red cloud before me, and a noise like thunder, and the mist seemed to steal away under the door."

His voice was becoming fainter and his breath more stertorous. Van Helsing stood up instinctively.

"He is here, and we know his purpose. It may not be too late."

We all hurried and took from our rooms the same things that we had when we entered the Count's house. The Professor said, "Be wise, my friends. It is no common enemy that we deal with Alas! Alas! That dear Madam Mina should suffer!" He stopped, his voice was breaking, and I do not know if rage or terror predominated in my own heart.

Outside the Harkers' door we paused. Art and Quincey held back, and the latter said, "Should we disturb her?"

"We must," said Van Helsing grimly. "If the door be locked, I shall break it in."

"May it not frighten her terribly? It is unusual to break into a lady's room!"

Van Helsing said solemnly, "You are always right. But this is life and death. All chambers are alike to the doctor. They are all as one to me tonight. Now!"

He turned the handle as he spoke, but the door did not yield. We threw ourselves against it. With a crash it burst open, and we almost fell headlong into the room. The Professor did actually fall. What I saw appalled me. I felt my hair rise like bristles on the back of my neck.

The moonlight was so bright that through the thick yellow blind the room was light enough to see. On the bed beside the window lay Jonathan Harker, his face flushed and breathing heavily as though in a stupor. Kneeling on the near edge of the bed facing outwards was the white-clad figure of his wife. By her side stood a tall, thin man, clad in black. His face was turned from us, but we all recognized the Count, in every way, even to the scar on his forehead. With his left hand he held both Mrs. Harker's hands, keeping them away with her arms at full tension. His right hand gripped her by the back of the neck, forcing her face down on his bosom. Her white night-dress was smeared with blood, and a thin stream trickled down the man's bare chest which was shown by his torn-open dress. The attitude of the two had a terrible resemblance to a child forcing a kitten's nose into a saucer of milk to compel it to drink. As we burst into the room, the Count turned his face, and a hellish look seemed to leap into it. His eyes flamed red with devilish passion. The nostrils of the white aquiline nose opened wide, and the white sharp teeth, behind the full lips of the blood dripping mouth, clamped together like those of a wild beast. With a wrench, which threw his victim back upon the bed, he turned and sprang at us. But by this time the Professor had gained his feet, and was holding towards him the envelope which contained the Sacred Wafer. The Count suddenly stopped, just as poor Lucy had done outside the tomb, and cowered back. Further and further back he cowered, as we, lifting our crucifixes, advanced. The moonlight suddenly failed, as a great black cloud sailed across the sky. And when the gaslight sprang up under Quincey's match, we saw nothing but a faint vapor. This trailed under the door. Van Helsing, Art, and I moved forward to Mrs. Harker, who had given a scream so wild, so ear-piercing, so despairing that it seems to me now that it will ring in my ears till my dying day. She lay in her helpless attitude and disarray. Her face was ghastly, with a pallor which was accentuated by the blood which smeared her lips and cheeks and chin. From her throat trickled a thin stream of blood. Her eyes were mad with terror. Then she put before her face her poor crushed hands, which bore on their whiteness the red mark of the Count's terrible grip, and from behind them came a low desolate wail. Van Helsing stepped forward and drew the coverlet gently over her body, whilst Art, ran out of the room.

Van Helsing whispered to me, "Jonathan is in a stupor such as we know the Vampire can produce. I must wake him!"

He dipped the end of a towel in cold water and with it began to flick him on the face, his wife all the while holding her face between her hands and sobbing. I looked out of the window. I could see Quincey Morris run across the lawn and hide himself in the shadow of a great yew tree. I heard Harker's quick exclamation as he woke, and turned to the bed. On his face was a look of wild amazement. He seemed dazed for a few seconds, and then he started up.

His wife turned to him with her arms stretched out, as though to embrace him. Instantly, however, she drew them in again, and putting her elbows together, held her hands before her face, and shuddered till the bed beneath her shook.

"In God's name what does this mean?" Harker cried out. "Dr. Seward, Dr. Van Helsing? What has happened? What is wrong? Mina, dear what is it? What does that blood mean? My God, my God!" And, raising himself to his knees, he beat his hands wildly together. "Good God help us! Help her! Oh, help her!"

He jumped from bed, and began to pull on his clothes. "What has happened?" he cried without pausing. "Dr. Van Helsing, do something. It cannot have gone too far yet. Guard her while I look for him!"

His wife, through her terror and horror and distress, saw some sure danger to him. Instantly forgetting her own grief, she seized hold of him and cried out.

"No! No! Jonathan, you must not leave me. You must stay with me. Stay with these friends who will watch over you!" Her expression became frantic as she spoke. And, he yielding to her, she pulled him down sitting on the bedside, and clung to him fiercely.

Van Helsing and I tried to calm them both. The Professor held up his golden crucifix, and said with wonderful calmness, "Do not fear, my dear. We are here, and whilst this is close to you no foul thing can approach."

She shuddered and was silent, holding down her head on her husband's breast. When she raised it, his white nightrobe was stained with blood where her lips had touched, and where the thin open wound in the neck had sent forth drops. The instant she saw it she drew back, with a low wail, and whispered, amidst choking sobs.

"Unclean, unclean! I must touch him or kiss him no more."

To this he spoke out resolutely, "Nonsense, Mina. It is a shame to me to hear such a word. And I shall not hear it from you!"

He put out his arms and folded her to his breast. And for a while she lay there sobbing. He looked at us over her bowed head, with eyes that blinked damply above his quivering nostrils. His mouth was set as steel.

"And now, Dr. Seward. Tell me all that has been."

I told him exactly what had happened and he listened with seeming impassiveness, but his eyes blazed. Just as I had finished, Quincey and Godalming knocked at the door. They entered in obedience to our summons. Van Helsing asked them what they had seen or done. To which Lord Godalming answered.

"I could not see him anywhere in the passage, or in any of our rooms. I looked in the study but, though he had been there, he had gone. He had, however . . ." He stopped suddenly, looking at the poor drooping figure on the bed.

Van Helsing said gravely, "Go on, friend Arthur. We want here no more concealments. Tell freely!"

So Art went on, "He made rare hay of the place. All the manuscript had been burned. The cylinders of your phonograph too were thrown on the fire."

Here I interrupted. "Thank God there is the other copy in the safe!"

His face lit for a moment, but fell again as he went on. "I ran downstairs then, but could see no sign of him. I looked into Renfield's room, but there was no trace there except . . ." Again he paused.

"Go on," said Harker hoarsely. So he added, "except that the poor fellow is dead."

Mrs. Harker said solemnly, "God's will be done!"

Art was keeping back something.

Van Helsing turned to Morris and asked, "And you, friend Quincey, have you any to tell?"

"A little," he answered. "It may be much eventually, but at present I can't say. I thought it well to know if possible where the Count would go when he left the house. I did not see him, but I saw a bat rise from Renfield's window, and flap westward. He evidently sought some other lair. He will not be back tonight, for the sky is reddening in the east, and the dawn is close. We must work tomorrow!"

He said the latter words through his shut teeth.

Then Van Helsing said, placing his hand tenderly on Mrs. Harker's head, "And now, Madam Mina, tell us exactly what happened."

The poor dear lady shivered, and I could see the tension of her nerves as she clasped her husband closer to her and bent her head lower and lower still on his breast. Then she raised her head proudly, and began.

"I took the sleeping draught which you had so kindly given me. I seemed to become more wakeful, and myriads of horrible fancies began to crowd in upon my mind. All of them connected with death, and vampires, with blood, and pain, and trouble." Her husband involuntarily groaned as she turned to him and said lovingly, "Do not fret, dear. You must be brave and strong, and help me through the horrible task. Sure enough sleep must soon have come to me, for I remember no more. Jonathan coming in had not waked me. There was in the room the same thin white mist that I had before noticed. I felt the same vague terror which had come to me before and the same sense of some presence. I turned to wake Jonathan, but found that he slept soundly. I tried, but I could not wake him. I looked around terrified. Then indeed, my heart sank within me. Beside the bed, as if he had stepped out of the mist, or rather as if the mist had turned into his figure, for it had entirely disappeared, stood a tall, thin man, all in black. I knew him at once from the description of the others. The waxen face, the high aquiline nose, the parted red lips, with the sharp white teeth showing between, and the red eyes that I had seemed to see in the sunset on the windows of St. Mary's Church at Witby. I knew, too, the red scar on his forehead where Jonathan had struck him. I would have screamed out, only that I was paralyzed. In the pause he spoke in a sort of keen, cutting whisper, pointing as he spoke to Jonathan.

"`Silence! If you make a sound I shall take him and dash his brains out before your very eyes.' I was appalled. With a mocking smile, he placed one hand upon my shoulder and, holding me tight, bared my throat with the other, saying as he did so, `First, a little refreshment to reward my exertions. You may as well be quiet. It is not the first time, or the second, that your veins have appeased my thirst!' I was bewildered, and strangely enough, I did not want to hinder him. I suppose it is a part of the horrible curse that such is, when his touch is on his victim. And oh, my God, my God, pity me! He placed his reeking lips upon my throat!" Her husband groaned again. She clasped his hand harder, and looked at him pityingly, as if he were the injured one, and went on.

"I felt my strength fading away, and I was in a half swoon. It seemed that a long time must have passed before he took his foul, awful, sneering mouth away. I saw it drip with the fresh blood!" The remembrance seemed for a while to overpower her, and she sunk down. With a great effort she recovered herself and went on.

"Then he spoke to me mockingly, `And so you, like the others, would play your brains against mine. You would help these men to hunt me and frustrate me in my design! You know now what it is to cross my path. They should have kept their energies for use closer to home. Whilst they played wits against me, against me who commanded nations, and intrigued for them, and fought for them, hundreds of years before they were born, I was countermining them. And you, their best beloved one, are now to me, flesh of my flesh, blood of my blood, kin of my kin, my bountiful wine-press for a while, and shall be later on my companion and my helper. But as yet you are to be punished for what you have done. You have aided in thwarting me. Now you shall come to my call. When my brain says "Come!" to you, you shall cross land or sea to do my bidding. And to that end this!'

With that he pulled open his shirt, and with his long sharp nails opened a vein in his breast. When the blood began to spurt out, he took my hands in one of his, holding them tight, and with the other seized my neck and pressed my mouth to the wound, so that I must either suffocate or swallow some to the . . . Oh, my God! My God! What have I done? What have I done to deserve such a fate, I who have tried to walk in meekness and righteousness all my days. God pity me!" Then she began to rub her lips as though to cleanse them from pollution.

As she was telling her terrible story, the eastern sky began to quicken, and everything became more and more clear. Harker was still and quiet. But over his face came a grey look.

We have arranged that one of us is to stay within call.

The sun rises today on no more miserable house in all the great round of its daily course.

Jonathan Harker's Journal, 3 October

It is now six o'clock. Poor Mina told me just now, tearfully, that it is in trouble and trial that our faith is tested. That God will aid us up to the end. The end! Oh my God! What end?

When Dr. Van Helsing and Dr. Seward had come back from seeing poor Renfield, we went gravely into what was to be done.

We decided that Mina should be in full confidence. That nothing should be kept from her.

"There must be no concealment," she said. "There is nothing in all the world that can give me more pain than I have already endured."

Van Helsing said, "But dear Madam Mina, are you not afraid?"

Her eyes shone with the devotion of a martyr as she answered, "Ah no! For my mind is made up!"

"To what?" he asked gently.

Her answer came with direct simplicity, "Because if I find in myself, a sign of harm to any that I love, I shall die!"

"You would not kill yourself?" he asked, hoarsely.

"I would!"

Van Helsing put his hand on her head as he said solemnly. "For myself I could hold it in my account with God to find such an euthanasia for you. Nay, were it safe! But my child . . ."

For a moment he seemed choked. He went on, "You must not die. You must not die by any hand, but least of all your own. Until the other, who has fouled your sweet life, is true dead you must not die. Your death would make you even as he is."

The poor dear grew white as death, and shivered. We were all silent. We could do nothing. At length she grew more calm and turning to him said sweetly, "I promise you, my dear friend, that if God will let me live, I shall strive to do so."

As usual Van Helsing had thought ahead.

"It is perhaps well," he said, "that after our visit to Carfax we decided not to do anything with the earth boxes that lay there. Had we done so, the Count must have guessed our purpose, and would doubtless have taken measures in advance to frustrate such an effort with regard to the others. But now he does not know our intentions. In all probability, he does not know that such a power exists to us as can sterilize his lairs, so that he cannot use them as of old.

"When we have examined the house in Piccadilly, we may track the very last of them. Until the sun sets tonight, that monster must retain whatever form he now has. He is confined within the limitations of his earthly envelope. He cannot melt into thin air nor disappear through cracks or chinks or crannies. If he go through a doorway, he must open the door like a mortal. And so we have this day to hunt out all his lairs and sterilize them."

Here I started up. But Van Helsing held up his hand warningly.

"Nay, friend Jonathan," he said, "The Count may have many houses which he has bought. Of them he will have deeds of purchase, keys, cheques. Why not in this place so central, so quiet, where he come and there is none to notice. We shall go there and search that house."

"Then let us come at once," I cried.

The Professor simply said, "And how are we to get into that house in Piccadilly?"

"Any way!" I cried. "We shall break in if need be."

"And your police? Where will they be, and what will they say?"

I was staggered. So I said, "Don't wait more than need be."

"Ah, my child, now we wish to get into the house, but we have no key. Is it not so?" I nodded.

"Now suppose you were the owner of that house, and could not still get in. What would you do?"

"I should get a respectable locksmith, and set him to work to pick the lock for me."

"And your police, they would interfere?"

"Oh no! Not if they knew the man was properly employed."

"Then," he looked at me as keenly as he spoke, "all that is in doubt is the conscience of the employer, and the belief of your policemen. We shall not go so early that the policemen who have then little to think of, shall deem it strange. But we shall go when there are many about, and such things would be done were we indeed owners of the house."

Van Helsing went on, "When once within that house we may find more clues. At any rate some of us can remain there whilst the rest find the other places where there be more earth boxes, at Bermondsey and Mile End."

Lord Godalming stood up. "I can be of some use here," he said. "I shall wire to my people to have horses and carriages."

"Look here, old fellow," said Morris, "We would attract too much attention. It seems to me that we ought to take cabs. And even leave them somewhere near the neighborhood we are going to."

"Friend Quincey is right!" said the Professor.

Mina took a growing interest in everything. She was very, very pale, almost ghastly, and so thin that her lips were drawn away, showing her teeth in somewhat of prominence. It made my blood run cold in my veins to think of what had occurred with poor Lucy when the Count had sucked her blood. As yet there was no sign of the teeth growing sharper, but the time as yet was short, and there was time for fear.

It was finally agreed that before starting for Piccadilly we should destroy the Count's lair close at hand. And his presence in his purely material shape, and at his weakest, might give us some new clue.

It was suggested we should all enter the house in Piccadilly. That the two doctors and I should remain there, whilst Lord Godalming and Quincey found the lairs at Walworth and Mile End and destroyed them. It was possible that the Count might appear in Piccadilly during the day, and that if so we might be able to cope with him then and there. I said that I intended to stay and protect Mina. Mina would not listen to my objection. She said that there might be some law matter in which I could be useful. That amongst the Count's papers might be some clue which I could understand out of my experience in Transylvania. And that all the strength we could muster was required to cope with the Count's extraordinary power. I had to give in, for Mina's resolution was fixed. She said that it was the last hope for her that we should all work together.

"As for me," she said, "I have no fear. Go, my husband! God can, if He wishes it, guard me."

So I started up crying out, "Then in God's name let us come at once, for we are losing time. The Count may come to Piccadilly earlier than we think."

"Not so!" said Van Helsing, holding up his hand.

"But why?" I asked.

"Do you forget," he said, with actually a smile, "that last night he banqueted heavily, and will sleep late?"

Did I forget! Shall I ever . . . can I ever! Mina put her hands before her face, and shuddered whilst she moaned. Van Helsing had not intended to recall her frightful experience.

"Oh, Madam Mina," he said, "dear, dear, Madam Mina, alas! These stupid old lips of mine, but you will forget it, will you not?" He bent low beside her as he spoke.

She took his hand, and looking at him through her tears, said hoarsely, "No, I shall not forget, for it is well that I remember. And with it I have so much in memory of you that is sweet, that I take it all together. Now, you must all be going soon. Breakfast is ready, and we must all eat that we may be strong."

Breakfast was a strange meal to us all. We tried to encourage each other, and Mina was the brightest of us. When it was over, Van Helsing stood up and said, "Now, my dear friends, we go forth to our terrible enterprise. Are we all armed against ghostly as well as carnal attack?"

We all assured him.

"Then it is well. Now, Madam Mina, you are in any case quite safe here until the sunset. I have prepared your chamber by the placing of things of which we know, so that He may not enter. Now let me guard yourself. On your forehead I touch this piece of Sacred Wafer in the name of the Father, the Son, and . . .

There was a fearful scream which almost froze our hearts to hear. As he had placed the Wafer on Mina's forehead, it had seared it . . . had burned into the flesh as though it had been a piece of whitehot metal. My poor darling.

The echo of the scream had not ceased to ring on the air when there came the reaction, and she sank on her knees on the floor in an agony of abasement. Pulling her beautiful hair over her face, as the leper of old his mantle, she wailed out.

"Unclean! Unclean! Even the Almighty shuns my polluted flesh! I must bear this mark of shame upon my forehead until the Judgement Day."

I had thrown myself beside her in an agony of helpless grief, and putting my arms around held her tight. The friends around us turned away their eyes that ran tears silently. Then Van Helsing turned and said gravely.

"That scar shall pass away when God sees right to lift the burden that is hard upon us."

There was hope in his words, and comfort. And we prayed for help and guidance. It was then time to start. So I said farewell to Mina, a parting which neither of us shall forget to our dying day, and we set out.

If we find out that Mina must be a vampire in the end, then she shall not go into that unknown and terrible land alone. I suppose it is thus that in old times one vampire meant many. Just as their hideous bodies could only rest in sacred earth, so the holiest love was the recruiting sergeant for their ghastly ranks.

We entered Carfax without trouble and found all things the same as on the first occasion. We found no papers, or any sign of use in the house. And in the old chapel the great boxes looked just as we had seen them last.

Dr. Van Helsing said, "And now, my friends, we must sterilize this earth. He has chosen this earth because it has been holy. Thus we defeat him with his own weapon, for we make it more holy still. It was sanctified to such use of man, now we sanctify it to God."

As he spoke he took from his bag a screwdriver and a wrench, and very soon the top of one of the cases was thrown open. The earth smelled musty and close. Taking from his box a piece of the Scared

Wafer he laid it reverently on the earth, and then shutting down the lid began to screw it home, we aiding him as he worked.

One by one we treated each of the great boxes, and left them as we had found them to all appearance. But in each was a portion of the Host.

As we passed across the lawn on our way to the station to catch our train we could see the front of the asylum. I looked eagerly, and in the window of my own room saw Mina. I waved my hand to her, and nodded to tell that our work there was successfully accomplished. She nodded in reply to show that she understood. The last I saw, she was waving her hand in farewell.

Piccadilly, 12:30 o'clock.--Just before we reached Fenchurch Street Lord Godalming said to me, "Quincey and I will find a locksmith. You had better not come with us in case there should be any difficulty. You are a solicitor and the Incorporated Law Society might tell you that you should have known better."

I demurred as to my not sharing any danger even of odium, but he went on, "Besides, it will attract less attention if there are not too many of us. My title will make it all right with the locksmith, and with any policeman that may come along."

"The advice is good!" said Van Helsing. Godalming and Morris hurried off in a cab, we following in another. At the corner of Arlington Street our contingent got out and strolled into the Green Park. My heart beat as I saw the house on which so much of our hope was centered, looming up grim and silent in its deserted condition amongst its more lively and spruce-looking neighbors. We sat down on a bench within good view, and began to smoke cigars so as to attract as little attention as possible.

At length we saw a four-wheeler drive up. Out of it, in leisurely fashion, got Lord Godalming and Morris. And down from the box descended a thick-set working man with his rush-woven basket of tools. Together the two ascended the steps, and Lord Godalming pointed out what he wanted done. The workman took off his coat leisurely and hung it on one of the spikes of the rail, saying something to a policeman who just then sauntered along. The policeman nodded acquiescence, and the man kneeling down placed his bag beside him. The man lifted a good sized bunch of keys and began to probe the lock. All at once the door opened under a slight push from him, and he and the two others entered the hall. We sat still. My own cigar burnt furiously, but Van Helsing's went cold altogether. We waited patiently as we saw the workman come out and bring his bag. He fitted a key to the lock and handed it to Lord Godalming, who took out his purse and gave him something. The man touched his hat, took his bag, put on his coat and departed. Not a soul took the slightest notice of the whole transaction.

When the man had fairly gone, we three crossed the street and knocked at the door. It was immediately opened by Quincey Morris, beside whom stood Lord Godalming lighting a cigar.

"The place smells so vilely," said the latter as we came in. It was plain to us that the Count had been using the place pretty freely. We moved to explore the house, all keeping together in case of attack, for as yet we did not know whether the Count might not be in the house.

In the dining room we found eight boxes of earth. Eight boxes only out of the nine which we sought! Our work was not over, and would never be until we should have found the missing box.

First we opened the shutters of the window which looked out across a narrow stone flagged yard at the blank face of a stable. We did not lose any time in examining the chests. We opened them, one by one, and treated them as we had treated those others in the old chapel. It was evident to us that the Count was not at present in the house, and we proceeded to search for any of his effects.

Only the dining room contained any effects which might belong to the Count. And so we proceeded to minutely examine them. They lay in a sort of orderly disorder on the great dining room table.

There were title deeds of the Piccadilly house, deeds of the purchase of the houses at Mile End and Bermondsey, notepaper, envelopes, and pens and ink. All were covered up in thin wrapping paper to keep them from the dust. There were also a clothes brush, a brush and comb, and a jug and basin. The latter containing dirty water which was reddened as if with blood. Last of all was a little heap of keys of all sorts and sizes, probably those belonging to the other houses.

When we had examined this last find, Lord Godalming and Quincey Morris taking accurate notes of the various addresses of the houses in the East and the South, took with them the keys in a great bunch, and set out to destroy the boxes in these places. The rest of us are, with what patience we can, waiting their return, or the coming of the Count.

Dr. Seward's Diary, 3 October

The time seemed terribly long whilst we were waiting. The Professor tried to keep our minds active. I could see his beneficent purpose, by the side glances which he threw from time to time at Harker. The poor fellow is overwhelmed in a misery that is appalling to see. Last night he was a frank, happy-looking man, with strong, youthful face, full of energy, and with dark brown hair. Today he is a drawn, haggard old man, whose white hair matches well with the hollow burning eyes and griefwritten lines of his face.

The Professor said, "I have studied all the papers relating to this monster, and the more I have studied, the greater seems the necessity to utterly stamp him out. He was in life a most wonderful man. Soldier, statesman, and alchemist. Which latter was the highest development of the science knowledge of his time. He had a mighty brain, a learning beyond compare, and a heart that knew no fear and no remorse. There was no branch of knowledge of his time that he did not essay.

"Well, in him the brain powers survived the physical death. Though memory was not all complete. In some faculties of mind he has been, and is, only a child. But he is growing, He is experimenting. And if it had not been that we have crossed his path he would be yet, the father or furtherer of a new order of beings."

Harker groaned and said, "But how is he experimenting? The knowledge may help us to defeat him!"

"He has all along been trying his power, slowly but surely. And a man who has centuries before him can afford to wait and to go slow."

"I fail to understand," said Harker wearily.

The Professor laid his hand tenderly on his shoulder as he spoke, "Do you not see how this monster has been creeping into knowledge experimentally. How he has been making use of the zoophagous patient to effect his entry into friend John's home. Do we not see how at the first all these so great boxes were moved by others. But he began to help. And then he try to move them all alone. And so he scatter these graves of him. And none but he know where they are hidden.

"He may have intend to bury them. So that only he use them in the night, or at such time as he can change his form, they do him equal well, and none may know these are his hiding place! But, this knowledge came to him just too late! Already all of his lairs but one be sterilize. Then he have no place where he can move and hide. By my clock it is one hour and already friend Arthur and Quincey are on their way to us."

We were startled by a knock at the hall door, the double postman's knock of the telegraph boy. Van Helsing, holding up his hand to us to keep silence, stepped to the door and opened it. The boy handed in a dispatch. The Professor closed the door again, opened it and read aloud.

"Look out for D. He has just now, 12:45, come from Carfax hurriedly and hastened towards the South: Mina."

There was a pause, broken by Jonathan Harker's voice, "We shall soon meet!"

Van Helsing turned to him quickly and said, "Do not fear."

"I care for nothing now," he answered hotly, "except to wipe out this brute from the face of creation. I would sell my soul to do it!"

"Oh, hush," said Van Helsing. "God does not purchase souls, and the Devil does not keep faith. Today this Vampire is limit to the powers of man, and till sunset he may not change. What we must hope for is that my Lord Arthur and Quincey arrive first."

About half an hour after we had received Mrs. Harker's telegram, there came a quiet, resolute knock at the hall door. An ordinary knock. We looked at each other, and together moved out into the hall. We each held ready to use our various armaments, the spiritual in the left hand, the mortal in the right. Van Helsing pulled back the latch. We saw Lord Godalming and Quincey Morris. They came quickly in and closed the door behind them.

"It is all right. We found both places. Six boxes in each and we destroyed them all."

"Destroyed?" asked the Professor.

"For him!" Then Quincey said, "There's nothing to do but to wait here. But we can't leave Mrs. Harker alone after sunset."

"He will be here before long now," said Van Helsing, who had been consulting his pocketbook. "Nota bene, in Madam's telegram he went south from Carfax. That means he went to cross the river, and he could only do so at slack of tide, which should be something before one o'clock. We should have ready some plan of attack. Hush, there is no time now. Have all your arms! Be ready!" We all could hear a key softly inserted in the lock of the hall door.

Quincey Morris, with a swift glance around the room, laid out our plan of attack. Van Helsing, Harker, and I were just behind the door. Godalming behind and Quincey in front stood just out of sight. We waited with nightmare slowness. The slow, careful steps came along the hall. The Count was evidently prepared for some surprise.

Suddenly with a single bound he leaped into the room. Winning a way past us. There was something so panther like in the movement, something so unhuman. Harker threw himself before the door. As the Count saw us, a horrible snarl passed over his face, showing the eyeteeth long and pointed. But the evil smile passed into a cold stare of lion-like disdain. We all advanced upon him. I wondered what we were to do. I did not myself know whether our lethal weapons would avail us anything.

Harker had ready his great Kukri knife and made a fierce and sudden cut at him. The blow was a powerful one. Only the diabolical quickness of the Count's leap back saved him. The trenchant blade had shorn through his coat, making a wide gap whence a bundle of bank notes and a stream of gold fell out. The expression of the Count's face was so hellish, I saw Harker throw the terrible knife aloft again for another stroke. Instinctively I moved forward with a protective impulse, holding the Crucifix and Wafer in my left hand. I saw the monster cower back. It would be impossible to describe the expression of hate and baffled malignity, of anger and hellish rage, which came over the Count's face. His waxen hue became greenish-yellow by the contrast of his burning eyes, and the red scar on the forehead showed on the pallid skin like a palpitating wound. The next instant he swept under Harker's arm and grasping a handful of the money from the floor, dashed across the room, threw himself at the window. Amid the crash and glitter of the falling glass, he tumbled into the flagged area below. Through the sound of the shivering glass I could hear the "ting" of the gold, as some of the sovereigns fell on the flagging.

We ran over and saw him spring unhurt from the ground. He crossed the flagged yard, and pushed open the stable door. There he turned and spoke to us.

"You think to baffle me, you are like sheep in a butcher's. My revenge is just begun! I spread it over centuries. Your girls that you all love are mine already. And through them you and others shall yet be mine, my creatures, to be my jackals when I want to feed."

With a contemptuous sneer, he passed quickly through the door, and we heard the rusty bolt creak as he fastened it behind him. The first of us to speak was the Professor. Realizing the difficulty of following him through the stable, we moved toward the hall.

"He fears us. He fears time, he fears want! For if not, why he hurry so? His very tone betray him. Why take that money? You follow quick. For me, I make sure that nothing here may be of use to him, if he returns."

As he spoke he put the money remaining in his pocket, took the title deeds, and swept the remaining things into the open fireplace, where he set fire to them with a match.

Godalming and Morris had rushed out into the yard, and Harker had lowered himself from the window to follow the Count. He had, however, bolted the stable door, and by the time they had forced it open there was no sign of him.

Sunset was not far off. Our game was up. With heavy hearts we agreed with the Professor when he said, "Let us go back to Madam Mina. Poor, poor dear Madam Mina. We can there, at least, protect her. There is but one more earth box, and we must try to find it."

He spoke as bravely as he could to comfort Harker.

With sad hearts we came back to my house, where we found Mrs. Harker waiting us, with an appearance of cheerfulness which did honor to her bravery and unselfishness.

She said cheerfully, "I can never thank you all enough. Oh, my poor darling!"

As she spoke, she took her husband's grey head in her hands and kissed it.

"All will yet be well, dear!" The poor fellow groaned. There was no place for words in his sublime misery.

We had a perfunctory supper together, and I think it cheered us all up somewhat.

We told Mrs. Harker everything which had passed.

Then without letting go her husband's hand she stood up amongst us and spoke. Oh, with the red scar on her forehead. And we, knowing that so far as symbols went, she with all her goodness and purity and faith, was outcast from God.

"Jonathan," she said, and the word sounded like music, "Jonathan dear, and you all my true, true friends, I want you to bear something in mind. I know that you must fight. But it is not a work of hate. That poor soul who has wrought all this misery is the saddest case of all. You must be pitiful to him."

As she spoke I could see her husband's face darken and draw together, his knuckles looked white.

He leaped to his feet, almost tearing his hand from hers as he spoke.

"If I could send his soul forever to burning hell I would do it!"

"Don't say such things, Jonathan. Just think, my dear . . . perhaps . . .some day . . . I, too, may need such pity, and that some other like you may deny it to me!"

Before they retired the Professor fixed up the room against any coming of the Vampire. The first watch falls to Quincey, so the rest of us shall be off to bed as soon as we can.

JONATHAN HARKER'S JOURNAL

3-4 October, close to midnight.--All we knew was that one earth box remained, and that the Count alone knew where it was. If he chooses to lie hidden, he may baffle us for years. If ever there was a woman who was all perfection, that one is my poor wronged darling. I love her more for her sweet pity of last night, a pity that made my own hate of the monster seem despicable. Faith is our only anchor. Mina is sleeping. I fear what her dreams might be like. She has not been so calm since the sunset. I am not sleepy myself, though I am weary . . . weary to death. For there is tomorrow to think of, and there is no rest for me until . . .

Later--I must have fallen asleep, for I was awakened by Mina. She had placed a warning hand over my mouth, and whispered in my ear, "There is someone in the corridor!" I got up and gently opened the door.

Just outside, stretched on a mattress, lay Mr. Morris, wide awake. He raised a warning hand for silence as he whispered to me, "One of us will be here all night. We don't mean to take any chances!"

4 October, morning.--Once again during the night I was wakened by Mina.

She said to me hurriedly, "Go, call the Professor. I want to see him at once."

"Why?" I asked.

"I have an idea. Go quick, dearest, the time is getting close."

I went to the door. Dr. Seward was resting on the mattress, and seeing me, he sprang to his feet.

"Is anything wrong?" he asked, in alarm.

"No," I replied. "But Mina wants to see Dr. Van Helsing at once."

"I will go," he said, and hurried into the Professor's room.

Two or three minutes later Van Helsing was in the room in his dressing gown, and Mr. Morris and Lord Godalming were with Dr. Seward at the door asking questions.

He rubbed his hands as he said, "And what am I to do for you?"

"I want you to hypnotize me!" she said. "Do it before the dawn, for I feel that then I can speak, and speak freely. Be quick, for the time is short!" Without a word he motioned her to sit up in bed.

Looking fixedly at her, he commenced to make passes in front of her, from over the top of her head downward, with each hand in turn. Mina gazed at him fixedly for a few minutes. Gradually her eyes closed, and she sat, stock still. Only by the gentle heaving of her bosom could one know that she was alive. The Professor made a few more passes, and I could see that his forehead was covered with great beads of perspiration. Mina opened her eyes, but she did not seem the same woman. There was a far-away look in her eyes, and her voice had a sad dreaminess which was new to me. The Professor motioned to me to bring the others in. They came on tiptoe. Mina appeared not to see them. The stillness was broken by Van Helsing's voice.

"Where are you?" The answer came in a neutral way.

"I do not know." For several minutes there was silence. Mina sat rigid, and the Professor stood staring at her fixedly.

The rest of us hardly dared to breathe. Dr. Van Helsing motioned me to pull up the blind. I did so, and the day seemed just upon us. A red streak shot through the room. On the instant the Professor spoke again.

"Where are you now?"

The answer came dreamily, but with intention.

"I do not know. It is all strange to me!"

"What do you see?"

"I can see nothing. It is all dark."

"What do you hear?" I could detect the strain in the Professor's patient voice.

"The lapping of water. It is gurgling by, and little waves leap. I can hear them on the outside."

"Then you are on a ship?'"

The answer came quick, "Oh, yes!"

"What else do you hear?"

"The sound of men stamping overhead as they run about. There is the creaking of a chain, and the loud tinkle as the check of the capstan falls into the ratchet."

"What are you doing?"

"I am still, oh so still. It is like death!" The voice faded away into a deep breath as of one sleeping, and the open eyes closed again.

By this time the sun had risen, and we were all in the full light of day. Dr. Van Helsing laid Mina's head down softly on her pillow. She lay like a sleeping child for a few moments, and then, with a long sigh, awoke and stared in wonder to see us all around her.

"Have I been talking in my sleep?" was all she said. The Professor repeated the conversation, and she said, "Then there is not a moment to lose. It may not be yet too late!"

Mr. Morris and Lord Godalming started for the door but the Professor's calm voice called them back.

"Stay, my friends. That ship, wherever it was, was weighing anchor at the moment in your so great Port of London. We can know now what was in the Count's mind, when he seize that money. He meant escape. Hear me, ESCAPE! He saw that with but one earth box left, and a pack of men following like dogs after a fox, this London was no place for him. He have take his last earth box on board a ship, and he leave the land. We follow him."

Mina looked at him appealingly as she asked, "But why need we seek him further, when he is gone away from us?"

"Because," he answered solemnly, "he can live for centuries, and you are but mortal woman. Time is now to be dreaded, since once he put that mark upon your throat."

She fell forward in a faint.

Dr. Seward's Phonograph Diary

SPOKEN BY VAN HELSING

This to Jonathan Harker.

You are to stay with your dear Madam Mina. We shall go to make our search. He, our enemy, have gone back to his Castle in Transylvania. That last earth box was ready to ship somewheres. For this he took the money. For this he hurry at the last, lest we catch him before the sun go down. He is clever, oh so clever! He know that his game here was finish.

We go off now to find what ship, and whither bound. This battle is but begun and in the end we shall win. So sure as that God sits on high to watch over His children.

VAN HELSING.

JONATHAN HARKER'S JOURNAL

4 October.--When I read to Mina, Van Helsing's message in the phonograph, the poor girl brightened up considerably. Already the certainty that the Count is out of the country has given her comfort. For my own part, now that his horrible danger is not face to face with us, it seems almost impossible to believe in it. Even my own terrible experiences in Castle Dracula seem like a long forgotten dream.

Alas! How can I disbelieve! My eye fell on the red scar on my poor darling's white forehead. Whilst that lasts, there can be no disbelief.

MINA HARKER'S JOURNAL

5 October, 5 p. m.--Our meeting for report. Present: Professor Van Helsing, Lord Godalming, Dr. Seward, Mr. Quincey Morris, Jonathan Harker, Mina Harker.

Dr. Van Helsing described what steps were taken during the day to discover on what boat and whither bound Count Dracula made his escape.

"As I knew that he wanted to get back to Transylvania, I felt sure that he must go by somewhere in the Black Sea, since by that way he come. Omme Ignotum pro magnifico. And so we go, by suggestion of Lord Godalming, to your Lloyd's, where are note of all ships that sail, however so small. There we find that only one Black Sea bound ship go out with the tide. She is the Czarina Catherine, and she sail from Doolittle's Wharf. `So!' said I, `this is the ship whereon is the Count.' So off we go to Doolittle's Wharf, and there we find a man in an office. From him we inquire of the goings of the Czarina Catherine.

"They make known to us among them, how last afternoon at about five o'clock comes a man so hurry. A tall man, thin and pale, with high nose and teeth so white, and eyes that seem to be burning. That he be all in black, except that he have a hat of straw which suit not him or the time. He come himself driving cart on which a great box. This he himself lift down, though it take several to put it on truck for the ship. He give much talk to captain as to how and where his box is to be place. But the captain like it not and swear at him in many tongues. Whereupon the captain tell him that he had better be quick for that his ship will leave the place before the turn of the tide. Then the thin man smile and say that of course he must go when he think fit. The captain swear again and the thin man make him bow, and thank him. Final the captain, more red than ever tell him that he doesn't want no Frenchmen. And so, after asking where he might purchase ship forms, he departed.

"It soon became apparent to all that the Czarina Catherine would not sail as was expected. A thin mist began to creep up from the river, and it grew, and grew. Till soon a dense fog enveloped the ship and all around her. The captain swore, but he could do nothing. The water rose and rose, and he began to fear that he would lose the tide altogether. He was in no friendly mood, when just at full tide, the thin man came up the gangplank again and asked to see where his box had been stowed. He must have come off by himself, for none notice him. Soon the fog begin to melt away, and all was clear again. The ship went out on the ebb tide, and was doubtless by morning far down the river mouth. She was then, when they told us, well out to sea.

"And so, my dear Madam Mina, it is that we have to rest for a time, for our enemy is on the sea, with the fog at his command, on his way to the Danube mouth. To sail a ship takes time, go she never so quick. And when we start to go on land more quick, and we meet him there. Our best hope is to come on him when in the box between sunrise and sunset. For then he can make no struggle, and we may deal with him as we should. The box we seek is to be landed in Varna, and to be given to an agent, one Ristics who will there present his credentials. He can telegraph and have inquiry made at Varna, we say `no,' for what is to be done is not for police or of the customs. It must be done by us alone and in our own way."

I asked Van Helsing if he were certain that the Count had remained on board the ship. He replied, "We have the best proof of that, your own evidence, when in the hypnotic trance this morning."

I asked him again if it were really necessary that they should pursue the Count.

"Yes, it is necessary, necessary, necessary! For your sake in the first, and then for the sake of humanity. Leaving his own barren land, and coming to a new land was the work of centuries. With this one, all the forces of nature that are occult and deep and strong must have worked together in some wonderous way. The very place, where he have been alive, Undead for all these centuries, is full of strangeness of the geologic and chemical world. There are deep caverns and fissures that reach none know whither. There have been volcanoes, of strange properties, and gases that kill or make to vivify. Doubtless, there is something magnetic or electric in some of these combinations of occult forces, and in himself were from the first some great qualities. In a hard and warlike time he was celebrate that he have more iron nerve, more subtle brain, more braver heart, than any man. In him some vital principle have in strange way found their utmost. And as his body keep strong and grow and thrive, so his brain grow too. He infect you in such wise, that even if he do no more, you have only to live, to live in your own old, sweet way, and so in time, death shall make you like to him. This must not be! We have sworn together that it must not."

He paused and I said, "Since he has been driven from England, will he not avoid it, as a tiger does the village from which he has been hunted?"

"Aha!" he said, "Your maneater, as they of India call the tiger who has once tasted blood of the human, care no more for the other prey, but prowl unceasing till he get him. Nay, in himself he is not one to retire and stay afar. In his life, his living life, he go over the Turkey frontier and attack his enemy on his own ground. He be beaten back, but did he stay? No! He come again, and again, and again. Look at his persistence and endurance. He that can smile at death, as we know him. For in this enlightened age, when men believe not even what they see, the doubting of wise men would be his weapons to destroy us."

I caught sight in the mirror of the red mark upon my forehead, and I knew that I was still unclean.

DR. SEWARD'S DIARY

5 October.--We all arose early. When we met at early breakfast there was more general cheerfulness than any of us had ever expected to experience again.

It is really wonderful how much resilience there is in human nature. It was only when I caught sight of the red blotch on Mrs. Harker's forehead that I was brought back to reality. We shall all have to speak frankly. And yet I fear that in some mysterious way poor Mrs. Harker's tongue is tied. I suppose it is some of that horrid poison which has got into her veins beginning to work. The Count had his own purposes when he gave her what Van Helsing called "the Vampire's baptism of blood." One thing I know, that if my instinct be true regarding poor Mrs. Harker's silences, then there is a terrible difficulty, an unknown danger, in the work before us. I dare not think further, for so I should in my thoughts dishonor a noble woman!

Later.--When the Professor came in, we talked over the state of things. After beating about the bush a little, he said, "Friend John, there is something that you and I must talk of alone."

Then he stopped, so I waited. He went on, "Our poor, dear Madam Mina is changing."

A cold shiver ran through me to find my worst fears thus endorsed. Van Helsing continued.

"I can see the characteristics of the vampire coming in her face. It is now but very, very slight. Her teeth are sharper, and at times her eyes are more hard. Now my fear is that she can, by our hypnotic trance, tell what the Count see and hear, is it not more true that he who have hypnotize her first should compel her mind to disclose to him that which she know?"

I nodded acquiescence. He went on, "Then, we must keep her ignorant of our intent, and so she cannot tell what she know not. This is a painful task!"

He wiped his forehead, which had broken out in profuse perspiration. I knew that it would be some sort of comfort to him if I told him that I also had come to the same conclusion.

Later.--Mrs. Harker had sent a message by her husband to say that she would not join us at present, as she thought it better that we should be free to discuss our movements without her presence to embarrass us. For my own part, I thought that if Mrs. Harker realized the danger herself, it was much pain as well as much danger averted. We went at once into our Plan of Campaign.

Van Helsing roughly put the facts before us first, "The Czarina Catherine left the Thames yesterday morning. It will take her at the quickest speed she has ever made at least three weeks to reach Varna. But we can travel overland to the same place in three days. Now, if we allow for delays, we have a margin of nearly two weeks.

"Thus, in order to be quite safe, we must leave here on 17th at latest. Then we shall at any rate be in Varna a day before the ship arrives, and able to make such preparations as may be necessary. Of course we shall all go armed, armed against evil things, spiritual as well as physical."

Here Quincey Morris added, "I propose that we add Winchesters to our armament."

"Good!" said Van Helsing, "Winchesters it shall be. Tonight and tomorrow we can get ready, and then if all be well, we four can set out on our journey."

"We four?" said Harker interrogatively, looking from one to another of us.

"Of course!" answered the Professor quickly. "You must remain to take care of your so sweet wife!"

Harker was silent for awhile and then said in a hollow voice, "Let us talk of that part of it in the morning. I want to consult with Mina."

I thought that now was the time for Van Helsing to warn him not to disclose our plan to her, but he took no notice. I looked at him significantly and coughed. For answer he put his finger to his lips and turned away.

JONATHAN HARKER'S JOURNAL

October, afternoon.--For some time after our meeting this morning I could not think. Mina's determination not to take any part in the discussion set me thinking. The way the others received it, too puzzled me. Mina is sleeping now, calmly and sweetly like a little child. Her lips are curved and her face beams with happiness.

Later.--How strange it all is. I sat watching Mina's happy sleep, and I came as near to being happy myself as I suppose I shall ever be. As the evening drew on, the silence of the room grew more and more solemn to me.

All at once Mina opened her eyes, and looking at me tenderly said, "Jonathan, I want you to promise me something on your word of honor. Quick, you must make it to me at once."

"Mina," I said, "a promise like that, I cannot make at once. I may have no right to make it."

"But, dear one," she said, with such spiritual intensity that her eyes were like pole stars, "it is I who wish it. And it is not for myself. You can ask Dr. Van Helsing."

"I promise!" I said, and for a moment she looked supremely happy. Though to me all happiness for her was denied by the red scar on her forehead.

She said, "Promise me that you will not tell me anything of the plans formed for the campaign against the Count. Not at any time whilst this remains to me!" And she solemnly pointed to the scar. I saw that she was in earnest, and said solemnly, "I promise!" and as I said it I felt that from that instant a door had been shut between us.

Later, midnight.--Mina has been bright and cheerful all the evening.
So much so that all the rest seemed to take courage, as if infected
somewhat with her gaiety. Mina is now sleeping like a little child. It is
wonderful thing that her faculty of sleep remains to her in the midst of
her terrible trouble. I shall try it. Oh! For a dreamless sleep.

6 October, morning.--Another surprise. Mina woke me early and
asked me to bring Dr. Van Helsing. I thought that it was another
occassion for hypnotism, and without question went for the Professor.
He had evidently expected some such call, for I found him dressed in his
room. He came at once. As he passed into the room, he asked Mina if
the others might come, too.

"No," she said quite simply, "it will not be necessary. You can tell
them just as well. I must go with you on your journey."

Dr. Van Helsing was as startled as I was. After a moment's pause he
asked, "But why?"

"You must take me with you. I am safer with you, and you shall be
safer, too."

"But why, dear Madam Mina? You know that your safety is our
solemnest duty. We go into danger, to which you are, or may be, more
liable than any of us from . . . from circumstances . . . things that have
been." He paused embarrassed.

As she replied, she raised her finger and pointed to her forehead. "I
know. That is why I must go. I can tell you now, whilst the sun is coming
up. I may not be able again. I know that when the Count wills me I must
go. I know that if he tells me to come in secret, I must by wile. By any
device to hoodwink, even Jonathan." God saw the look that she turned
on me as she spoke. I could only clasp her hand. My emotion was too
great for even the relief of tears.

She went on. "Besides, you can hypnotize me and so learn that which
even I myself do not know."

Dr. Van Helsing said gravely, "Madam Mina, you are, as always, most
wise. You shall with us come."

Mina had fallen back on her pillow asleep. Van Helsing motioned to
me to come with him quietly. We went to his room, and within a minute
Lord Godalming, Dr. Seward, and Mr. Morris were with us also.

He told them what Mina had said, and went on. "In the morning we
shall leave for Varna. We have now to deal with a new factor, Madam
Mina. Oh, but her soul is true. It is to her an agony to tell us so much as
she has done. But it is most right, and we are warned in time. There must
be no chance lost, and in Varna we must be ready to act the instant when
that ship arrives."

"What shall we do exactly?" asked Mr. Morris laconically.

The Professor paused before replying, "We shall board that ship. Then, when we have identified the box, we shall place a branch of the wild rose on it. This we shall fasten, for when it is there none can emerge, so that at least says the superstition. And to superstition must we trust at the first. Then, when we get the opportunity that we seek, when none are near to see, we shall open the box, and . . . and all will be well."

"I shall not wait for any opportunity," said Morris. "When I see the box I shall open it and destroy the monster!" I grasped his hand instinctively and found it as firm as a piece of steel. I think he understood my look. I hope he did.

"Good boy," said Dr. Van Helsing. "For none of us can tell what, or when, or how, the end may be."

There was nothing further to be said, and we parted. I shall now settle up all my affairs of earth, and be ready for whatever may come.

Later.--It is done. My will is made, and all complete. Mina if she survive is my sole heir. If it should not be so, then the others who have been so good to us shall have remainder.

It is now drawing towards the sunset. Mina's uneasiness calls my attention to it. I am sure that there is something on her mind which the time of exact sunset will reveal. She is calling to me.

Dr. Seward's Diary, 11 October

Evening-We have of late come to understand that sunrise and sunset are to Mrs. Harker times of freedom. When her old self can be manifest without any controlling force subduing or restraining her, or inciting her to action. At first there is a sort of negative condition, as if some tie were loosened, and then the absolute freedom quickly follows. When, however, the freedom ceases the change back or relapse comes quickly, preceeded only by a spell of warning silence.

Tonight she was somewhat constrained, and bore all the signs of an internal struggle or a violent effort.

A very few minutes, however, gave her complete control of herself. Then, motioning her husband to sit beside her on the sofa where she was half reclining, she made the rest of us bring chairs up close.

Taking her husband's hand in hers, she began, "We are all here together in freedom, for perhaps the last time! I know that you will always be with me to the end. I know that all that brave earnest men can do for a poor weak woman, whose soul perhaps is lost, you will do. There is a poison in my blood, in my soul, which may destroy me, which must destroy me, unless some relief comes. And though I know there is one way out for me, you must not and I must not take it!" She looked appealingly to us all in turn, beginning and ending with her husband.

"What is that way?" asked Van Helsing in a hoarse voice.

"That I may die now, either by my own hand or that of another, before the greater evil is entirely wrought. I know you could and would set free my immortal spirit, even as you did my poor Lucy's."

We were all silent. The faces of the others were set, and Harker's grew ashen grey.

She continued, "What will you give to me?" She looked questionly, but avoided her husband's face. Quincey seemed to understand, he nodded, and her face lit up. "Then I shall tell you plainly what I want. You must promise me, one and all, even you, my beloved husband, that should the time come, you will kill me."

"What is that time?" The voice was Quincey's, but it was low and strained.

"When I am so changed that it is better that I die that I may live. Without a moment's delay, drive a stake through me and cut off my head, or do whatever else may be wanting to give me rest!"

Quincey knelt down before her and taking her hand in his said solemnly, "I swear to you by all that I hold sacred and dear that I shall not flinch from the duty that you have set us."

"My true friend!" was all she could say amid her fastfalling tears, as she kissed his hand.

"I swear the same, my dear Madam Mina!" said Van Helsing. "And I!" said Lord Godalming, each of them in turn kneeling to her to take the oath. I followed, myself.

Then her husband turned to her.

"You too, my dearest," she said, with infinite yearning of pity in her voice and eyes. "It is men's duty. Dr. Van Helsing, if that time shall come again, make it a happy memory."

"Again I swear!" came the Professor's resonant voice.

Mrs. Harker positively smiled, as with a sigh of relief she leaned back and said, "And now one word of warning. This time, if it ever come, may come quickly and unexpectedly, and in such case you must lose no time in using your opportunity. At such a time I shall be leagued with your enemy.

"One more request," she became very solemn as she said this. "I want you to read the Burial Service." She was interrupted by a deep groan from her husband.

"But oh, my dear one," he pleaded, "death is afar off from you."

"Nay," she said, holding up a warning hand. "I am deeper in death at this moment than if the weight of an earthly grave lay heavy upon me!"

"Oh, my wife, must I read it?" he said, before he began.

"It would comfort me, my husband!" was all she said, and he began to read when she had got the book ready.

How can I, how could anyone, tell of that strange scene, its solemnity, its gloom, its sadness, its horror, and its sweetness. I cannot go on . . . words . . . and v-voices . . . f-fail m-me!

She was right in her instinct. Strange as it was, it comforted us much. And the silence, which showed Mrs. Harker's coming relapse from her freedom of soul, did not seem so full of despair to any of us as we had dreaded.

JONATHAN HARKER'S JOURNAL

15 October, Varna.--We left Charing Cross on the morning of the 12th, got to Paris the same night, and took the places secured for us in the Orient Express. We traveled night and day, arriving here at about five o'clock. Lord Godalming went to the Consulate to see if any telegram had arrived for him, whilst the rest of us came on to this hotel, "the Odessus." Until the Czarina Catherine comes into port there will be no interest for me in anything in the wide world. Mina sleeps a great deal. Before sunrise and sunset, however, she is very wakeful and alert. And it has become a habit for Van Helsing to hypnotize her at such times. At

first, some effort was needed. But now, she seems to yield at once, as if by habit. He seems to have power at these particular moments to simply will, and her thoughts obey him. He always asks her what she can see and hear.

She answers to the first, "Nothing, all is dark."

And to the second, "I can hear the waves lapping against the ship, and the water rushing by. Canvas and cordage strain and masts and yards creak. The wind is high . . . I can hear it in the shrouds, and the bow throws back the foam."

It is evident that the Czarina Catherine is still at sea, hastening on her way to Varna. Lord Godalming has just returned. He had four telegrams, one each day since we started, and all to the same effect. That the Czarina Catherine had not been reported to Lloyd's from anywhere.

Tomorrow we are to see the Vice Consul, and to arrange, if we can, about getting on board the ship as soon as she arrives. Van Helsing says that our chance will be to get on the boat between sunrise and sunset. The Count, even if he takes the form of a bat, cannot cross the running water of his own volition, and so cannot leave the ship. As he dare not change to man's form without suspicion he must remain in the box. Thank God! This is the country where bribery can do anything, and we are well supplied with money.

16 October.--Mina's report still the same. Lapping waves and rushing water, darkness and favoring winds. When we hear of the Czarina Catherine we shall be ready. As she must pass the Dardanelles we are sure to have some report.

17 October.--Godalming told the shippers that he fancied that the box sent aboard might contain something stolen from a friend of his. The owner gave him a paper telling the Captain to give him every facility in doing whatever he chose on board the ship, and also a similar authorization to his agent at Varna.

We have already arranged what to do in case we get the box open. Van Helsing and Seward will cut off the Count's head at once and drive a stake through his heart. Morris and Godalming and I shall prevent interference, even if we have to use the arms. The Professor says that if we can so treat the Count's body, it will soon after fall into dust. In such case there would be no evidence against us, in case any suspicion of murder were aroused. But even if it were not, we should stand or fall by our act, and perhaps someday this very script may be evidence to come between some of us and a rope.

24 October.--A whole week of waiting. Daily telegrams to Godalming, but only the same story. "Not yet reported." Mina's morning and evening hypnotic answer is unvaried. Lapping waves, rushing water, and creaking masts.

TELEGRAM, OCTOBER 24TH RUFUS SMITH, LLOYD'S, LONDON, TO LORD GODALMING, CARE OF
H. B. M. VICE CONSUL, VARNA
"Czarina Catherine reported this morning from Dardanelles."

DR. SEWARD'S DIARY
25 October.--I know now what men feel in battle when the call to action is heard. We all tried not to show any excitement when we were in Mrs. Harker's presence. She is greatly changed during the past three weeks. Van Helsing and I talk of her often. We have not said a word to the others. It would break poor Harker's heart, certainly his nerve, if he knew that we had even a suspicion on the subject. Van Helsing examines her teeth very carefully for he says that so long as they do not begin to sharpen there is no active danger of a change in her. If this change should come, it would be necessary to take steps! "Euthanasia" is an excellent and a comforting word! I am grateful to whoever invented it.

It is only about 24 hours' sail from the Dardanelles to here, at the rate the Czarina Catherine has come from London. She should therefore arrive sometime in the morning. We shall get up at one o'clock, so as to be ready.

25 October, Noon.--No news yet of the ship's arrival. Mrs. Harker's hypnotic report this morning was the same as usual. We men are all in a fever of excitement, except Harker, who is calm. His hands are cold as ice, and an hour ago I found him whetting the edge of the great Ghoorka knife which he now always carries with him.

Van Helsing and I were a little alarmed about Mrs. Harker today. About noon she got into a sort of lethargy which we did not like. Poor girl, she has so much to forget that it is no wonder that sleep, if it brings oblivion to her, does her good.

Later.--Our opinion was justified, for when after a refreshing sleep of some hours she woke up, she seemed brighter and better than she had been for days. At sunset she made the usual hypnotic report. Wherever he may be in the Black Sea, the Count is hurrying to his destination. To his doom, I trust!

26 October.--Another day and no tidings of the Czarina Catherine. She ought to be here by now. That she is still journeying somewhere is apparent, for Mrs. Harker's hypnotic report at sunrise was still the same. The vessel may be lying by, at times, for fog. Some of the steamers which came in last evening reported patches of fog both to north and south of the port.

27 October, Noon.--Most strange. No news yet of the ship we wait for. Mrs. Harker reported last night and this morning as usual. "Lapping waves and rushing water," though she added that "the waves were very faint." The telegrams from London have been the same, "no further report." Van Helsing is terribly anxious, and told me just now that he fears the Count is escaping us.

28 October.--Telegram. Rufus Smith, London, to Lord Godalming, care H. B. M. Vice Consul, Varna "Czarina Catherine reported entering Galatz at one o'clock today."

DR. SEWARD'S DIARY

28 October.--When the telegram came announcing the arrival in Galatz I do not think it was such a shock. Van Helsing raised his hand over his head for a moment. But he said not a word, and in a few seconds stood up with his face sternly set.

Lord Godalming grew very pale. I was myself half stunned. Quincey Morris tightened his belt with that quick movement which I knew so well. In our old wandering days it meant "action." Mrs. Harker grew ghastly white, so that the scar on her forehead seemed to burn, but she folded her hands meekly and looked up in prayer. Harker smiled, actually smiled, the dark, bitter smile of one who is without hope, but at the same time his hands instinctively sought the hilt of the great Kukri knife and rested there.

"When does the next train start for Galatz?" said Van Helsing to us generally.

"At 6:30 tomorrow morning!" We all started, for the answer came from Mrs. Harker.

"How on earth do you know?" said Art.

"I am the train fiend. At home in Exeter I always used to make up the time tables, so as to be helpful to my husband. I knew that to Castle Dracula we should go by Galatz, or at any rate through Bucharest, so I learned the times very carefully."

"Wonderful woman!" murmured the Professor.

Van Helsing said, "You, friend Arthur, go to the train and get the tickets. Friend Jonathan, go to the agent of the ship and get from him letters with authority to make a search of the ship. Quincey Morris, you see the Vice Consul, and get his aid with his fellow in Galatz and all he can do to make our way smooth. John will stay with Madam Mina and me, and we shall consult."

"And I," said Mrs. Harker brightly, "shall think and write for you as I used to do. Something is shifting from me in some strange way, and I feel freer than I have been of late!"

The three younger men looked happier at the moment as they seemed to realize the significance of her words. But Van Helsing and I, turning to each other, met each a grave and troubled glance. We said nothing at the time, however.

When the three men had gone out to their tasks Van Helsing asked Mrs. Harker to look up the copy of the diaries and find him the part of Harker's journal at the Castle. She went away to get it.

"Do you know why I asked her to get the manuscript?"

"No!" said I.

"In the trance of three days ago the Count sent her his spirit to read her mind. He learn then that we are here. Now he make his most effort to escape us.

"He is sure with his so great knowledge that she will come at his call. But he cut her off, take her out of his own power, that so she come not to him. Ah! Here comes Madam Mina. Not a word to her of her trance! I fear, as I never feared before. We can only trust the good God. Silence! Here she comes!"

I thought that the Professor was going to break down and have hysterics, just as he had when Lucy died, but with a great effort he controlled himself. As Mrs. Harker came in, she handed a number of sheets of typewriting to Van Helsing. He looked over them gravely, his face brightening up as he read.

Then holding the pages between his finger and thumb he said, "Here is a lesson. Do not fear ever to think. See I read here what Jonathan have written.

"That other of his race who, in a later age, again and again, brought his forces over The Great River into Turkey Land, who when he was beaten back, came again, and again, and again, though he had to come alone from the bloody field where his troops were being slaughtered, since he knew that he alone could ultimately triumph.

"What does this tell us? Not much? No! The Count's child thought see nothing, therefore he speak so free. My man thought see nothing, till just now. No! There is this peculiarity in criminals. In all countries and at all times, the criminal always work at one crime. This criminal has not full man brain. He is clever and cunning and resourceful, but he be not of man stature as to brain. He be of child brain in much. Now this criminal of ours is pre-destinate to crime also. He, learn not by principle, but empirically."

He went on, "Now you shall speak. Tell us two dry men of science what you see with those so bright eyes." He took Mrs. Harper's hand and held it whilst he spoke. His finger and thumb closed on her pulse as she spoke.

"The Count is a criminal and of criminal type. He is of an imperfectly formed mind. Thus, in a difficulty he has to seek resource in habit. His past is a clue, once before, when in what Mr. Morris would call a `tight place,' he went back to his own country from the land he had tried to invade and prepared himself for a new effort. He came again better equipped for his work, and won. So he came to London to invade a new land. He was beaten, and when all hope of success was lost, and his existence in danger, he fled home. Just as formerly he had fled back over the Danube from Turkey Land."

"Good, good! Oh, you so clever lady!" said Van Helsing, enthusiastically, as he stooped and kissed her hand. A moment later he said to me, as calmly as though we had been having a sick room consultation, "Seventy-two only, and in all this excitement. I have hope."

Turning to her again, he said with keen expectation, "But go on. Go on!"

"Then, as he is criminal he is selfish. And as his intellect is small, he confines himself to one purpose. That purpose is remorseless. As he fled back over the Danube, leaving his forces to be cut to pieces, so now he is intent on being safe, careless of all. So his own selfishness frees my soul somewhat from the terrible power which he acquired over me on that dreadful night. My soul is freer than it has been since that awful hour. All that haunts me is a fear he may have used my knowledge for his ends."

The Professor stood up, "He has so used your mind, and by it he has left us here in Varna, whilst the ship rushed through enveloping fog up to Galatz. But his child mind only saw so far. For now that he think he is free from every trace of us all. There is where he fail! That terrible baptism of blood which he give you makes you free to go to him in spirit. At such times you go by my volition and not by his. This is now all more precious that he know it not, and to guard himself have even cut himself off from his knowledge of our where. We shall follow him."

Dr. Seward's Diary, 29 October

This is written in the train from Varna to Galatz. We are prepared for the whole of our journey, and for our work when we get to Galatz. When the usual time came round Mrs. Harker prepared herself for her hypnotic effort. Usually she speaks on a hint, but this time the Professor had to ask her questions. At last her answer came.

"I can see nothing. We are still. No waves lapping, but only a steady swirl of water softly running against the hawser. I can hear men's voices, and the roll and creak of oars in the rowlocks. A gun is fired somewhere, the echo of it seems far away. There is tramping of feet overhead, and ropes and chains are dragged along. What is this? There is a gleam of light. I can feel the air blowing upon me."

Here she stopped. She had risen, as if impulsively, from where she lay on the sofa, and raised both her hands, palms upwards, as if lifting a weight. Van Helsing and I looked at each other with understanding. Quincey raised his eyebrows, whilst Harker's hand instinctively closed round the hilt of his Kukri. There was a long pause.

Suddenly she sat up, and as she opened her eyes said sweetly, "Would none of you like a cup of tea? You must all be so tired!"

We could only make her happy, and so acquiesced. She bustled off to get tea. When she had gone Van Helsing said, "He is close to land. He has left his earth chest. But he has yet to get on shore. If he be not carried on shore, or if the ship do not touch it, he cannot achieve the land. And if he be carried, then the customs men may discover what the box contain. Thus, in fine, if he escape not on shore tonight, or before dawn, there will be the whole day lost to him. We may then arrive in time. For if he escape not at night we shall come on him in daytime, boxed up and at our mercy. For he dare not be his true self, awake and visible, lest he be discovered."

There was no more to be said, so we waited in patience until the dawn, at which time we might learn more from Mrs. Harker.

Early this morning we listened, with breathless anxiety, for her response in her trance. The hypnotic stage was even longer in coming than before. Van Helsing seemed to throw his whole soul into the effort. At last, in obedience to his will she made reply.

"All is dark. I hear lapping water, level with me, and some creaking as of wood on wood." She paused, and the red sun shot up. We must wait till tonight.

We are three hours late, so we cannot possibly get in till well after sunup. Thus we shall have two more hypnotic messages from Mrs. Harker!

Later.--Sunset has come and gone. Mrs. Harker yielded to the hypnotic influence even less readily than this morning. I am in fear that her power may die away. It seems to me that her imagination is beginning to work. Whilst she has been in the trance hitherto she has confined herself to the simplest of facts. If I thought that the Count's power over her would die away equally with her power of knowledge it would be a happy thought. But I am afraid that it may not be so.

Her words were enigmatical, "Something is going out. I can feel it pass me like a cold wind. I can hear, far off, confused sounds, as of men talking in strange tongues, fierce falling water, and the howling of wolves." A shudder ran through her, increasing in intensity for a few seconds, till at the end, she shook as though in a palsy. She said no more, even in answer to the Professor's imperative questioning. When she woke from the trance, she was cold, and exhausted, and languid, but her mind was all alert. She could not remember anything, but asked what she had said.

30 October, 7 a. m.--We are near Galatz now. Sunrise this morning was anxiously looked for by us all. Knowing of the increasing difficulty of procuring the hypnotic trance, Van Helsing began earlier than usual. She yielded with a still greater difficulty, only a minute before the sun rose. The Professor lost no time in his questioning.

Her answer came with equal quickness, "All is dark. I hear water swirling by, level with my ears. Cattle low far off. There is another sound, a queer one like . . ." She stopped and grew white, and whiter still.

"Go on, go on! Speak, I command you!" said Van Helsing in an agonized voice. At the same time there was despair in his eyes, for the risen sun was reddening even Mrs. Harker's pale face. She opened her eyes, and we all started as she said, sweetly and seemingly with the utmost unconcern.

"Oh, Professor, why ask me to do what you know I can't? I don't remember anything." Then she said, "What have I said? What have I done? It seemed so funny to hear you order me about, as if I were a bad child!"

The whistles are sounding. We are nearing Galatz. We are on fire with anxiety and eagerness.

MINA HARKER'S JOURNAL
30 October.--Mr. Morris took me to the hotel. The forces were distributed much as they had been at Varna, except that Lord Godalming went to the Vice Consul, as his rank might serve as an immediate

guarantee of some sort to the official. Jonathan and the two doctors went to the shipping agent to learn particulars of the arrival of the Czarina Catherine.

Later.--Lord Godalming has returned. The Consul is away, and the Vice Consul sick. So the routine work has been attended to by a clerk. He was very obliging, and offered to do anything in his power.

JONATHAN HARKER'S JOURNAL

30 October.--At nine o'clock Dr. Van Helsing, Dr. Seward, and I called on Messrs. Mackenzie & Steinkoff, the agents of the London firm of Hapgood. They had received a wire from London, in answer to Lord Godalming's telegraphed request, asking them to show us any civility in their power. They were more than kind and courteous, and took us at once on board the Czarina Catherine, which lay at anchor out in the river harbor. There we saw the Captain, Donelson by name, who told us of his voyage. He said that in all his life he had never had so favorable a run.

"Man!" he said, "but it made us afeard. As though the Deil himself were blawin' on yer sail for his ain purpose. A fog fell on us and travelled wi' us."

This mixture of simplicity and cunning, of superstition and commercial reasoning, aroused Van Helsing, who said, "Mine friend, that Devil is more clever than he is thought by some, and he know when he meet his match!"

The skipper was not displeased with the compliment, and went on, "The men began to grumble. Some o' them, the Roumanians, came and asked me to heave overboard a big box which had been put on board by a queer lookin' old man just before we had started frae London. I had seen them speer at the fellow, and put out their twa fingers when they saw him, to guard them against the evil eye. Man! but the supersteetion of foreigners is pairfectly rideeculous! Well, on we went, and as the fog didn't let up I joost let the wind carry us. The Roumanians were wild, and wanted me right or wrong to take out the box and fling it in the river. I had to argy wi' them aboot it wi' a handspike. But in the mornin', braw an' airly, an hour before sunup, a man came aboard wi' an order, written to him from England, to receive a box marked for one Count Dracula."

"What was the name of the man who took it?" asked Dr. Van Helsing with restrained eagerness.

He produced a receipt signed "Immanuel Hildesheim." Burgenstrasse 16 was the address. We found out that this was all the Captain knew, so with thanks we came away.

We found Hildesheim in his office, a Hebrew of rather the Adelphi Theatre type, with a nose like a sheep, and a fez. With a little bargaining he told us what he knew. He had received a letter from Mr. de Ville of London, telling him to receive, if possible before sunrise so as to avoid customs, a box which would arrive at Galatz in the Czarina Catherine. This he was to give in charge to a certain Petrof Skinsky.

We then sought for Skinsky, but were unable to find him. One of his neighbors, who did not seem to bear him any affection, said that he had gone away two days before. We were at a standstill again.

Whilst we were talking one came running and breathlessly gasped out that the body of Skinsky had been found inside the wall of the churchyard of St. Peter, and that the throat had been torn open as if by some wild animal. Those we had been speaking with ran off to see the horror, the women crying out. "This is the work of a Slovak!"

We were all convinced that the box was on its way, by water, to somewhere, but where that might be we would have to discover. With heavy hearts we came home to the hotel to Mina.

When we met together, the first thing was to consult as to taking Mina again into our confidence.

MINA HARKER'S JOURNAL

30 October, evening.--They were so tired and worn out and dispirited that there was nothing to be done till they had some rest.

Poor dear, dear Jonathan, what he must have suffered, what he must be suffering now. He lies on the sofa hardly seeming to breathe, and his whole body appears in collapse. His brows are knit. His face is drawn with pain. Oh! if I could only help at all. I shall do what I can.

Whilst they are resting, I shall go over all carefully, and perhaps I may arrive at some conclusion. I shall try to follow the Professor's example, and think without prejudice on the facts before me . . .

I do believe that under God's providence I have made a discovery. I shall get the maps and look over them.

MINA HARKER'S MEMORANDUM
(ENTERED IN HER JOURNAL)

Ground of inquiry.--Count Dracula's problem is to get back to his own place.

(a) He must be brought back by someone. This is evident. For had he power to move himself as he wished he could go either as man, or wolf, or bat, or in some other way. He evidently fears discovery or interference, in the state of helplessness in which he must be, confined as he is between dawn and sunset in his wooden box.

(b) How is he to be taken?--Here a process of exclusions may help us. By road, by rail, by water?

1. By Road.--There are endless difficulties, especially in leaving the city.

(x) There are people. And people are curious, and investigate. A hint, a surmise, a doubt as to what might be in the box, would destroy him.

(y) There are, or there may be, customs and octroi officers to pass.

(z) His pursuers might follow. This is his highest fear. And in order to prevent his being betrayed he has repelled, so far as he can, even his victim, me!

2. By Rail.--There is no one in charge of the box. It would have to take its chance of being delayed, and delay would be fatal, with enemies on the track. True, he might escape at night. But what would he be, if left in a strange place with no refuge that he could fly to? He does not mean to risk it.

3. By Water.--Here is the safest way, in one respect, but with most danger in another. On the water he is powerless except at night. Even then he can only summon fog and storm and snow and his wolves. But were he wrecked, the living water would engulf him, helpless, and he would indeed be lost. He could have the vessel drive to land, but if it were unfriendly land, wherein he was not free to move, his position would still be desperate.

We know from the record that he was on the water, so what we have to do is to ascertain what water.

Firstly.--We must differentiate between what he did in London as part of his general plan of action, when he was pressed for moments and had to arrange as best he could.

Secondly we must see what he has done here.

As to the first, he evidently intended to arrive at Galatz, and sent invoice to Varna to deceive us lest we should ascertain his means of exit from England. His immediate and sole purpose then was to escape. The proof of this, is the letter of instructions sent to Immanuel Hildesheim to clear and take away the box before sunrise. There is also the instruction to Petrof Skinsky. There must have been some letter or message, since Skinsky came to Hildesheim.

The Czarina Catherine made a phenomenally quick journey. So much so that Captain Donelson's suspicions were aroused. That the Count's arrangements were well made, has been proved. Hildesheim cleared the box, took it off, and gave it to Skinsky. Skinsky took it, and here we lose the trail. We only know that the box is somewhere on the water, moving along. The customs and the octroi, if there be any, have been avoided.

—

Now we come to what the Count must have done after his arrival, on land, at Galatz.

The box was given to Skinsky before sunrise. At sunrise the Count could appear in his own form. Here, we ask why Skinsky was chosen at all to aid in the work? In my husband's diary, Skinsky is mentioned as dealing with the Slovaks who trade down the river to the port. And the man's remark, that the murder was the work of a Slovak, showed the general feeling against his class. The Count wanted isolation.

My surmise is this, that in London the Count decided to get back to his castle by water, as the most safe and secret way. He was brought from the castle by Szgany, and probably they delivered their cargo to Slovaks who took the boxes to Varna, for there they were shipped to London. Thus the Count had knowledge of the persons who could arrange this service. When the box was on land, before sunrise or after sunset, he came out from his box, met Skinsky and instructed him what to do as to arranging the carriage of the box up some river. When this was done, and he knew that all was in train, he blotted out his traces, as he thought, by murdering his agent.

I have examined the map and find that the river most suitable for the Slovaks to have ascended is either the Pruth or the Sereth. I read in the typescript that in my trance I heard cows low and water swirling level with my ears and the creaking of wood. The Count in his box, then, was on a river in an open boat, propelled probably either by oars or poles, for the banks are near and it is working against stream. There would be no such if floating down stream.

Of course it may not be either the Sereth or the Pruth, but we may possibly investigate further. Now of these two, the Pruth is the more easily navigated, but the Sereth is, at Fundu, joined by the Bistritza which runs up round the Borgo Pass. The loop it makes is manifestly as close to Dracula's castle as can be got by water.

MINA HARKER'S JOURNAL--CONTINUED

When I had done reading, Jonathan took me in his arms and kissed me. The others kept shaking me by both hands, and Dr. Van Helsing said, "Our dear Madam Mina is once more our teacher. Now we are on the track once again. Now men, to our Council of War."

"I shall get a steam launch and follow him," said Lord Godalming.

"And I, horses to follow on the bank lest by chance he land," said Mr. Morris.

"Good!" said the Professor, "both good. But neither must go alone. The Slovak is strong and rough, and he carries rude arms." All the men smiled, for amongst them they carried a small arsenal.

Said Mr. Morris, "I have brought some Winchesters. They are pretty handy in a crowd, and there may be wolves."

Dr. Seward said, "I think I had better go with Quincey. We have been accustomed to hunt together, and we will be a match for whatever may come along. You must not be alone, Art. It may be necessary to fight the Slovaks. We shall not rest until the Count's head and body have been separated."

He looked at Jonathan as he spoke, and Jonathan looked at me. I could see that the poor dear was torn about in his mind. Of course he wanted to be with me. But then the boat service would, most likely, be the one which would destroy the . . . the . . . Vampire. (Why did I hesitate to write the word?)

He was silent awhile, and during his silence Dr. Van Helsing spoke, "Friend Jonathan, this is to you for twice reasons. First, because you are young and brave and can fight. And again that it is your right to destroy him. Be not afraid for Madam Mina. She will be my care, if I may. I am old. But I can be of other service. While you, my Lord Godalming and friend Jonathan go in your steamboat up the river, and whilst John and Quincey guard the bank, I will take Madam Mina right into the heart of the enemy's country. Whilst the old fox is tied in his box, floating on the running stream whence he cannot escape to land, we shall go in the track where Jonathan went, to the Castle of Dracula. Here, Madam Mina's hypnotic power will surely help, and we shall find our way. There is much to be done, and other places to be made sanctify, so that that nest of vipers be obliterated."

Here Jonathan interrupted him hotly, "You would bring Mina right into the jaws of his deathtrap? Not for the world! Not for Heaven or Hell!"

He became almost speechless for a minute, and then went on, "Do you know what the place is? Have you seen that awful den of hellish infamy, with the very moonlight alive with grisly shapes, and ever speck of dust that whirls in the wind a devouring monster? Have you felt the Vampire's lips upon your throat?"

Here he turned to me, and as his eyes lit on my forehead he threw up his arms with a cry, "Oh, my God, what have we done to have this terror upon us?" and he sank down on the sofa in a collapse of misery.

The Professor's voice, as he spoke in clear, sweet tones, which seemed to vibrate in the air, calmed us all.

"Oh, my friend, it is because I would save Madam Mina from that awful place that I would go. There is work, wild work, to be done before that place can be purify. If the Count escape us he may choose to sleep him for a century, and then in time our dear one," he took my hand, "would come to him to keep him company, and would be as those others that you, Jonathan, saw. You have told us of their gloating lips. You heard their ribald laugh as they clutched the moving bag that the Count threw to them."

"Do as you will," said Jonathan, with a sob that shook him all over, "we are in the hands of God!"

Later.--How can women help loving men when they are so earnest, and so true, and so brave! And, too, it made me think of the wonderful power of money! What can it not do when basely used. I felt so thankful that Lord Godalming is rich, and both he and Mr. Morris, who also has plenty of money, are willing to spend it so freely. For if they did not, our little expedition could not start. And now Lord Godalming and Jonathan have a lovely steam launch, with steam up ready to start at a moment's notice. Dr. Seward and Mr. Morris have half a dozen good horses, well appointed. We have all the maps and appliances of various kinds that can be had. Professor Van Helsing and I are to leave by the 11:40 train tonight for Veresti, where we are to get a carriage to drive to the Borgo Pass. We are bringing a good deal of ready money, as we are to buy a carriage and horses. We shall drive ourselves, for we have no one whom we can trust in the matter. The Professor knows something of a great many languages, so we shall get on all right. We have all got arms, even for me a large bore revolver. Jonathan would not be happy unless I was armed like the rest. Dear Dr. Van Helsing comforts me by telling me that I am fully armed as there may be wolves. The weather is getting colder every hour, and there are snow flurries which come and go as warnings.

Later.--It took all my courage to say goodby to my darling. We may never meet again. Courage, Mina! The Professor is looking at you keenly. His look is a warning. There must be no tears now.

JONATHAN HARKER'S JOURNAL

30 October, night.--I am writing this in the light from the furnace door of the steam launch. Lord Godalming is firing up. He is an experienced hand at the work, as he has had for years a launch of his own on the Thames, and another on the Norfolk Broads. Regarding our plans, we finally decided that Mina's guess was correct, the Bistritza at its junction, would be the one. We have no fear in running at good speed up the river at night. Lord Godalming tells me to sleep for a while. But I cannot sleep, how can I with the terrible danger hanging over my darling, and her going out into that awful place . . .

My only comfort is that we are in the hands of God. Mr. Morris and Dr. Seward were off on their long ride before we started. They are to keep up the right bank. They have, for the first stages, two men to ride and lead their spare horses, four in all, so as not to excite curiosity. When they dismiss the men, which shall be shortly, they shall themselves look after the horses. It may be necessary for us to join forces. If so they can mount our whole party. One of the saddles has a moveable horn, and can be easily adapted for Mina, if required.

Here, as we are rushing along through the darkness, with the cold from the river seeming to rise up and strike us, with all the mysterious voices of the night around us, it all comes home. We seem to be drifting into unknown places and unknown ways. Into a whole world of dark and dreadful things. Godalming is shutting the furnace door . . .

31 October.--Still hurrying along. The day has come, and Godalming is sleeping. I am on watch. The morning is bitterly cold, the furnace heat is grateful, though we have heavy fur coats. As yet we have passed only a few open boats, but none of them had on board any box or package of anything like the size of the one we seek. The men were scared every time we turned our electric lamp on them, and fell on their knees and prayed.

1 November, evening.--No news all day. We have found nothing of the kind we seek. We have now passed into the Bistritza. We got a Roumanian flag which we now fly conspicuously. Some of the Slovaks tell us that a big boat passed them, going at more than usual speed as she had a double crew on board. At Fundu we could not hear of any such boat, so she must have passed there in the night. I am feeling very sleepy. The cold is perhaps beginning to tell upon me, and nature must have rest some time. Godalming insists that he shall keep the first watch. God bless him for all his goodness to poor dear Mina and me.

2 November, morning.--It is broad daylight. That good fellow would not wake me. It seems brutally selfish to me to have slept so long, and let him watch all night, but he was quite right. I am a new man this morning. And, as I sit here and watch him sleeping, I can do all that is necessary both as to minding the engine, steering, and keeping watch. I wonder where Mina is now, and Van Helsing. They should have got to Veresti about noon on Wednesday. I am afraid to think what may happen. If we could only go faster. But we cannot. The engines are throbbing and doing their utmost. I wonder how Dr. Seward and Mr. Morris are getting on. The horsemen may not have met much obstruction. I hope that

before we get to Strasba we may see them. For if by that time we have not overtaken the Count, it may be necessary to take counsel together what to do next.

DR. SEWARD'S DIARY

2 November.--Three days on the road. No news. We have had only the rest needful for the horses. We must push on. We shall never feel happy till we get the launch in sight again.

3 November.--We heard at Fundu that the launch had gone up the Bistritza. I wish it wasn't so cold. There are signs of snow coming. And if it falls heavy it will stop us. In such case we must get a sledge and go on, Russian fashion.

4 November.--Today we heard of the launch having been detained by an accident when trying to force a way up the rapids. The Slovak boats get up all right, by aid of a rope and steering with knowledge. Some went up only a few hours before. Godalming is an amateur fitter himself, and evidently it was he who put the launch in trim again.

Finally, they got up the rapids all right, with local help, and are off on the chase afresh. I fear that the boat is not any better for the accident, the peasantry tell us that after she got upon smooth water again, she kept stopping every now and again so long as she was in sight. We must push on harder than ever. Our help may be wanted soon.

MINA HARKER'S JOURNAL

31 October.--Arrived at Veresti at noon. The Professor tells me that this morning at dawn he could hardly hypnotize me at all, and that all I could say was, "dark and quiet." He is off now buying a carriage and horses. We have something more than 70 miles before us. The country is lovely, and most interesting. If only we were under different conditions, how delightful it would be to see it all. But, alas!

Later.--Dr. Van Helsing has returned. He has got the carriage and horses. We are to have some dinner, and to start in an hour. The landlady is putting us up a huge basket of provisions. It seems enough for a company of soldiers. The Professor encourages her, and whispers to me that it may be a week before we can get any food again. He has been shopping too, and has sent home such a wonderful lot of fur coats and wraps, and all sorts of warm things. There will not be any chance of our being cold.

We shall soon be off. I am afraid to think what may happen to us. We are truly in the hands of God.

Mina Harker's Journal, 1 November

All day long we have travelled, and at a good speed. Dr. Van Helsing is laconic, he tells the farmers that he is hurrying to Bistritz, and pays them well to make the exchange of horses. We get hot soup, or coffee, or tea, and off we go. It is a lovely country. Full of beauties of all imaginable kinds, and the people seem full of nice qualities. They are very, very superstitious. In the first house where we stopped, when the woman who served us saw the scar on my forehead, she crossed herself and put out two fingers towards me, to keep off the evil eye. I believe they went to the trouble of putting an extra amount of garlic into our food, and I can't abide garlic. Ever since then I have taken care not to take off my hat or veil, and so have escaped their suspicions. We are travelling fast, and as we have no driver with us to carry tales, we go ahead of scandal. But I daresay that fear of the evil eye will follow hard behind us all the way. The Professor seems tireless. All day he would not take any rest, though he made me sleep for a long spell. At sunset time he hypnotized me, and he says I answered as usual, "darkness, lapping water and creaking wood." So our enemy is still on the river. I am afraid to think of Jonathan, but somehow I have now no fear for him, or for myself. I write this whilst we wait in a farmhouse for the horses to be ready. Dr. Van Helsing is sleeping. Poor dear, he looks very tired and old and grey, but his mouth is set as firmly as a conqueror's. Even in his sleep he is intense with resolution. When we have well started I must make him rest whilst I drive . . . All is ready. We are off shortly.

2 November, morning.--We took turns driving all night. Now the day is on us, bright though cold. There is a strange heaviness in the air. It oppresses us both. Only our warm furs keep us comfortable. At dawn Van Helsing hypnotized me. He says I answered "darkness, creaking wood and roaring water," so the river is changing as they ascend.

2 November, night.--All day long driving. The country gets wilder as we go, and the great spurs of the Carpathians, which at Veresti seemed so far, now seem to tower in front. I think we make an effort each to cheer the other, in the doing so we cheer ourselves. Dr. Van Helsing says that by morning we shall reach the Borgo Pass. The houses are very few here now. We are not worried with other travelers, and so even I can drive. We shall get to the Pass in daylight. We do not want to arrive before. So we take it easy, and have each a long rest in turn. God watch over my husband and those dear to us. As for me, I am unclean to His eyes.

MEMORANDUM BY ABRAHAM VAN HELSING

4 November.--This to my old and true friend John Seward, M. D., of Purefleet, London, in case I may not see him. It may explain. It is morning, and I write by a fire which all the night I have kept alive, Madam Mina aiding me. It is cold, cold. So cold that the grey heavy sky is full of snow. It seems to have affected Madam Mina. She has been so heavy of head all day that she was not like herself. She sleeps, and sleeps, and sleeps! Something whisper to me that all is not well. However, her long sleep all day have refresh and restore her, for now she is all sweet and bright as ever. At sunset I try to hypnotize her, but alas! with no effect.

We got to the Borgo Pass just after sunrise yesterday morning. When I saw the signs of the dawn I got ready for the hypnotism. I made a couch with furs, and Madam Mina, lying down, yield herself as usual, but more slow and more short time than ever, to the hypnotic sleep. As before, came the answer, "darkness and the swirling of water." Then she woke, bright and radiant and we go on our way and soon reach the Pass. At this time and place, she become all on fire with zeal. Some new guiding power be in her manifested, for she point to a road and say, "This is the way."

"How know you it?" I ask.

"Of course I know it,' she answer, and with a pause, add, "Have not my Jonathan travelled it and wrote of his travel?"

At first I think somewhat strange. The road is used but little.

So we came down this road. By and by we find all the things which Jonathan have note in that wonderful diary of him. Then we go on for long, long hours and hours. At the first, I tell Madam Mina to sleep. She sleep all the time, till at the last, I feel myself to suspicious grow, and attempt to wake her. But she sleep on. I do not wish to try too hard lest I harm her. For I know that she have suffer much, and sleep at times be all-in-all to her. I think I drowse myself, for all of sudden I feel guilt, as though I have done something. I find myself bolt up, with the reins in my hand. We are going up, and up, and all is oh, so wild and rocky, as though it were the end of the world.

Then I arouse Madam Mina. I try to put her to hypnotic sleep. But she sleep not, being as though I were not. Still I try and try, till I find her and myself in dark, so I look round, and find that the sun have gone down. Madam Mina laugh, and I turn and look at her. She is now quite awake, and look so well as I never saw her since that night at Carfax when we first enter the Count's house. I am amaze, and not at ease then. But she is so bright and tender and thoughtful for me that I forget all fear. I light a fire, and she prepare food. I go to help her, but she smile, and tell me that she have eat already. That she was so hungry that she would not wait. I have grave doubts. She help me and I eat alone, and then we wrap in fur and lie beside the fire, and I tell her to sleep while I watch. But presently I find her lying quiet, but awake, and looking at me with so bright eyes. Once, twice more the same occur, and I get much sleep till before morning. When I wake I try to hypnotize her, but alas! Though she shut her eyes obedient, she may not sleep. The sun rise up, and up, and up, and then sleep come to her too late, but so heavy that she will not wake. I have to lift her up, and place her sleeping in the carriage when I have harnessed the horses and made all ready. Madam still sleep, and she look in her sleep more healthy than before. And I like it not. And I am afraid, afraid, afraid! But I must go on my way. The stake we play for is life and death, or more than these, and we must not flinch.

5 November, morning.--Though I have seen some strange things, you may at the first think that I, Van Helsing, am mad. That the many horrors and the so long strain on nerves has at the last turn my brain.

All yesterday we travel, always getting closer to the mountains, and moving into a more and more wild and desert land. There are great, frowning precipices and much falling water. Madam Mina still sleep and sleep. I began to fear that the fatal spell of the place was upon her, tainted as she is with that Vampire baptism. "Well," said I to myself, "if it be that she sleep all the day, it shall also be that I do not sleep at night." As we travel on the rough road, for a road of an ancient and imperfect kind there was, I held down my head and slept.

Again I waked. The frowning mountains seemed further away, and we were near the top of a steep rising hill, on summit of which was such a castle as Jonathan tell of in his diary. At once I exulted and feared. For now, for good or ill, the end was near.

I woke Madam Mina, and again tried to hypnotize her, but alas! unavailing till too late. Then, ere the great dark came upon us. Then, with the fear on me of what might be, I drew a ring so big for her comfort, round where Madam Mina sat. And over the ring I passed some of the wafer, and I broke it fine so that all was well guarded. She sat still all the time, so still as one dead. And she grew whiter and even whiter till the snow was not more pale, and no word she said. But when I drew near, she clung to me, and I could know that the poor soul shook her from head to feet with a tremor that was pain to feel.

I said to her presently, "Will you not come over to the fire?" for I wished to make a test of what she could. She rose obedient, but when she have made a step she stopped, and stood as one stricken.

"Why not go on?" I asked. She shook her head, and coming back, sat down in her place. Then, looking at me with open eyes, as of one waked from sleep, she said simply, "I cannot!" and remained silent. I rejoiced. Though there might be danger to her body, yet her soul was safe!

Presently the horses began to scream, and tore at their tethers till I came to them and quieted them. When they did feel my hands on them, they whinnied low as in joy, and licked at my hands and were quiet for a time. Many times through the night did I come to them. In the cold hour the fire began to die. Even in the dark there was a light of some kind, as there ever is over snow, and it seemed as though the snow flurries and the wreaths of mist took shape as of women with trailing garments. All was in dead, grim silence only that the horses whinnied and cowered, as if in terror of the worst. I began to fear, horrible fears. But then came to me the sense of safety in that ring wherein I stood. For the snow flakes and the mist began to wheel and circle round, till I could get as though a shadowy glimpse of those women that would have kissed Jonathan. And then the horses cowered lower and lower, and moaned in terror as men do in pain. I feared for my dear Madam Mina when these weird figures drew near and circled round. I looked at her, but she sat calm, and smiled at me. When I would have stepped to the fire to replenish it, she caught me and held me back, and whispered, like a voice that one hears in a dream, so low it was.

"No! No! Do not go without. Here you are safe!"

I turned to her, and looking in her eyes said, "But you? It is for you that I fear!"

Whereat she laughed, a laugh low and unreal, and said, "Fear for me! Why fear for me? None safer in all the world from them than I am," and as I wondered at the meaning of her words, a puff of wind made the flame leap up, and I see the red scar on her forehead. Then, alas! I knew. The wheeling figures of mist and snow came closer, but keeping ever without the Holy circle. Then they began to materialize. There were before me in actual flesh the same three women that Jonathan saw in the room, when they would have kissed his throat. I knew the swaying round forms, the bright hard eyes, the white teeth, the ruddy color, the voluptuous lips. They smiled ever at poor dear Madam Mina. And as their laugh came through the silence of the night, they twined their arms and pointed to her, and said in those so sweet tingling tones that Jonathan said were of the intolerable sweetness of the water glasses, "Come, sister. Come to us. Come!"

In fear I turned to my poor Madam Mina, and my heart with gladness leapt like flame. For oh! the terror in her sweet eyes, the repulsion, the horror, told a story to my heart that was all of hope. God be thanked she was not, yet of them. I seized some of the firewood which was by me, and holding out some of the Wafer, advanced on them towards the fire. They drew back before me, and laughed their low horrid laugh. I fed the fire, and feared them not. For I knew that we were safe within the ring, which she could not leave no more than they could enter. The horses had ceased to moan, and lay still on the ground. The snow fell on them softly, and they grew whiter. I knew that there was for the poor beasts no more of terror.

I was desolate and afraid, and full of woe and terror. At the first coming of the dawn the horrid figures melted in the whirling mist and snow. The wreaths of transparent gloom moved away towards the castle, and were lost.

Instinctively, with the dawn coming, I turned to Madam Mina, intending to hypnotize her. But she lay in a deep and sudden sleep, from which I could not wake her. I tried to hypnotize through her sleep, but she made no response, none at all, and the day broke. I fear yet to stir. I have made my fire and have seen the horses, they are all dead. Today I have much to do here, and I keep waiting till the sun is up high. For there may be places where I must go, where that sunlight, though snow and mist obscure it, will be to me a safety.

I will strengthen me with breakfast, and then I will do my terrible work. Madam Mina still sleeps, and God be thanked! She is calm in her sleep . . .

JONATHAN HARKER'S JOURNAL

4 November, evening.--The accident to the launch has been a terrible thing for us. Only for it we should have overtaken the boat long ago, and by now my dear Mina would have been free. We have got horses, and we follow on the track. I note this whilst Godalming is getting ready. We have our arms. The Szgany must look out if they mean to fight. Oh, if only Morris and Seward were with us. We must only hope! If I write no more Goodby Mina! God bless and keep you.

DR. SEWARD'S DIARY

5 November.--With the dawn we saw the body of Szgany before us dashing away from the river with their leiter wagon. They surrounded it in a cluster, and hurried along as though beset. The snow is falling lightly and there is a strange excitement in the air. It may be our own feelings, but the depression is strange. Far off I hear the howling of wolves. The snow brings them down from the mountains, and there are dangers to all of us, and from all sides. The horses are nearly ready, and we are soon

off. We ride to death of some one. God alone knows who, or where, or what, or when, or how it may be . . .

DR. VAN HELSING'S MEMORANDUM

5 November, afternoon.--I am at least sane. Though the proving it has been dreadful. When I left Madam Mina sleeping within the Holy circle, I took my way to the castle. The blacksmith hammer which I took in the carriage from Veresti was useful, though the doors were all open I broke them off the rusty hinges, lest some ill intent or ill chance should close them, so that being entered I might not get out. Jonathan's bitter experience served me here. By memory of his diary I found my way to the old chapel, for I knew that here my work lay. The air was oppressive. It seemed as if there was some sulphurous fume, which at times made me dizzy. Either there was a roaring in my ears or I heard afar off the howl of wolves. Then I bethought me of my dear Madam Mina, and I was in terrible plight. The dilemma had me between his horns.

Her, I had not dare to take into this place, but left safe from the Vampire in that Holy circle. And yet even there would be the wolf! I resolve me that my work lay here, and that as to the wolves we must submit, if it were God's will.

I knew that there were at least three graves to find, graves that are inhabit. So I search, and search, and I find one of them. She lay in her Vampire sleep, so full of life and voluptuous beauty that I shudder as though I have come to do murder. Ah, I doubt not that in the old time, when such things were, many a man who set forth to do such a task as mine, found at the last his heart fail him, and then his nerve. So he delay, and delay, and delay, till the mere beauty and the fascination of the wanton Undead have hypnotize him. And he remain on and on, till sunset come, and the Vampire sleep be over. Then the beautiful eyes of the fair woman open and look love, and the voluptuous mouth present to a kiss, and the man is weak. And there remain one more victim in the Vampire fold. One more to swell the grim and grisly ranks of the Undead! . . .

There is some fascination, surely, though there be that horrid odor such as the lairs of the Count have had. Yes, I was moved. I, Van Helsing, with all my purpose and with my motive for hate. I was moved to a yearning for delay which seemed to paralyze my faculties and to clog my very soul. Certain it was that I was lapsing into sleep, when there came a long, low wail, so full of woe and pity that it woke me. For it was the voice of my dear Madam Mina that I heard.

Then I braced myself again to my horrid task, and found by wrenching away tomb tops one other of the sisters, the other dark one. I dared not pause to look on her as I had on her sister, lest once more I should begin to be enthrall. But I go on searching until, presently, I find in a high great tomb as if made to one much beloved that other fair sister which, like Jonathan I had seen to gather herself out of the atoms of the mist. She was so fair to look on, so radiantly beautiful, so exquisitely voluptuous, that the very instinct of man in me, made my head whirl with new emotion. But God be thanked, that soul wail of my dear Madam Mina had not died out of my ears. And, before the spell could be wrought further upon me, I had nerved myself to my wild work. By this time I had searched all the tombs in the chapel, so far as I could tell. And as there had been only three of these Undead phantoms around us in the night, I took it that there were no more of active Undead existent. There was one great tomb more lordly than all the rest. Huge it was, and nobly proportioned. On it was but one word.

DRACULA

This then was the Undead home of the King Vampire, to whom so many more were due. Its emptiness spoke eloquent to make certain what I knew. Before I began to restore these women to their dead selves through my awful work, I laid in Dracula's tomb some of the Wafer, and so banished him from it, Undead, for ever.

Then began my terrible task, and I dreaded it. Had it been but one, it had been easy, comparative. But three! To begin twice more after I had been through a deed of horror. For it was terrible with the sweet Miss Lucy, what would it not be with these strange ones who had survived through centuries, and who had been strengthened by the passing of the years. Who would, if they could, have fought for their foul lives . . .

Oh, my friend John, but it was butcher work. Had I not been nerved by thoughts of other dead, and of the living over whom hung such a pall of fear, I could not have gone on. I tremble and tremble even yet, though till all was over, God be thanked, my nerve did stand. Had I not seen the gladness that stole over it just ere the final dissolution came, as realization that the soul had been won, I could not have endured the horrid screeching as the stake drove home, the plunging of writhing form, and lips of bloody foam. I should have fled in terror and left my work undone. But it is over! And the poor souls, I can pity them now and weep. For, friend John, hardly had my knife severed the head of each, before the whole body began to melt away and crumble into its native dust!"

Before I left the castle I so fixed its entrances that never more can the Count enter there Undead.

When I stepped into the circle where Madam Mina slept, she woke from her sleep and, seeing me, cried out in pain that I had endured too much.

"Come!" she said, "come away from this awful place! Let us go to meet my husband who is, I know, coming towards us." She was looking thin and pale and weak. But her eyes were pure and glowed with fervor. I was glad to see her paleness and her illness, for my mind was full of the fresh horror of that ruddy vampire sleep.

And so with trust and hope, and yet full of fear, we go eastward to meet our friends, and him, whom Madam Mina tell me that she know are coming to meet us.

MINA HARKER'S JOURNAL

6 November.--It was late in the afternoon when the Professor and I took our way towards the east whence I knew Jonathan was coming. We did not go fast, though the way was steeply downhill, for we had to take heavy rugs and wraps with us. We had to take some of our provisions too, for there was not even the sign of habitation. When we had gone about a mile, I was tired with the heavy walking and sat down to rest. Then we looked back and saw where the clear line of Dracula's castle cut the sky. For we were so deep under the hill whereon it was set that the angle of perspective of the Carpathian mountains was far below it. We saw it in all its grandeur, perched a thousand feet on the summit of a sheer precipice. We could hear the distant howling of wolves. The sound, even though coming muffled through the deadening snowfall, was full of terror. I knew from the way Dr. Van Helsing was searching about that he was trying to seek some strategic point, where we would be less exposed in case of attack. The rough roadway still led downwards.

In a little while the Professor had found a sort of natural hollow in a rock, with an entrance like a doorway between two boulders. He took me by the hand and drew me in.

"See!" he said, "here you will be in shelter. And if the wolves do come I can meet them one by one."

He brought in our furs, and made a snug nest for me, and got out some provisions and forced them upon me. But I could not eat, to even try to do so was repulsive to me. He looked very sad, but did not reproach me. Taking his field glasses from the case, he stood on the top of the rock, and began to search the horizon.

Suddenly he called out, "Look! Madam Mina, look! Look!"

I sprang up and stood beside him on the rock. He handed me his glasses and pointed. The snow was now falling more heavily, and a high wind was beginning to blow. From the height where we were it was possible to see a great distance. Straight in front of us and not far off came a group of mounted men hurrying along. In the midst of them was a cart, a long leiter wagon which swept from side to side, like a dog's tail wagging, with each stern inequality of the road. Outlined against the snow as they were, I could see from the men's clothes that they were peasants or gypsies of some kind.

On the cart was a great square chest. My heart leaped as I saw it, for I felt that the end was coming. The evening was now drawing close, and well I knew that at sunset the Thing, which was till then imprisoned there, would take new freedom and could in any of many forms elude pursuit. In fear I turned to the Professor. To my consternation, however, he was not there. An instant later, I saw him below me. Round the rock he had drawn a circle, such as we had found shelter in last night.

When he had completed it he stood beside me again saying, "At least you shall be safe here from him!" He took the glasses from me, and at the next lull of the snow swept the whole space below us. "See," he said, "they come quickly. They are flogging the horses, and galloping as hard as they can."

He paused and went on in a hollow voice, "They are racing for the sunset. We may be too late. God's will be done!" Down came another blinding rush of driving snow, and the whole landscape was blotted out. It soon passed, however, and once more his glasses were fixed on the plain.

Then came a sudden cry, "Look! Look! Look! See, two horsemen follow fast, coming up from the south. It must be Quincey and John. Take the glass. Look before the snow blots it all out!" I took it and looked. The two men might be Dr. Seward and Mr. Morris. At the same time I knew that Jonathan was not far off. Looking around I saw on the north side of the coming party two other men, riding at breakneck speed. One of them I knew was Jonathan, and the other I took, of course, to be Lord Godalming. They too, were pursuing the party with the cart. When I told the Professor he laid his Winchester rifle ready for use against the boulder at the opening of our shelter.

"They are all converging," he said. "When the time comes we shall have gypsies on all sides." I got out my revolver ready to hand, for whilst we were speaking the howling of wolves came louder and closer. When the snow storm abated a moment we looked again. Sweeping the glass all around us I could see here and there dots moving singly and in twos and threes and larger numbers. The wolves were gathering for their prey.

Every instant seemed an age whilst we waited. The wind came now in fierce bursts, and we knew that before long the sun would set. We waited in that rocky shelter before the various bodies began to converge close upon us. We could distinguish clearly the individuals of each party, the pursued and the pursuers. Strangely enough those pursued did not seem to realize, or at least to care, that they were pursued. They seemed, however, to hasten with redoubled speed as the sun dropped lower and lower on the mountain tops.

Closer and closer they drew. The Professor and I crouched down behind our rock, and held our weapons ready. I could see that he was determined that they should not pass. One and all were quite unaware of our presence.

All at once two voices shouted out to, "Halt!" One was my Jonathan's, raised in a high key of passion. The other Mr. Morris' strong resolute tone of quiet command. The gypsies may not have known the language, but there was no mistaking the tone. Instinctively they reined in, and at the instant Lord Godalming and Jonathan dashed up at one side and Dr. Seward and Mr. Morris on the other. The leader of the gypsies, a splendid looking fellow who sat his horse like a centaur, waved them back, and in a fierce voice gave to his companions some word to proceed. They lashed the horses which sprang forward. But the four men raised their Winchester rifles, and in an unmistakable way commanded them to stop. At the same moment Dr. Van Helsing and I rose behind the rock and pointed our weapons at them. Seeing that they were surrounded the men tightened their reins and drew up. The leader turned to them and gave a word at which every man of the gypsy party drew what weapon he carried, knife or pistol, and held himself in readiness to attack. Issue was joined in an instant.

The leader, with a quick movement of his rein, threw his horse out in front, and pointed first to the sun, now close down on the hill tops, and then to the castle, said something which I did not understand. For answer, all four men of our party threw themselves from their horses and dashed towards the cart. Seeing the quick movement of our parties, the leader of the gypsies gave a command. His men instantly formed round the cart in a sort of undisciplined endeavor, each one shouldering and pushing the other in his eagerness to carry out the order.

In the midst of this I could see that Jonathan on one side of the ring of men, and Quincey on the other, were forcing a way to the cart. It was evident that they were bent on finishing their task before the sun should set. Nothing seemed to stop or even to hinder them. Neither the levelled weapons nor the flashing knives of the gypsies in front, nor the howling of the wolves behind, appeared to even attract their attention. Jonathan's impetuosity seemed to overawe those in front of him. Instinctively they cowered aside and let him pass. In an instant he had jumped upon the cart, and with a strength which seemed incredible, raised the great box, and flung it over the wheel to the ground. In the meantime, Mr. Morris had had to use force to pass through his side of the ring of Szgany. All the time I had been breathlessly watching Jonathan I had, with the tail of my eye, seen him pressing desperately forward, and had seen the knives of the gypsies flash as he won a way through them, and they cut at him. He had parried with his great bowie knife, and at first I thought that he too had come through in safety. But as he sprang beside Jonathan, who had by now jumped from the cart, I could see that with his left hand he was clutching at his side, and that the blood was spurting through his fingers. He did not delay notwithstanding this, for as Jonathan, with desperate energy, attacked one end of the chest, attempting to prize off the lid with his great Kukri knife, Mr. Morris attacked the other frantically with his bowie. Under the efforts of both men the lid began to yield. The nails drew with a screeching sound, and the top of the box was thrown back.

By this time the gypsies, seeing themselves covered by the Winchesters, and at the mercy of Lord Godalming and Dr. Seward, had given in and made no further resistance. The sun was almost down on the mountain tops, and the shadows of the whole group fell upon the snow. I saw the Count lying within the box upon the earth, some of which the rude falling from the cart had scattered over him. He was deathly pale, just like a waxen image, and the red eyes glared with the horrible vindictive look which I knew so well.

As I looked, the eyes saw the sinking sun, and the look of hate in them turned to triumph.

But, on the instant, came the sweep and flash of Jonathan's great knife. I shrieked as I saw it shear through the throat. Whilst at the same moment Mr. Morris's bowie knife plunged into the heart.

It was like a miracle, but before our very eyes, and almost in the drawing of a breath, the whole body crumbled into dust and passed from our sight.

I shall be glad as long as I live that even in that moment of final dissolution, there was in the face a look of peace, such as I never could have imagined might have rested there.

The Castle of Dracula now stood out against the red sky, and every stone of its broken battlements was articulated against the light of the setting sun.

The gypsies, taking us as in some way the cause of the extraordinary disappearance of the dead man, turned, without a word, and rode away as if for their lives. Those who were unmounted jumped upon the leiter wagon and shouted to the horsemen not to desert them. The wolves, which had withdrawn to a safe distance, followed in their wake, leaving us alone.

Mr. Morris, who had sunk to the ground, leaned on his elbow, holding his hand pressed to his side. The blood still gushed through his fingers. I flew to him, for the Holy circle did not now keep me back, so did the two doctors. Jonathan knelt behind him and the wounded man laid back his head on his shoulder. With a sigh he took, with a feeble effort, my hand in that of his own which was unstained.

He must have seen the anguish of my heart in my face, for he smiled at me and said, "I am only too happy to have been of service! Oh, God!" he cried suddenly, struggling to a sitting posture and pointing to me. "It was worth for this to die! Look! Look!"

The sun was now right down upon the mountain top, and the red gleams fell upon my face, so that it was bathed in rosy light. With one impulse the men sank on their knees and a deep and earnest "Amen" broke from all as their eyes followed the pointing of his finger.

The dying man spoke, "Now God be thanked that all has not been in vain! See! The snow is not more stainless than her forehead! The curse has passed away!"

And, to our bitter grief, with a smile and in silence, he died, a gallant gentleman.

NOTE

Seven years ago we all went through the flames. And the happiness of some of us since then is, we think, well worth the pain we endured. It is an added joy to Mina and to me that our boy's birthday is the same day as that on which Quincey Morris died. His mother holds, I know, the secret belief that some of our brave friend's spirit has passed into him. His bundle of names links all our little band of men together. But we call him Quincey.

In the summer of this year we made a journey to Transylvania, and went over the old ground which was, and is, to us so full of vivid and terrible memories. Every trace of all that had been was blotted out. The castle stood as before, reared high above a waste of desolation.

When we got home we were talking of the old time, which we could all look back on without despair, for Godalming and Seward are both happily married. I took the papers from the safe where they had been ever since our return so long ago. We were struck with the fact, that in all the mass of material of which the record is composed, there is hardly one authentic document. Nothing but a mass of typewriting, except the later notebooks of Mina and Seward and myself, and Van Helsing's memorandum. We could hardly ask anyone to accept these as proofs of so wild a story. Van Helsing summed it all up as he said, with our boy on his knee.

"We want no proofs. We ask none to believe us! This boy will some day know what a brave and gallant woman his mother is. Already he knows her sweetness and loving care. Later on he will understand how some men so loved her, that they did dare much for her sake.

JONATHAN HARKER

Printed in Great Britain
by Amazon

36908301R00128